MW01129861

To Owen—

SHARK BAIT

AN ARISTOTLE "SOC" SOCARIDES MYSTERY

PAUL KEMPRECOS

SUSPENSE PUBLISHING

Best wishes,
Paul Kemp
Cape Cod, Aug., 2018

ALSO BY PAUL KEMPRECOS

Aristotle "Soc" Socarides Series
Grey Lady
Bluefin Blues
The Mayflower Murder
Feeding Frenzy
Death in Deep Water
Neptune's Eye
Cool Blue Tomb

Matinicus "Matt" Hawkins Series
The Minoan Cipher
The Emerald Scepter

SHARK BAIT
by
Paul Kemprecos

PAPERBACK EDITION
* * * * *
PUBLISHED BY:
Suspense Publishing

Paul Kemprecos
Copyright 2018 Paul Kemprecos

PUBLISHING HISTORY:
Suspense Publishing, Paperback and Digital Copy, April 2018

Cover Design: Shannon Raab
Cover Photographer: iStockphoto.com/Ramon Carretero
Cover Photographer: iStockphoto.com/Michael Zeigler

ISBN-13: 978-1986671095
ISBN-10: 1986671097

All rights reserved. Without limiting the rights under copyright reserved above, no part of this publication may be reproduced, stored in or introduced into a retrieval system, or transmitted, in any form, or by any means (electronic, mechanical, photocopying, recording, or otherwise) without the prior written permission of both the copyright owner and the above publisher of this book.

This is a work of fiction. Names, characters, places, brands, media, and incidents are either the product of the author's imagination or are used fictitiously. The author acknowledges the trademarked status and trademark owners of various products referenced in this work of fiction, which have been used without permission. The publication/use of these trademarks is not authorized, associated with, or sponsored by the trademark owners.

For my wife Christi, who is always there for me.

ACKNOWLEDGEMENTS

My thanks to Greg Burns, proprietor of The Oyster Company, for showing me around his oyster farm on the flats of Cape Cod Bay. My nephew, Eric Munk, works in the film production business, and was a ready source of information on how a movie scene is shot. Michelle Wciesel, program manager at the Atlantic White Shark Conservancy Center, filled me in on the dining habits of the Great White Shark.

A manuscript is only a pile of pages until an editor digs into it. I was fortunate to have my words seen by several sets of eyes, belonging to Shannon Raab and Amy Lignor, my editors at *Suspense Publishing*, my wife Christi, and writer-editor Rose Connors.

PRAISE FOR
PAUL KEMPRECOS

"Solidly written and elegantly structured, *Shark Bait* crackles with energy, authenticity and vibrance. #1 *New York Times* bestselling author Paul Kemprecos employs his seasoned hand to stir the ingredients of a perfectly-toned tale that's equal parts dark and light, as long-time series hero Aristotle 'Soc' Socarides faces danger from sharks who roam the land as well as the sea. *Shark Bait* is storytelling at its level best, the very definition of what a great read is all about, certain to take a bite out of the competition for the best beach book of the year."
—Jon Land, *USA Today* bestselling author of the *MURDER SHE WROTE* series

"In a wonderfully descriptive fashion we are treated to, as Soc would say, a novel of the *finestkind, cap'n* and learn that the most dangerous sharks are not those trolling Buzzards Bay, but the ones with two feet that are ready to ambush you on shore."
—Mark P. Sadler, author of "Kettle of Vultures"

"A brilliant mystery that combines suspense with exciting adventure. Intriguing plot twists from beginning to end, shrouded under genuine history."
—Clive Cussler, *New York Times* Bestselling Author

"Absorbing...Soc is an appealing, witty protagonist...and the Cape Cod locale is rendered with panache in this fast-paced enjoyable yarn."
—*Publisher's Weekly*

"To live without evil belongs only to the gods."
—Sophocles

Shark Bait: A person who swims far from shore in dangerous waters.

SHARK BAIT

PAUL KEMPRECOS

CHAPTER 1

The first time I met Howie Gill he was standing in my driveway next to a high-lift pickup truck that looked like it had been used as a paintball target. He stood there with his legs planted wide apart and his hands glued to his hips, elbows akimbo in a "wanna fight" pose. The frown that decorated a face the color of a ripe carrot would have put a bull-dog to shame. If his square head were bent any lower, his chin would have rested on the top of his substantial belly. When a guy built like a haystack glares at you that way, you know he's trouble.

I ran down the mental list of people who might have a reason to be ticked off at me. It was longer than I would have liked. The stranger didn't fit the profile of anyone I had offended or owed money to, but I kept a wary eye peeled as I got out of my pickup truck, strolled over and asked if I could help him.

The frown deepened. Not a good sign.

"You Aristotle Socarides?" he growled, making the question sound like an accusation.

"Yup," I said. "That's me. Have we met?"

Dumb question. It was unlikely that I'd forget meeting the man blocking the path to my front door. He was a couple inches over six feet tall. His shoulders strained the seams of a faded denim shirt.

The sleeves had been inexpertly cut off to accommodate his beefy biceps. His gut hung over mud-speckled blue jeans. His v-shaped unibrow and brush-cut hair were matching orange, as if someone had used the top of his head for a juicer.

He squinted at me with baby-blue eyes that were too small for his face. We had a squinting contest for about ten seconds. I gave him the full-on Clint Eastwood. All that was missing were the electric guitar chords, the chewed-up cigar and the echoing whistle.

I must have out-squinted him, because after ten seconds he blinked and said, "Name is Gill. I want to hire you."

Gill's rough-and-tumble looks didn't fit the profile of my usual charter fishing customers, who tend to be white-collar workers or professionals. Gill wore the knee-high black rubber boots of someone who made his living along the shore, and he gave off an odor that was a mixture of sweat, booze and low tide. Ordinarily, I wouldn't turn away a paying customer as long as his money didn't smell, but I shook my head and gave him the bad news.

"Sorry, Mr. Gill. I'm not taking anyone out fishing right now."

"Who said anything about going fishing? I want to hire a private detective. That's what you do, right?"

"That's only part of what I do when I'm not running a charter fishing boat."

The tips of his wide mouth drooped. "Maybe you're not the one I want."

Gill was starting to bore me. "Maybe I'm not," I said. "Pleasure meeting you, Mr. Gill. Have a nice day."

I stepped around his wide-beamed body and headed for the front door.

"Hey," he called after me. "Maybe we should talk anyway."

I paused with my hand on the doorknob. *What the heck*, I thought. Talking to Gill might take my mind off my own problems. I turned and pointed to the stairs that ran from the driveway onto the deck that wrapped around three sides of the converted boathouse

I call home.

"Make yourself comfortable. Be with you in a couple of minutes."

Kojak, the Maine Coon cat, greeted me as soon as I stepped inside. Kojak shares rooms with me, as Dr. Watson used to say about his friend Sherlock Holmes. He's getting on in years, moves more slowly and sleeps a lot. The one thing that hasn't failed is his appetite. He rubbed against my leg and practically knocked me over until I tossed a handful of tuna flavored Greenies into his favorite bowl—the one with the kitten face on it. While he munched on his snacks, I got a growler of Cape Cod Red beer out of the fridge, grabbed a couple of mismatched mugs from the cupboard and pushed open the screen door to the deck.

Gill was sitting on an unpainted wooden Adirondack chair that was practically invisible under his bulky body. I plunked down in the chair next to his, tilted the bottle and handed a foaming mug to him. Then I poured one for myself. Gill was gazing with half-lidded eyes at a couple of sailboats cutting twin wakes through the green jade waters of the bay. He grunted something that could have been a thank you, or simply a grunt, slurped down half his beer in a single gulp, and said, "Nice view."

I sipped from my mug, letting the cold liquid trickle down my throat, and gazed off at the narrow barrier beach that separated the bay from the Atlantic Ocean.

"It's the reason I bought this place, even though it was pretty much a wreck. It was part of an old estate and the heirs wanted to unload the old eyesore to pay inheritance taxes on the main property."

He shook his head. "Not what I expected."

"The wind used to whistle in through one wall and out the other before I plugged the leaks, but even with all the work I've put into it the house isn't exactly a McMansion."

"Talking about *you*, not the house. You're not what I expected in a private detective. I was thinking you'd be in an office and wearing a suit."

"Like I said, the detective stuff is a sideline. My day job is taking people out to catch fish. I only take cases that interest me. I don't advertise. How did you hear about me?"

"A guy named Frank Martin in the DA's office said I should talk to you."

"Assistant District Attorney Martin?"

Francis Xavier Martin was a young ADA I'd met on a murder case. Frank is covertly angling for the DA's job. We've been secret friends ever since I made his boss look bad.

"That's the one. What's this going to cost me?"

I could have told Gill that he wouldn't have to spend a nickel because I wasn't going to take his case, but I was curious why Martin had sent him my way.

So I said, "The first consultation is free. I can't tell you how much I'm going to charge until I know why you want to hire a private detective. What's going on?"

He drained the second half of the beer mug as if he were trying to douse some inner fire and wiped his mouth with the back of his hand. I filled the mug again.

"I'm an oyster farmer. Got a grant on Cape Cod Bay. I was doing pretty good until some bastards ripped off my oyster beds."

I'd heard coffee shop talk about poachers hitting some of the oyster farms that have sprouted up along the shore of the bay in recent years, but I'd had a busy summer with my charter business and didn't know the details. "Bring me up to date on what's been happening."

He nodded. "Started late spring. It wasn't just me who lost stock and gear. Buncha guys with farms got hit, but I got slammed the hardest. Twenty thousand oysters got taken in one raid. Top dollar crop ready for market, meaning I got hurt big-time. Ten grand gone in one night."

I sympathized with Gill. After I left my job as a Boston cop

I, too, became a commercial fisherman and I learned from hard experience that working on or around the water is a tough way to make a living. Oyster farmers plant seed shellfish, tend the crop and harvest it. I've never done the work, but I've talked to a few farmers and know that bad weather or the forces of nature can wipe out months of investment in both time and money. No oyster farmer should have to worry about someone coming in and stealing his crop.

"Sorry to hear that," I said, meaning every word. "When did the poaching start?"

"I got hit the first time in June. Farmers near me had losses around the same time. We took turns patrolling the flats and hid cameras to see if we could catch these weasels. Even offered a reward. Nothing. By then the poachers had moved on to other towns along the bay."

"Do the police have any leads?"

Gill sounded like a sump pump as he slurped down his beer. He plunked the empty mug down hard on the table.

"Those guys are nothing but welfare in uniform," Gill huffed. "I've gone to the town cops, the shellfish warden, the harbormaster, the natural resources officer and the environmental police. Everyone says the same thing." He gave me a humorless smile that displayed the gap between his two front teeth. "They say it's under investigation," he said, drawing out the sentence in a lazy drawl.

"With all those people chasing after the poachers, it's only a matter of days or weeks before someone drops a dime. Why spend money hiring a private cop?"

"Cuz I'm running out of time and oysters. My grant got hit again last night. They didn't take a lot of shellfish, so it wasn't a huge money loss, but they grabbed big breeding oysters that are tough to replace. Hell, I didn't even report it to the cops. Done with those dead-brained screw-offs. I went directly to the DA's office. Just another clown show. Your friend was the only one who'd talk to me."

I made a mental note to thank Frank for fobbing Gill off on me. The last thing I needed in my life was a short-tempered oyster farmer. I fetched another growler of beer from my fridge and poured our mugs full.

"Okay, Mr. Gill, let's back it up a bit. What's your first name?"

He scowled. "It's Howland. But don't call me that if you want to live. Howie will do."

"Fair enough. Same goes for me. Call me Soc."

"Deal, Soc."

"Now that's settled, I'm going to be up front, Howie. I've got other things on my plate. One of the outboards on my party boat has crapped out and the other is close to receiving last rites. I'll have some time available while I figure out how to salvage the rest of the charter season, but I can't do a full investigation."

"Not asking for one, Soc. Just need you for a few hours. I think the poachers are going to try again tonight."

"What makes you so sure of that?"

"These guys like to come in on the new moon, when it's darker than a clam's asshole. I told the cops, but now they say they don't have the manpower. Guess they're all tired out from standing around drinking coffee on road jobs."

"I get it, Howie. You don't like the boys in blue, but how can I help?"

"Your pal at the DA's office said it's not just getting a look at the poachers. I need a pro to collect evidence that will stand up in court."

"He's right. An amateur would mess things up. Okay, I'll do a stake-out. My normal fee is a hundred-fifty bucks an hour. I'll give you the fisherman's discount and knock it down to a hundred. Figure a five-hour minimum between midnight and sunrise."

Gill glowered. "That's five hundred bucks."

"I usually get a five hundred dollar retainer. I'll pass it up in this case. Pay me when the job is done. The beer is on the house."

"I don't have that kind of money, especially after the latest hit," Gill said. "But the reward's five thousand bucks. If you catch someone the money's all yours."

I raised an eyebrow. Five grand was a tidy sum.

"I'll have to check out the crime scene to make sure I can do the job."

"That's fair," he said. "When do you want to go?"

"No time like the present."

CHAPTER 2

Six Hours Earlier

When the blind poet Homer said that 'our fortunes lie on the knees of the gods,' he was probably thinking about a frisky young goddess named Tyche. If Tyche smiles, you bump into a friend who invites you to a party where you meet the love of your life. When Tyche is feeling cranky, you miss your pal by a second, spend the night alone tossing shots down in a gin mill only to kiss a tree on the drive home.

I don't know what Tyche was doing in my neighborhood. Maybe she was on Cape Cod to take in the sea air. And maybe Lady Luck, as we call her, got tired of the lobster stews and ocean views Patti Page used to croon about. But if she hadn't decided to spice up my life, I would not have driven up to my house to find Howie Gill waiting on my doorstep. I would never have met a great white shark named Emma. I wouldn't have been drawn into the love affair between a long-dead pirate and a reputed witch. Nor would I have gone into the movie business and met the most beautiful woman in the world. I might have lived what some people would consider a boring and safe existence as a charter boat captain.

Tyche and I go way back. She had let me survive a combat

stint as a Marine and gave me a promising career as a detective with the Boston Police Department. I was engaged to a beautiful and intelligent woman who was much better than I deserved. Then Tyche had a bad day and shared it with me. A kid from the Charlestown projects stole a car in what was a rite of passage for young punks. He T-boned my fiancée's mini-van and killed her. It was a chance encounter, but it sent me skittering off in search of a new life. In my grief, I looked for solace where I had found it after coming home from war. I headed for the sea.

Still in a daze after the funeral, I drove away from Boston and wound up on a deserted Cape Cod beach. I threw stones into the breaking waves and yelled myself hoarse over the crashing surf, which helped a little. I stopped at a coffee shop to warm up and that's where I met Sam. He ran a fishing boat, needed a crewman, and was desperate enough to offer me a job. I was desperate enough to take it. I quit the BPD, signed on to the *Millie D.* and learned how to catch fish.

Sam and I made a good team. We were high-liners, which meant we caught more fish than anyone else in the fleet, until years of toil in the toughest of elements caught up with Sam. After he survived a major heart episode, his doctor told him he was done fishing. Sam and his wife Mildred moved to Florida, where the most stressful part of their day was and still remains deciding where to go to enjoy the Early Bird Dinner special.

All I knew when I got up with the sun that golden September morning was that the day was full of promise. I ate a hearty breakfast, said goodbye to Kojak, and headed toward the Hyannis Marina in my 1987 GMC pickup. Shortly after eight o'clock I eased the charter boat *Thalassa II* out of its slip and pointed the bow into the Hyannis Harbor channel.

As the 36-foot-long, blue-hulled Grady-White joined the slow-moving line of traffic into Lewis Bay, I pictured Sam beside me at the wheel, his sun-toasted nose raised to the heavens like a hound's.

Yup, Sam would declare, *any fisherman worth his salt can sniff out codfish miles away*. Sam confessed after he retired that he didn't use his nose to find fish; he had simply figured out when and where they fed over decades of chasing the finny critters around the ocean. Then he used the fish finder.

Sam got a nice retirement cushion when I bought the *Millie D.* but the days of full fish holds were a thing of the past. Fish were becoming scarce and the cod fishery was circling the drain. I sold the *Millie D.* for short money and got into the party boat business. Now all I had to do to earn my pay was take folks out on the *Thalassa II*, find a school of fish, make sure the clients hooked a few, then snap photos of them and their catch for the family album.

Instead of the boots, faded jeans, work shirt and slickers that go with commercial fishing, I wear tan shorts or slacks, depending on the weather, boat shoes and a spiffy sky-blue polo shirt inscribed with a boat logo over my name: *Captain Aristotle Socarides*. I shaved off the mustache because it was going gray along with my hair. I still wear a gold earring and a shark's tooth pendant hangs from a cord around my neck, only because that's the kind of thing clients like to see on us "salty" types.

It had been a great summer. The weather was superb and the fish were so eager to jump into the boat I practically had to bat them off. Fall was looking good. Clear sunny skies were forecast for the next few weeks.

The boat had been hired by a CPA named Mike from Somerville, Massachusetts, for a reunion with three buddies who'd gone to school with him at Northeastern University. As the *Thalassa II* came abreast of the Kennedy Compound, where dreams were born and died, Mike sidled up to the helm and asked about the boat's name. I gave him the standard answer.

"It's the Greek word for the sea."

Thalassa does mean the sea, but it's more than that. The word evokes the spirit, the mysticism of the realm of gods and goddesses, the great deep, the abyss from which all things come. I told Mike to whisper the word and he'd hear the hiss of breaking waves. He gave it a try and a smile came to his face.

"Cool," Mike said. "I like it. What happened to the first *Thalassa*?"

I could have told Mike the whole story—that a Russian gangster I'd offended had his goons torch the boat, but I didn't want to make him nervous. I cut it down to the basics: "I had a fire on board."

Mike must have been satisfied with the explanation because he rejoined his classmates. We cleared the harbor and I goosed the twin 250-horsepower outboard motors. I set a southwest course toward Horseshoe Shoals, a patch of shallow water that lies south of Cape Cod between the islands of Nantucket and Martha's Vineyard.

More than a dozen boats had their lines in the water when we arrived at the shoals. I steered the boat to a reliable honey-hole I had marked on the GPS. The fish finder screen showed a thicket of silhouettes directly below the hull. I cut the engine and we drifted in the easy swells. I handed around the rods and reels. Most clients have little or no experience at fishing, but these guys knew exactly how to cast and troll without getting a fishhook caught in their thumbs. I didn't have to untangle lines, and even had time to make a few casts myself.

It only took a few minutes before someone shouted, "Fish on."

Soon, a big bluefish was flopping around on the deck. Then another. It went like that all morning. Over the next couple of hours, we hauled in dozens of blues and bonito. We kept only enough to eat; the rest went back into the water. Around noon I broke open the cooler and passed out the sandwiches that were part of the package deal.

The charter was for a half day, so we headed home after lunch. By then the classmates were re-creating the drunken memories of the night Northeastern whomped Harvard at the Beanpot hockey Tournament. Noses were getting red, only partly from the sun.

I poured coffee all around, reminded the revelers that they had to stay sober enough to drive once we reached the marina, then hauled anchor and started the motors. We made a quick trip back to the harbor entrance. As the boat passed the long breakwater that sticks out from Kalmus Beach, I cut speed in the no-wake zone. Which is when I discovered that Tyche had hitched a ride between the fishing grounds and the harbor.

The blue-black smoke coming from under the starboard motor cover smelled like a burning toxic waste dump. I put the throttle on forward idle, slid the boat into the slip and cut power. The smoke diminished but the odor still hung in the air. I hustled my passengers off the boat and laid the fish out on the dock for the mandatory post-trip photos. The party gave me a generous tip, we shook hands all around and they thanked me for a nice day. As soon as they left I removed the engine cover.

The oil on the dipstick was milky in color. Not good. I walked over to the marine repair shop and talked to a mechanic named Len who said he'd take a look at it. Len came over and checked the oil, clucked like a mother hen, took a closer look at the motor and clucked again.

"Sorry to ruin your day. You've got a cracked engine block."

"I don't know how that could be, Len. I make sure the motor is maintained."

"Not a question of maintenance. Block's been that way for a while. Someone filled in the crack. Take a look here." He ran his finger down the side of the block to show where the seam had been caulked. "Let's check out the other motor." It took only seconds to find another patched block. "This one is still holding, but it'll blow with some hard use."

"Damn," I said. "Guy who sold me the boat and motors didn't say anything about the patches."

"Maybe he forgot."

"Yeah. Right. Maybe I should give him a call."

I found the bill of sale tucked in with the boat registration. The number I called was out of service. I told Len. He sighed. "You got any warranty on those outboards?"

"The warranty expired this spring. What are my options?"

None of the choices he offered made me jump for joy. It was like picking out my casket from a line-up of coffin models. New motors were out of the question, so I would have to look for refurbished ones or buy reconditioned blocks and rebuild the motors. All options were expensive. All except for new motors would take time. And I would end the *Thalassa*'s charter season with a big fat repair bill. I told Len I would have to think about it. He said he was sorry to be the bearer of bad news.

Len had a better bedside manner than many of the doctors I've met, but there was no sugar-coating the diagnosis. I went back to the boat, hosed down the deck and stowed the fishing rods in the cabin. After piling some personal items into a canvas bag, I got into my truck, headed out of Hyannis and drove east on Route 6, the Mid-Cape Highway. There was no way to minimize it. This was an unexpected disaster.

I had borrowed family money to go into the charter fishing business. I would have preferred a bank loan, but I had already borrowed against my house to buy Sam's boat and sold it at a loss when the fishery went down the drain. Like the bank robber Willie Sutton said, "You go where the money is." Working hundred-hour weeks, the Socarides family had built a mom-and-pop pizza and sub joint into a frozen pizza and sub empire. The business is run by my younger brother George. Sister Chloe does the marketing.

My dad retired after dementia set in and spends his days quietly in a rest home room decorated with photos of his hometown of Athens. George voted against the loan and my younger sister Chloe was in favor. My mother is nearly ninety years old, but she still calls the shots. Her vote in favor of the loan was the tie-breaker. It was her idea to name the boat *Thalassa* as part of the deal. If I reneged on the loan, my mother would lose face. George would make a power play for the company, and Chloe would fight him with every ounce of stubbornness in her body. A family mess, in other words.

There's another reason I was worried about being beholden to the family. To put it kindly, my mother is a benevolent loan shark. She won't knock my teeth out or leave me senseless in an alley. She will call in the chits, the obligations that I should be carrying out as the eldest son in a Greek-American family. It would come as a softball. 'Aristotle,' my mother would say, 'I have a favor to ask of you.' The words strike cold fear in my heart. For years, I never carried a cell phone. I've got one now, a Flintstones model flip-phone, because of the business, but every time it rings I worry that it's my mother needing my help with the family.

I was still stewing about my bad luck when I turned onto my driveway and saw Howie Gill waiting to offer me a job chasing oyster thieves. Tyche was a fickle god, but until she brought Gill into my life, I didn't know she was also infused with a sense of humor.

CHAPTER 3

Jouncing over the potholes in my clamshell driveway behind a truck that looked like something out of the *Dukes of Hazzard* jarred my brain back to reality. By the time we reached the end of the road, I had decided I needed this job the way an undertaker needs a *Life Is Good* T-shirt. I felt sorry for Gill, but that didn't mean I liked him. He would never win a personality contest. He smelled bad. And I had problems of my own. I decided to blow him off with a quick tap dance. First I'd check out the crime scene. Then I'd scratch my head, admit that the job was too big for me to take on and suggest that he let the cops do their thing. Then I'd tappity-tap my way off stage-right.

Less than a half hour after leaving my place, we turned onto Old King's Highway, the road that runs along the curving shoreline of Cape Cod Bay, passed through a quiet village of antique houses, and followed a narrow road past a cemetery whose occupants would have had a great view of the velvety marsh—if they had been able to see it. The paved road ended a short distance beyond the lichen-covered gravestones, changing to hard-packed dirt flanked by dense thickets of stunted oak and scrub pine.

After a mile or so, the road popped out of the woods into the open. Gill stopped his truck and I pulled the Jimmy alongside. He poked his head out the window. "Does your pickup have 4-wheel drive?" he said.

"It's barely got two-wheel drive."

He waved me over. "Hop in. Track gets sandy, so only off-road vehicles are allowed from here."

I parked the Jimmy and got into Gill's truck. We followed the track for about fifty yards and popped out behind a grassy ridge of dunes. He steered the truck off the sand road through an opening in the dunes, then across a sloping stretch of beach and onto the flats.

At low tide the water level in the bay drops as if someone has pulled a plug, leaving flats that stretch out almost two miles from shore. The currents had sculpted rippling furrows into the mud that were cast into sparkling relief by the slanting rays of the sun. The striated expanse was broken here and there by shallow streams and sparkling pools of tidal water. The flats smelled just like Gill.

He drove across the mud to the edge of an oval-shaped tidal lagoon measuring around two hundred feet across. Clusters of rectangular dark objects were lined up in parallel rows in and around the pool, extending to the east and west, and north on the bay side. A couple of pickup trucks were parked on the flats next to the lagoon. Some men were mucking around on the mud near the edge of the shallows.

Gill parked the truck. We got out and walked across the mud to the nearest of a dozen rows of black plastic trays, each about a yard square, that were stacked on legs made of white PVC piping. Each platform held three perforated trays full of oysters.

"Here's my oyster farm," Gill said with a sweep of his arm. "I've got about an acre under cultivation. The trays get the full tidal wash. Seawater goes in and out and the oysters get happy and grow."

Other stacks of black trays were clustered in and around the lagoon. "This is a busy patch of farmland, Howie."

"Right about that. We're looking at about twenty grants. Each farmer works one grant, except for a couple of guys who've got two operations going."

"Where does the stuff go after it's harvested?"

"Local restaurants and markets for the most part. Some stock goes to Boston. Harvesting is done in phases. A crop takes two years to mature. You buy seed shellfish and separate them by size into three batches: zero to six months, six months to one year, and harvest at two years. Once a batch gets to the three-inch market size, you harvest it to make room for another batch. Not rocket science."

"Who else got hit by the poachers?"

"Everyone. The creeps also grabbed some contaminated shellfish from a town-owned grant."

Towns sometimes allowed shellfish to be planted in off-limits' areas where the tide can flush away the toxins. The contaminated shellfish added a new dimension to the case. The oysters could end up in a fish market or on a plate in a restaurant. People who ate contaminated shellfish could become very sick, or maybe even fatally ill.

"That's serious," I said.

He gave me his bifurcated grin. "Poachers don't follow the safety regulations. With legal produce, you chill the oysters as soon as they're off the beds. Got ten hours to get them down to fifty degrees. Every detail gets reported to the state."

"Any idea how the thieves came in?" I asked.

Gill shook his head. "That's the big mystery, Soc. Coming in the way we did, through the village, they might have been seen. They could have landed a boat at the edge of the flats and walked in, but they'd have to lug the stolen goods over the sand. That would be risky, too."

"You say *they*."

"Whoever hit my farm took a lot of stock. The stuff's heavy. They stole trays, too. So they'd need muscle to haul it away. Probably had lookouts on shore, too."

I spun slowly around on one heel, imprinting an image of the crime scene on my brain.

The blue line marking the edge of the bay to the north was at least a quarter mile from the farms. The water is inches deep where it meets the flats. A shallow draft boat could come close, but Gill was right. The stolen stock would have to be transported the distance to the water. I turned to face the land. A truck could drive in along the beach to the east or the west.

"Any public access to the beach?" I said.

"Not for miles. Truck would have had to drive by shorefront houses to get here. Risky again."

"Everything okay, Howie?"

While I was casing the scene, one of the oyster men who'd been visible from the dunes had walked over to Gill's farm. He was tall, maybe a couple of inches above my six-foot-one, and in his late fifties or early sixties. He had a long horsey face. His jaw was decorated with a neatly trimmed white goatee that looked even whiter against his tanned skin. The hair tucked under the wide-brimmed tan Tilley hat was worn long over the ears.

"I got hit again last night," Gill said with a shrug of his shoulders.

"Sorry to hear that," the man said. "I haven't seen any police poking around."

"You're not going to see any. I didn't report it this time. I'm through with the law. What about you? Lose anything?"

"No one touched my stock since spring" he said with a slight touch of a prep school accent. "So far, that is." He slipped a work glove off and extended his hand.

"My name is Guy Rich," he said, giving me a toothy smile.

"Nice to meet you, Guy," I said.

His palm was surprisingly smooth for a working man. His jeans and tan work shirt were spotless. Except for a few mud splatters on his boots, nothing suggested he'd been messing around in the shellfish beds. He removed his aviator sunglasses and his razor-sharp blue eyes glanced at the front of my shirt. Pointing to the logo that had my name on it, he said, "Are you Aristotle Socarides?"

"That's me. I usually tell people to call me by my nickname. Soc."

He nodded. "You're in the charter fishing business, Soc?"

"That's right. I run a boat out of Hyannis Harbor."

"Your boat has an interesting name, *Thalassa*. The sea."

"You sound like you know Greek."

"I've picked up a few languages here and there in my travels. Is that how you know Howie, through fishing?"

I glanced at Gill and saw him give a slight wag of his head.

"Actually, I'm an oyster aficionado. I tasted his oysters at a restaurant and tracked him down. He was nice enough to give me a tour of the farm. They're the best I've ever had. The delicate flavor is amazing."

"We're fortunate to grow our stock in this section of the bay," Rich said. "The combination of conditions is just right for producing the best. Come over and give my oysters a try next time you're in the neighborhood. Sorry you got hit again last night, Howie. Let me know if you need any seed."

I watched him slosh back across the flats.

"Did I give him the right answer?" I said.

"Yeh. I don't want it to get around that I hired a private detective."

"Understandable. Guy said he got hit this past spring."

"Early in the season he lost a pile of market oysters, but he's not hurting like some of us. He made major bucks in real estate before he retired to a big house on the shore not far from here. He was looking for something to do and got two grants. The other farmers call him Rich Guy, but he's been generous sharing stock. He even put up the reward you're gonna get when you catch these bastards."

The reward Gill kept waving under my nose seemed like a sketchy proposition. The crime scene covered a lot of ground and water. I could see why the police might have a hard time catching the poachers in the act. The investigation needed dozens of lawmen to keep an eye on dozens of oyster farms, not just a part-time shamus trying to pay for outboard motor repairs. It was time to give Gill the bad news.

"This case might not be so easy to handle," I said. "There's a lot of territory to stake out."

He made an unpleasant throaty sound that didn't match his smile. He opened the door to his truck, reached under the driver's seat and pulled out a 9mm Glock semi-automatic. "You herd the bastards my way and I'll take care of them."

"That's not the way it happens, Howie."

"I got a permit to carry. You worried you might have to split the reward?"

"Naw. I'm worried about someone out here shooting at shadows. One of them might be me. You want me to take this case, I do it *my* way. On my own. I don't want you anywhere near here."

Gill gave it a thought, then said, "Okay. We'll do it your way."

He put the pistol back where he found it. I took one last look around and said I had seen enough. On the ride back to my truck I realized that either Gill was very smart or I'd been very dumb, because one thing was undeniable. My big, fat, Greek mouth had talked me *into* the case, not out of it.

CHAPTER 4

Gill dropped me off at the parking area and I said I'd call him in the morning. After he left, I trudged back to the dunes and plunked belly-down in a hollow the wind had carved out in the sand. I wanted to imprint the scene in my head while it was still daylight. I watched Guy Rich unloading plastic trays onto the flats for a couple of minutes, then I got to my feet and picked up a yard-long piece of driftwood, sticking it upright into the sand to use as a marker.

When I got home a short time later, I called Len, the doleful mechanic. I told him to go ahead with the outboard motor repairs using reconditioned blocks. I said I'd drop off five hundred dollars the next morning as a down payment. I'd call my family in the morning, ask for a loan extension from the Parthenon Pizza treasury to pay for the full repairs and argue that I was simply protecting their original investment. George would do his annoying 'I-told-you-so' bit, but if I could sway my mother, sister Chloe would come along.

Next, I called the District Attorney's office.

"I'd like to speak to Frank Martin," I said. The receptionist asked who was calling and I replied, "My name is Peter Ho*nay*."

Martin came on the line seconds later. "Hello Mr. Pho*nay*. When did you become a Frenchman?"

"I thought P. Honay had more class than P. Hony."

"Too cute for words. What ever happened to Fred Raud?"

"I tossed F. Raud in the discard pile with S. Purious and B. Ogus."

"Spurious and Bogus. Your cleverness is making my head explode."

"I wouldn't want your exploding head to mess up the district attorney's lair. The next time I call I'll use my real name."

"Not a good idea, Monsieur Honay." He cleared his throat. "I suppose you're calling to thank me for sending a client your way."

"Thanks isn't the word I had in mind. Gill showed up at my house and said everyone's been jerking him around except for his new best friend Assistant District Attorney Francis Xavier Martin, who told him to hire a private detective. Me."

"Guy's been driving everyone crazy. Town cops. Staties. He's been a real pain in the ass. He smells bad, too. I almost passed out when he was in my office."

"So naturally, you sent the bad-smelling pain in the ass to see me."

"Consider it a compliment, Soc. You were the only one I could think of who could defuse a nutcase like that. Did you, um…take the job?"

"Before I answer that, I'll ask you a question. Did you know the nutcase is packing a Glock?"

"No. Crap. *Oh shit*. How do you know?"

"He shoved it under my nose. Says he has a permit. I was afraid he'd shoot himself or someone else if I didn't calm him down. I said I'd stake out the oyster farm for one night. He thinks the farm is due for another hit."

"Yeah, he told me the same thing. It had to do with the moon."

"He may be onto something. The moon will be in its dark phase. It'll be pitch black. Prime conditions for poaching."

"I dunno. Doesn't make sense that the poachers would hit the same farm time after time, though. What's your plan?"

"I'll sit in the dark until the mosquitoes and no-see-ums drain me of my life's blood. Then I'll go home. If I see or hear something suspicious while I'm out there, I'll call the police."

"Where will Gill be in the grand scheme?"

"At home taking a bubble bath, I hope. I told him to get lost or the deal's off. Tell me this, Marty. Is he right about the cops giving him the run-around?"

"That's how he sees it. The situation is more complicated," Martin said. "There were a half dozen thefts in different towns over several months.

Which means we're dealing with separate jurisdictions. On top of that, you've got state and local environmental police, and street crimes units involved, too."

"I'm surprised the five thousand dollar reward hasn't shaken some fruit off the informant tree."

"It'll happen, but even if the cops hook onto a lead, you're not going to see an immediate arrest."

"Why not, if they've got the evidence?"

"Again, mainly because of the territorial question. The grand jury will consider charges after we nail someone. The indictment will go directly into the hands of the superior court. That avoids the jurisdictional conflict."

"Has anyone checked on where the oysters might go when they leave the flats? We're talking perishable goods. The poachers have to dump their loot somewhere before it starts smelling worse than Gill."

"We're looking into possible buyers. The goods may be moving off-Cape. Even out of state. It would take no time to load the stolen shellfish on a truck and drive directly to New York. The stuff could be in markets or on restaurant tables the day after a heist."

"That's a scary thought, Frank. Some of the stolen shellfish was contaminated. Which leaves open the chance that someone could be served industrial waste with his order of Oysters Rockefeller."

"We've been in contact with the health departments in Boston and New York. We've asked them to tell us about any problems involving bad shellfish."

"Let's hope it doesn't get to the stomach pump level. Or worse."

"Jeez. Thinking about something like that happening gives me the shivers. I really appreciate you doing this, Soc. Gill could mess up the whole investigation. I owe you."

"Yes you do. As a start, maybe you can put in a good word with your boss so I can use my real name when I call the DA's office."

"Ha, ha. Better buy a new dictionary. Mr. District Attorney would fire my ass if he knew I was talking to you."

"Suit yourself. The next time I call I'll use the name I. M. Faiken."

I hung up on his groan and rummaged in a closet for the brown leather satchel I bought for two bucks at a Methodist church thrift shop. I opened the bag on the kitchen table and laid out night vision goggles and a halogen flashlight. I made sure the batteries were in working order. Then I put everything in a canvas rucksack along with a can of deep woods strength bug spray. Snacks and water would go in later.

Kojak is a great pal, but our conversations tend to be one-sided. The closest thing to human company was the clientele bellying up to the bar at the 'Hole, a local purveyor of spirits and hangovers. If my deal with Gill had been a normal case, I would have stayed dry. I expected there would be nothing demanding about the job. I'd done dozens of stake-outs, and after years as a fisherman I was used to working when most people are tucked in their beds.

The Red Sox were playing the Yankees that night. Over a burger and beer, I watched the bar's TV with satisfaction as the Sox whipped the Evil Empire. I was about to head home when someone tapped me on the shoulder. I turned and saw the olive-skinned face of a lobster fisherman named Tommy Avellar.

"Hi Tommy," I said. "How's the big bug business?"

"Can't complain. Catches have been holding up, and the weather's been good. What about you?"

"It was a great season until today. An outboard on my charter boat crapped out and the other motor is about to do the same. But maybe I'll get back on the water in a few days."

"Well, good luck with that. Just stay away from Cape Cod Bay."

"I fish Nantucket Sound. What's with the Bay?"

"Didn't you hear? Guy was killed by a great white shark in the bay, near Great Island."

"I was in a 7-11 and saw the headline in *The Cape Cod Times*, but that's all I know. I guess it was bound to happen with all the shark activity we've been seeing, but I figured an attack would come at an Atlantic side beach. Anyone we know?"

"Naw. It was a guy running a boat for on the crew that's filming a pirate movie. They showed up a few weeks ago. They've got a casting office for pirate extras at the Wequassett Inn near where you live. Surprised you haven't heard."

"I've been busy with the charters out of Hyannis Harbor. I fish, sleep and fish some more, so I haven't caught up on local news."

"Too bad," he said with a grin. "You'd make a great-looking pirate if you grew your mustache back."

I gave Avellar an *argh*, said goodnight to him and my fellow barflies, and went home. I set the alarm for two o'clock in the morning, crawled into bed and fell asleep dreaming sweet dreams of Red Sox home runs soaring over the left field wall known as the Green Monster.

Four hours later I was pouring dark coffee into a thermos which I then packed in the rucksack with bottles of water, a bag of Cape Cod potato chips and a couple of protein bars. The snacks would carry me through to dawn's early light. Next, I put a low-slung beach chair into the back of the truck.

I was wearing jeans, a wool sweater and windbreaker, and had my faded Red Sox cap plunked down on my head. Even though it was still summer, a fall coolness had crept into the night air. I tucked my cell phone in my rucksack, gave Kojak a snack and told him I'd be home in time for breakfast.

The roads were practically deserted. Less than a half hour after leaving my house I arrived at the parking area near the oyster farms. I pulled my truck into a set of sand tracks that led off from the parking area, grabbed my rucksack and hiked out to the dunes.

The flashlight beam picked out the driftwood marker I'd planted in the sand. I climbed through an opening between two grassy hillocks. Slipping the beach chair off my shoulder, I set it in the hollow I had chosen as my spy perch. I settled onto the chair, gazed at the wall of darkness and inhaled the rank smell of dead sea plants and marine life. Next, I slipped the night vision goggles on my head for a test. The change from inky darkness to a glowing green almost blew out my retinas. The shoreline was bathed in a Land of Oz luminosity.

I removed the goggles from my head, set them on my lap and waited for the tide to go out. I figured I would hear any unusual activity over the hum of mosquitoes looking for a patch of skin unprotected by Deet. About an hour after I'd set up shop, I washed down a handful of potato chips with water, stood up to stretch and put the goggles on. The expanse of rippling mudflats was expanding with the approach of low tide. I started checking the scene through my night vision goggles every fifteen minutes. I had just about decided that I was wasting my time when I saw a flicker of movement off to the left. My heartbeat ratcheted up a couple of notches. A truck was moving along the beach. Near the lagoon, it veered out onto the flats and headed toward the oyster farms. There was no sound of an engine.

The truck stopped near Gill's oyster trays. Two people got out and began loading oyster trays into the back of the truck. They worked fast.

I went to pull the phone from my rucksack to call the police, but I hesitated, thinking the poachers would be gone by the time the law arrived. Instead, I slung the bag onto my shoulders got out of my chair and started toward the flats, hoping to get close enough to pick out the license plate on the truck.

I figured that the total blackness of the night insulated me from unfriendly eyes. Turned out, I was dead wrong about that. Two poachers stepped out from behind the truck. The glow from their night vision goggles made them look like aliens from another planet. But there was nothing other-worldly about the muzzle flashes that lit up the flats like strobe lights. Or the stutter of automatic weapons. Or the splat of mud around ten feet in front of me.

I was a sitting duck in the open expanse. The next burst would find its mark. I spun around and bolted toward the beach, zigzagging to throw off the shooters' aim. The mud was as slick as butter. The zig was fine, but the zag was a disaster. On one change of direction my foot slipped out from under me. I landed on my left hip. Cursed. Another burst of gunfire. Rounds shredded the air above my head. I scrambled to my feet. The beach was only yards away. Bending low, I limped across the sand, dove behind the dune, then crawled back and peered through the grass at the flats.

The poachers were back in the truck and the vehicle was moving fast back the way it had come. I still couldn't hear the motor, although it might have been drowned out by the noise I made expelling air from my lungs.

I wiped the mud and sand off my knees and elbows, gathered up my beach chair and rucksack, and headed away from the flats. My botched stake-out wasn't a total failure, however. I had partially answered the question of the poachers' methods. Somehow, they had made their way undetected along the beach. As I trekked along the sand road I soon discovered that there must have been more than one team. The second had been keeping watch from shore.

The first hint of my miscalculation was a noxious smell in the air. The second was a flickering yellow glow above the trees. I began to run. As I neared the woods where I'd parked the truck, I got the strongest sign of all. The Jimmy had erupted into flames.

CHAPTER 5

Where my 1987 GMC pickup had been, a greasy plume of orange and red soared hundreds of feet into the air. By the time the tank truck lumbered out of the access road with lights flashing, my pickup was fully enveloped.

The firefighters jumped out; as they uncoiled the hose, another fire truck arrived. A third vehicle from the neighboring town came in as back-up. The pump trucks were going to need every drop of water in their tanks. The burning pickup was throwing off sparks like a July 4th sparkler and the fiery shower was landing in the woods. Tendrils of fire licked at the underbrush.

The fire crews quickly swung into action and poured hundreds of gallons of water on and around the truck. Once the firefighters tamped down the flames, a glowing silhouette of the truck's cab could be seen through the choking clouds of billowing smoke.

A cruiser pulled up to where I was standing, my shoulders hunched like a mourner at a wake. A police officer got out, and said, "That your vehicle, sir?"

"Yeah. That is, it *was* my vehicle."

"Any idea what happened?"

"Only that the truck was on fire when I got here."

Pause. He eye-balled me from head to toe. My jacket and

jeans were caked with mud. I had more mud on my hands. I had a backpack hanging from my shoulders. I was holding a folded beach chair. It was in the wee hours of the morning. I could practically hear the gears of suspicion grinding in his head.

"Where did you come from, sir?" Less friendly now.

"I walked over from the beach."

Another pause. More gears spinning. He would have known that poachers had been hitting the oyster farms, so the next question was no surprise.

"Are you an oyster farmer, sir?"

"Nope."

He squinted at me, then at the fire, and back to me.

"If you're not an oysterman, what were you doing in this area at this time of night?"

I noticed that he had stopped calling me 'sir.' His right hand went to the side of his belt that had the holster on it. Not exactly the signs of a developing friendship.

"Long story," I said.

"Maybe you'd like to tell me about it at the station house. First, I want you to remove your backpack, drop it on the ground, and step away from it. Slowly."

Actually, I didn't want to tell him about it at the station house. I wanted to go home. But I had no other means of transportation. I accepted his offer, even though I rode in the backseat with the doors locked. On the ride from the beach I filled the police officer in on who I was and what I was doing there. He must have believed me because instead of a cell I ended up in a nondescript room furnished with a couple of chairs and a table. I was placed in the hands of a sergeant named Nolan. He had wide shoulders and his dark hair was shaved close to the sides of his head, military style. He reeked of after-shave.

While I washed the mud off my hands and face, the police officer conferred with Nolan, then left me in the hands of the sergeant, who said, "You say you're a private investigator?"

"That's right. As I told the other officer, I'm a retired Boston homicide detective. My day job is being a charter boat captain, but I take a case now and then to keep my hand in. Howie Gill hired me to keep an eye on his oyster farm."

At the mention of Howie's name he gave a little jerk of his head and his eyes narrowed. "I'm acquainted with Mr. Gill," he said.

"Then you know he's very upset about his stolen oysters."

He smirked. "I've heard something to that effect. The officer you came in with said you mentioned a shooting."

"I was staked out in the dunes, watching the flats through night vision goggles. I saw the poachers' truck arrive. They drove along the beach and onto the flats. Two guys got out and ripped into Gill's oyster trays."

"Do you have a cell phone?"

"It was in my backpack."

"Why didn't you call the police?"

"I planned to give you a ring, but the thieves worked faster than I expected. I was afraid they'd leave before back-up arrived. I moved in for a closer look. I wasn't the only one wearing night vision goggles. The poachers started shooting. Automatics! I was too busy dodging bullets to make a call."

"Automatics? That fits in with some of the noise complaints we got. People said it sounded like a popcorn cooker. Crap! These guys have been hit-and-run up till now. Shooting doesn't fit with their MO."

"All I can tell you is that the bullets were real. I would have called you after I got off the beach, but I was distracted. When I tried to get to my truck, I discovered that it had been torched. I had a gas tank for an outboard motor in the back of the truck. Someone could have used the gas to start the fire."

"Are you saying the shooters had confederates on shore?"

"That's how it looks to me. The fire could have been used as a distraction or to send me a message."

"No sign of anyone?"

"Nothing."

He furrowed his brow. "We've assumed that the poaching was the work of a couple of guys at the most. You're talking about a sophisticated operation, using some heavy muscle."

"Seems that way. That's for the cops to figure out. All I know is that someone owes me a replacement for my pickup truck."

Nolan leaned back in his chair and folded his arms across his chest. From the worried look on his face, I guessed that it had occurred to him that big time crime had come to his quiet little tourist town. He let out a low whistle and popped the lid on his laptop.

"Okay. I've got to prepare an incident report."

I knew the drill because I had been on the other side of the table many times. Starting with my name and address, I went on from there, describing the sequence of events right up until the police officer started asking me questions at the truck fire.

After about an hour, Nolan said, "Thanks. I'll get investigators out to the crime scene to check it out."

"They may want to bring their scuba gear," I said, pointing to the wall clock. "Tide's coming in."

"Hell," he said. "We'll check out the beach and woods near the flats. You got someone who can give you a ride home?"

It only took a second to decide who I should wake up from a sound sleep. I smiled, asked to borrow a phone and punched out the number. There was a pause before a groggy male voice came on the line and said hello.

"Hi Frank," I said. "Sorry to interrupt your beauty sleep."

"Christ! Do you know what time it is, Soc?"

"Yep. It's time to crawl out of your warm bed, get in your car, and give me a ride home from the police station."

"Aw, crap. Did you get nailed for DUI?"

"Sorry to disappoint you; I'm not drunk. But you might want to be after I tell you what happened with the job you sent my way. I got shot at and someone set my truck on fire."

"Holy Mother of God!"

"I'll fill you in on the details when you pick me up."

"I'll be there in thirty minutes, Soc."

Martin actually made it in twenty-five. He must have jumped from his bed, into his jeans and sweatshirt, and broken the speed limit. He bustled into the interrogation room just as Nolan and I were winding up our dissection of Red Sox pitching and who we'd hire to improve it. I thanked the sergeant for his time, and coffee, gave him my home phone number, and strolled with Martin out into the gray light of the pre-dawn.

We got into Martin's SUV, and on the drive home I told him about the shoot-out on the oyster flats. Whenever I paused for a breath, he'd say, "Holy shit."

"Yeah, there was a lot of that—up to my chin, in fact—but none of it was holy," I said as we bumped down my driveway and stopped at the boathouse.

He leaned on the steering wheel and stared off at the yellow disk of the sun starting to rise over the barrier beach.

"This is huge," he said. "These aren't a bunch of small-time guys. We're dealing with an organization that's carrying heavy weaponry. The fact that they were willing to kill someone indicates a higher level of criminal than we thought we were dealing with."

"Frank, I can't tell you how happy I am to know that the guys shooting at me were not low-class criminals, but unless it has slipped your mind, the *someone* they wanted to kill happened to be me."

"Of course. Glad you're not hurt. But this is a big deal. If I can break this case, I'll have the street cred to take on my boss in the next election."

"*Street cred*? You've been watching too much cop TV."

"Hell, you know what I mean. The tougher the crooks, the tougher I look. I don't know how to thank you, Soc."

Martin was sounding far too giddy over my near-death experience and the positive effect it would have on his career track.

"I can suggest one way to pay me back. Find out who burned my truck."

"That's a given, Soc. Sorry about that. Insurance should take care of it. I'll keep you posted."

"You do that." I opened the door to get out. "Thanks for the ride."

"You're welcome." Martin came down momentarily from his dreams of moving into the DA's office. "What are you going to do now?"

I rubbed my eyes and opened my mouth in a major yawn.

"The only thing I *can* do at this point. I'm going to get out of my muddy clothes. Then I'm going to crawl into bed."

CHAPTER 6

In late summer, the prevailing southwest breeze shifts more to the east and when that happens, it floods my bedroom with the salty scent of the mighty Atlantic. There is no better way to wake up. But not today. My nostrils wrinkled at an unpleasant smell. My eyelids snapped up like window shades. A jack o' lantern face peered at me through the screen. Which presented a couple of problems: It was not Halloween, and the pumpkin was actually talking to me.

"Hey Soc," Gill said. "You awake?"

"I am now," I croaked. "What are you doing here?"

"I heard about the crap that went down on the flats last night. Came over to see how you're doing."

I closed my eyes and opened them again. It wasn't a bad dream. Gill's face was still framed in the window.

"Why are you peeking in my bedroom window?"

"There was no answer when I knocked on the front door so I started poking around."

"Of course. Go around to the deck," I said. "I'll be out in a minute."

I yanked the shade down. Then I rolled out of bed, pulled on work-out pants and a sweatshirt, and went into the kitchen. The hands on the wall clock were both almost vertical. Noon. Kojak was giving me the bad eye. I poured a double order of munchies into his dish to make up for his late breakfast, brewed a pot of coffee and filled two mugs. I went out onto the deck and handed a mug to Gill, who started to say something. I shushed him until a couple of sips started my transition back to humanity.

"Now we can talk," I said. "How'd you hear about last night?"

"Cops called to tell me that the poachers hit my farm again." He flashed me a smug grin. "Looks like you could have used my friend Mr. Glock."

"You call your gun *Mr.*?"

"It's a sign of respect. Like they say, nothing beats a bad guy with a gun like a little ol' good guy with a gun."

I drummed my fingers on the chair armrest, then turned to Gill. "Let me explain a few things, Howie. There was more than one bad guy with a gun out there, and they were wearing night vision goggles. They were also using machine guns. The bad guys would have filled your little ol' good guy with little ol' holes."

"Maybe," he said, but he didn't seem to mean it.

"No maybe about it. You and your friend Mr. Glock would have been out of your league. *I* was out of my league. The only difference is, I admit it. Looking on the bright side, they were too busy shooting at me to do much damage to your farm."

"Thanks for keeping watch, Soc. Sorry about the bastards wrecking your truck."

"So am I. It was a bucket of bolts but it got me around."

He grunted. "Speaking of money, Soc. About that five hundred bucks I was going to pay you."

"I messed up, so you're off the hook for the dough."

"That's damned decent of you. What are you going to do now?"

"Try to find myself some cheap wheels. In the meantime, I'd suggest that you play ball with the cops and the DA's office and let them do their jobs."

"Maybe you're right," he said, minus his earlier bluster.

"I'm right, Howie. I'll let you know if I hear anything."

"Okay. Thanks for the coffee." He reached down next to his chair for a plastic bag, which he handed to me. "Maybe this will make you feel better. Consider it partial payment."

"What is it?"

He gave me his gap-toothed grin.

"Oysters."

After Gill left, I put the oysters in the refrigerator, took a shower and got dressed for the day. Then I made an Egg McMykonos—fried egg on an English muffin with sliced tomato, sprinkled with feta cheese and oregano. I carried breakfast out onto the deck. Kojak always knows when I'm down. He followed me, jumped onto my lap and emitted the creaking door sound that passes for his purr.

After a few munches, I said, "Okay, pal, let me lay out our options. My boat is out of commission. My truck is a pile of ashes. So this is what will have to happen. I'll call the insurance company and maybe get a loaner. I'll tell Len to put the motor repairs on hold. Then I'll call my family and grovel to George." I thought about it. "Instead of that last thing, I'll sharpen up a stick and poke it in my eye. Got a better idea?"

Kojak isn't one for words. He yawned and stared off across the bay at a flock of gulls wheeling over a point of land that sticks out into the bay around a half mile from the boathouse. Years ago, someone built an inn out on the point. Now it's the location of a sprawling resort with a swimming pool, high-end restaurant, and water view bars. On quiet summer evenings, when the wind is right, jazz music glides across the water. I followed Kojak's gaze and a cartoon lightbulb went on over my head.

"Dammit Kojak! You're a genius."

I carried him into the house and gave him some special treats that were the feline equivalent of junk food. Then I went down to the dock where I keep a wooden skiff with a 25-horsepower Evinrude outboard. Sometimes I'll take the skiff out onto the bay and throw a fishing line over the side. I rarely catch anything, but it's a great way to relax. I got into the skiff, started the motor, cast off the line and headed for the point.

Ten minutes later I tied up at the resort dock behind the boat that takes guests to the outer beach, and climbed the stairs to a terrace. A chambermaid was walking by with a load of towels. Before I had the chance to ask where the movie people were, she smiled and said, "Go up to the pavilion."

I climbed another set of stairs. Coming my way were two young guys who both had scruffy beards and long hair. One pointed back the way they'd come. I must have stumbled on to a convention of psychics. Everyone seemed to know where I was supposed to go except me.

At the top of the stairs, under a big open structure that served as a permanent tent, were dozens of round tables covered with white tablecloths. A woman sat at one table, bent over paperwork. She wore a black baseball hat that had a skull and crossbones decorating the brim.

I went over and said hello.

She looked up and immediately shook her head. "Sorry, but we've filled the last two openings for pirates," she said.

I jerked my thumb over my right shoulder. "I passed Blackbeard and Captain Kidd on the way in."

She nodded. "They were the last extras we hired. There was no shortage of applicants. I guess everyone wants to be Johnny Depp. I can put you on a waitlist."

"Thanks, but I'm not here to apply for a pirate role."

She cocked her head and gave me a sunny smile, showing perfect white teeth.

"My name is Cait Lassiter. I'm the casting director. If you're not here looking to be a pirate extra, what can I do for you?"

I gave her a business card for my charter business.

"We already have a boat," she said after reading the card.

"I know. I'm looking for a job running it."

The smile faded and she gave me a hard stare.

"Sit down and fill out an application, if you don't mind, Mr. Socarides. Then we'll chat."

I pulled up a chair and she handed me a form. While she organized her paperwork, I filled in the spaces for address and phone number.

"I'm a retired Boston cop. Do you need that on the form?"

"Not necessary. We're only interested in your boating experience."

I completed filling out the rest of the form and, as an afterthought, mentioned that I had done commercial diving jobs.

Cait scanned the application form, then looked up at me. "Why are you interested in this job if you're running a charter boat?"

"Good question. My charter fishing business went on temporary hold this week after one outboard motor blew a gasket and the other went on life support." I pointed to the boathouse. "That's where I live. I was sitting on my deck, trying to figure out how to pay for the repairs, when Kojak looked in this direction."

"Kojak? Like the old TV series with Telly Savalas?"

"Yes. Kojak is my cat."

"Your cat?"

"Yes."

"*Okaaay*," she said, drawing the word out. "Go on."

"When he did that, I remembered that a friend told me you might be looking for a boat captain."

"That's right. Unfortunately, our boat captain died unexpectedly."

"I heard. I may be able to help you." I pointed to the application. "As you can see, I've worked on commercial and charter fishing boats. I've got a captain's license. And I know the local waters."

She parted her lips, and a thoughtful expression came to her hazel eyes.

"Hold on," she said. She picked her cell phone off the table and made a call.

"I'm about done here, Max," she said. "We've got a full pirate crew. But I've got someone here you might like to talk to. He's a boat captain. He's a diver, too. Yes. Okay."

She hung up, and said, "That was our director. He'd like to talk to you."

"Sure. Any time would be fine."

"Great. He's on location. Let's go for a ride."

She gathered up her things and walked out to the parking lot where she'd left her sky blue two-seater Mini Cooper convertible.

"Nice car," I said.

"When I tried it on for size it fit me perfectly," she said.

Cait was joking about her height. She was about five feet tall. She wore baggy tan shorts and a shapeless tie-dye T-shirt. The round face under the visor of the baseball cap had freckled cheeks, a turned-up nose and a perfect mouth that seemed to be set in a permanent smile.

We got in the Mini and headed off the resort. On the ride to the set, she told me how she'd ended up as the movie's casting director. She was a California girl, born in Irvine, and went a couple of years to the University of California before she got bored and left school to look for a job in movies. She lived in a house in Studio City with five young people who were breaking into film, and worked as a short-order cook in between low-end movie work. This was her first job as Casting Director. She was in her forties and hoped it would be her big break.

"What's the name of the movie?" I asked.

Cait removed the skull and crossbones cap, revealing a sunburst of short, reddish-blonde hair. She handed the cap to me so I could see the words printed in white on the back of the crown:

THE PIRATE'S DAUGHTER.

I returned the cap and she plunked it on her head.

"Intriguing title," I said. "Makes me want to know more about the story."

"I'll give it to you in Hollywood-speak. In Tinseltown, everyone talks in comparisons. You pitch a project by comparing it to big hits, like saying a screenplay is a combination of *Gone with the Wind* and *Casablanca*."

"What's the pitch on your pirate project?"

"Our director calls it a combo of *Romeo and Juliet*, *The Scarlet Letter* and *Captain Blood*. It's a tale of unrequited love, witchcraft and swashbuckler extraordinaire."

"I'd buy a ticket to see something like that, but I'm having a hard time picturing it."

"Don't worry," she said, "Max will tell you all about it. And *more*."

CHAPTER 7

Cait was a brisk driver, and she didn't have to contend with the slow-moving traffic that clogs the roads in the summer. She wheeled the Mini along Route 6, the highway that follows the curving arm of the outer Cape.

Less than half an hour after leaving the resort, she turned off Route 6 at an earth-brown National Park Service sign that informed us we were entering the Cape Cod National Seashore Marconi Area. At a fork in the road, she veered to the left. After we'd gone less than a mile, she pulled to the side of the road at the end of a line of vehicles that included a couple of panel trucks, a passenger van and a pickup. She parked behind a white SUV that had the words "Park Ranger" printed in green letters on the door.

We got out of the Mini and walked across the road to where a park ranger stood in front of a split-rail fence with a handful of people. Just beyond the fence, a sandy path meandered a couple of hundred yards through sparse, ground-hugging vegetation to the cliffs that overlooked the Atlantic Ocean.

The ranger was a slightly-built young woman wearing a tan uniform and broad-brimmed Smokey the Bear hat. She must have known Cait, because she smiled and gestured toward a green-roofed pop-up canopy set up near the cliffs.

"Good timing," the ranger said. "Just chatting with these folks who wondered what's going on. Your gang's been here a while getting ready."

Cait glanced past the ranger. "And from the looks of things, they're about to start shooting."

Cait told me to follow her, then led the way around the fence and we walked along the path until we neared the canopy. She stuck her arm out in a signal to stop, then put her finger to her lips and pointed at a cameraman. He stood next to his camera, which was on a tripod, lens aimed at a figure in a hooded red cloak who stood at the top of a bluff, facing the ocean. I deduced, from the full beige skirt whipping in the breeze that the figure was a woman. A breeze tossed the folds of the cloak, which she pulled close to her body. Then, without warning, she whirled around and started running.

The cameraman panned the camera, keeping the lens pointed at the cloaked woman as she made her way along the edge of the cliffs.

A man wearing a lurid Hawaiian shirt and baggy cargo shorts came out from under the canopy, cupped his hands to his mouth and yelled, "Cut!"

The cloaked woman stopped and turned around to wave. The man returned her wave, then ducked back under the canopy. The woman made her way toward the film crew. A few yards from where I stood, she threw her hood back onto her shoulders. My heart skipped a beat. Let me correct that. My heart danced and gamboled like a drunken faun. Okay, I'm exaggerating, but only a little bit. I had seen that face before, but at the time it was thirty feet high and projected onto the movie screen. I was still working with the Boston PD. My fiancée had dragged me to a multiplex to see a World War I romance starring Ana Roman. She played a Belgian farm girl searching for her loved one, a French soldier who'd been wounded in the trenches. My fiancée was head-turning pretty, but as I gazed at the soulful eyes and lush mouth up on the big screen, I had thought, without guilt, that Ana Roman must be the most beautiful woman in the world.

She was one of those talented actors, like Meryl Streep, who could move with ease from one role to another. Ana made a pile of movies, and I saw most of them before she started fading from the Hollywood scene. I heard she was going through some hard times. But by then I was drowning in my own sea of troubles.

Now here she was, years later, at the top of a high dune overlooking the Atlantic, standing so close I could touch her. The flaxen-haired Belgian girl who had trekked through the war-torn Belgian countryside trying to find her lover was now middle-aged. Gray strands were woven into platinum hair that was pulled back and tied in a knot. Her cheeks were slightly fuller than I remembered, and she had smile wrinkles at the corners of her extraordinary green eyes. But her skin was creamy and unblemished. In a nutshell, she was still the most beautiful woman I had ever seen.

"Hi Cait," she said. She flicked a curious glance in my direction. "I see you've recruited yet another pirate to the cast." Her slightly-accented voice had always been cool and low, but the years had given it a husky sultriness.

"The pirate crew is full up, Ana. Mr. Socarides has applied for the job running our boat."

I wouldn't have noticed Ana's smile weaken slightly if I hadn't been staring at her perfect mouth.

"Nice to meet you, Mr. Socarides. My name is Ana Roman."

We shook hands. "Nice to meet you too, Ms. Roman. I've seen practically every movie you've ever made."

She arched a brow and continued holding my hand in her warm grip.

"I'm very pleased to hear that, Mr. Socarides. But if you're joining our crew, please get used to calling me Ana."

"Only if you call me Soc. It's easier on the ear and the tongue."

"I understand completely, Soc. Have you met Max yet?"

"That's why we're here," Cait said. "Max asked me to bring Soc onto the set so he could talk to him."

"If you'll allow me, I'll make the introductions," Ana said.

She gave my hand a quick clench before letting go, then took me by the arm. The man in the wild shirt had come out from under the canopy and was talking to the camera operator. He gave Ana a beaming smile.

"We've reviewed the scene, Ana. It's perfect. Great job as usual."

"Thank you. The hardest part was trying not to get lifted in the air like Mary Poppins when the wind got under my skirt. This is Mr. Socarides, the man who's applying for the boat job. Soc, this is Max Corman, our brilliant director."

We shook hands. Corman had a strong grip. He was about six feet tall and had the wide shoulders and the thick arms and legs of a weightlifter. Judging from the puffiness of his face, though, the heaviest things he'd been lifting lately were cheeseburgers and pizzas. With his plump round cheekbones, a puckerish mouth, and the wreath of curly brown hair and beard that framed his features, he looked like a young Santa Claus.

"Thanks for coming to the set, Mr. Socarides. Hope I didn't mess up your schedule."

"My schedule is already messed up. My charter fishing boat is down for repairs. I'm looking around for work until it's back in the water."

"He's got all the necessary licenses and permits," Cait said.

She handed Corman my job application. He gave it a quick scan, then said, "This is incredible timing. I've had to put off the water shoots until we had someone to handle the boat. Wow! You're a diver, too."

"Please excuse me," Ana said. "While you two get to know each other, I'd like to slip out of the 18th century garb. God, I don't know how women wore all this stuff!" She took her cloak off, shimmied out of the skirt and pulled the cotton blouse over her head. She was wearing a blue bathing suit underneath and she looked good in it.

Ana handed the clothes to a woman I assumed was her assistant because she folded the costume and placed it into a wardrobe suitcase.

"See you back at the Big House," Corman said.

She pecked him on the cheek. "Bye, Cait. Nice meeting you, Soc. Perhaps I'll see you later."

Then Ana and her assistant started off on the path that led to the road. A husky guy who was one of the crew grabbed the wardrobe suitcase and trailed after them. Cait excused herself to help the film crew pack its gear.

Corman turned back to me. "Tell me, Soc. How did you know we needed a boat handler? We haven't officially advertised the job opening."

"A friend told me what happened to your last boat guy. Hope you don't think I'm a ghoul for applying."

"Hell, no! We really need someone for the boat." Max shook his head. "I still can't believe Kirk's lousy luck. Eaten by a freaking shark."

"I haven't heard the whole story."

"It's pretty sad. Kirk had a substance abuse problem. He got stoned one night, took the boat out to go fishing and fell overboard. The next morning I discovered that the boat and Mike were missing. I called the Coast Guard. They found it adrift not far from where the shark got Kirk. It's the boat you'll be using. Hope you're not superstitious about stuff like that."

"I come from a Mediterranean background, so of course I'm superstitious. On the other hand, I don't mean to tempt fate by going for a nighttime swim in shark-infested waters."

"Very relieved to hear that. Did Cait fill you in on our project?"

"She said the name of the movie is, *The Pirate's Daughter*."

"Correct. *The Pirate's Daughter* is a historical romance, but it's also a tale of adventure, witchcraft and revenge." He took off his round-framed blue sunglasses. "You said you were a little superstitious. Does that extend to a belief in ghosts?"

"I liked Casper when I was a kid. I've never met a ghost in person, but I've learned to keep an open mind no matter how weird things get."

"I'm glad to hear you've got an open mind. Because if you sign on to this project, you'll need it. Let's go for a stroll in Satan's Meadow."

CHAPTER 8

Max threw his arm around my shoulders and herded me toward the road, talking non-stop about what a great actress Ana Roman was. Which wasn't exactly news to me. If Max had even a slightly more kinetic energy, he'd be jumping out of his own skin. He didn't take a breath until we got into one of the vehicles lined up on the side of the road. He drove the red GMC pickup around a quarter of a mile to the site of the station where Guglielmo Marconi tapped out the first trans-Atlantic wireless message ever sent from the U.S. winging across the big pond to England. The message was from Teddy Roosevelt to the king of England. Most people don't remember what it said, or even care, but the transmission went down in the history books.

Erosion has chewed away at the cliffs where the station and its four tall transmission towers used to be. The National Park Service has set up plaques to commemorate the historic site. A few tourists strolled around taking photos. I followed Max up a ramp to a circular observation platform built on a low hill. From the platform, there's a spectacular view to the east of the Atlantic Ocean stretching out to the horizon. The great outer beach curves north and south as far as the eye can see. The upland gradually slopes down from forty-foot cliffs, a couple of hundred yards across

60

heathlands covered with vegetation called poverty grass, because it grows in only the most impoverished soil, to a stunted forest of pitch pine and oak.

We were the only ones on the platform, which was probably just as well, because Max stepped to the center and spun slowly around, sweeping his arm in the air like the needle of a compass.

"Welcome to the set of *The Pirate's Daughter*," he said.

"I'm new to the movie business, so maybe this is a dumb question, but didn't we just come from the set?

He stopped rotating and dropped his arm to his side.

"Sorry about the confusion. *That* scene was shot on only a small part of the set. Have a seat and I'll explain." We plunked down on the bench that goes around the inside perimeter of the platform. "What do you know about Samuel Bellamy?" he said.

"You'd have to have washed up on shore five minutes ago not to know about Captain Sam Bellamy." I pointed toward the ocean. "His pirate ship, *Whydah*, went down a few hundred yards from where we're sitting."

Max gazed off at the sea and nodded his head. "So you know what an amazing story it is."

"I've read a couple of books. There's a *Whydah* pirate museum not far from here that I've been meaning to visit."

"I've been there. They do a pretty good job laying out the story. Bellamy arrives on Cape Cod in 1716. Hoping to make his fortune, he buys a sloop and sails to the Caribbean to salvage sunken Spanish treasure galleons. When that plan fizzles, he turns to piracy. He's a natural at capturing ships. He becomes so successful he needs a bigger ship. He captures the merchant slaver *Whydah*, and it becomes the flagship of his three-ship fleet. He is the richest pirate in the Caribbean by March of the following year when his fleet sails north. In April, he encounters a fierce storm off Cape Cod and his ship breaks up on the shoals out there."

"So Bellamy is the pirate in the film's title?"

"One and the same. There's a lot of contemporary documentation on Bellamy's exploits. But this story actually starts after his death."

"And the daughter?"

"The facts are sketchy. For the purposes of this story she existed, if only as a figment of my imagination."

"The Bellamy saga is already pretty powerful. Why add a figment when the real life characters were so compelling?"

"I didn't want this to be another *Pirates of the Caribbean* with guys in puffy-sleeved shirts swinging down from the rigging."

"I liked *Pirates of the Caribbean.*"

"Me too," he said. "In fact, it's the kind of movie I was *going* to make."

"What made you change your mind?"

"Not what. *She.* Mary Hallett changed my mind. Mary was Bellamy's young lover. According to the legend, they met when he was looking for a ship to buy. Nature took its course, and she was pregnant when he left on his treasure hunt. The lore says he promised to return once he had made his fortune, and that's what brought him back to these parts. By then, Mary had delivered his baby. I've called the kid Mehitabel, which was a common name back then."

"I'll take a wild guess. Mehitabel *is* the pirate's daughter."

"Right. The story picks up after Sam has left the scene. With him gone, Mary is in a pickle.

The townspeople know the baby's father is a bad dude, so she must be the spawn of the devil. They drive Mary and the girl into exile and mother and daughter end up out here in the lonely moors where they live in a crude hut. The locals avoid the place, which becomes known as Goody Hallett's Meadow. Some legends say Mary practiced witchcraft and that's how this area got even more sinister names, like Lucifer's Land and Satan's Meadow." He leaned forward and lowered his voice. "You're going to think I'm crazy, Soc."

"Why would I think that?"

"Because when I stood here for the first time, I could feel Goody's presence. As if she wanted her story told. Scenes started flashing in my mind."

"Maybe Goody cast a witchy spell on you, Max."

Max chuckled, and his voice returned to normal. "You know, I've thought the same thing, believe me. Sometimes she comes to me in my dreams. I see her roaming across the moors. Standing at the edge of the cliffs in her scarlet cloak, watching for the return of her lover."

"Ana Roman. The woman in scarlet."

"Yes, Ana Roman plays Goody Hallett, the Witch of Eastham or the Witch of the Red Heels. Some say her real name was Maria Hallett, although that's a Catholic name and that would be unlikely in Protestant Massachusetts. I'm sticking with Mary or Goody."

"Where did Goody come from? Seems like an odd name for a witch."

"Yeah, that's crazy. Goody was short for "goodwife," a term commonly used back in colonial times. The whole story is filled with contradictions. And there are different versions of the tale. In one legend, the child lives. In another, it dies during birth. Some say it was a boy. One legend says Mary went mad when she saw the ship go down, and her wailing ghost still wanders the moors waiting for Sam to return as promised. In another narrative, she sold her soul to the devil in exchange for witchy powers she uses to raise the storm that drowns the lover who abandoned her."

"None of those sound like Hollywood endings."

"It's like they say on the TV infomercials: 'But wait, that's not all!' There's a more romantic telling of the story, too. She keeps watch for her lover, Sam, only to see his ship sink. In that version Bellamy survives, retrieves his treasure, and reunites with Mary."

"What if the narrator is Max Corman? What version did *you* go with?"

"I patched together elements from all the stories. I liked the one where the girl baby lives."

"I do, too. What happens to Mary and Mehitabel?"

"Not saying. You'll have to wait and see the movie." He grinned like a mischievous kid. "Just kidding. I'll give you a copy of the treatment when you come to the house tonight for cocktails. We're having an informal party."

"Does that mean I've got the job?"

"If you want it. This is a low-budget film, but we try to pay a good wage. How about a hundred-fifty bucks an hour?"

"How many hours do you figure?"

"Maybe twenty? Maybe more. We'll probably need you for a week. Some days will be short, others long. I may add in scenes that aren't in the screenplay right now."

I did a quick mental calculation. "How about two-hundred an hour? I'll throw in my services as a diver if needed."

"That would be a godsend. Your underwater skills could come in handy."

"It's a deal, except for one thing. My truck is out of commission. I'm going to need wheels."

"No problem. You can use Kirk's truck. Take it home with you now. We'll talk again at the Big House, where the crew is bunking out. Cait can show you how to get there."

"I'm looking forward to the party, and working with you," I said.

"Wonderful! You can't imagine how exciting this is for me as a director. This is the culmination of a very long film project. Most of the village scenes were shot in Canada. We hired a talented actress and a kid to play the younger Goody and her daughter. They're looking for a big break, so they worked for cheap. We used a stage set to portray the village and villagers, but I wanted to film the final scenes where it all happened. We lucked out. This place could have been all house lots, but there was an army base here and later the feds acquired it for the National Seashore."

"Maybe that was Mary's doing, too," I suggested.

"Hey, you may be right. The area still has a haunted feel to it. Sometimes when the fog rolls in you think you see things in the shadows."

I happened to look inland toward the woods and saw a dark figure in the trees. Thinking it was a tall bush, I turned to Max and joked: "Is that one of your *things* hiding in the woods?"

He looked to where I was pointing, "I don't see anything except for the trees," he said.

He was right. The shadow had disappeared.

"It must have been my imagination," I said, although I wasn't sure. Bushes don't usually move from one place to another.

"Like I said, this place can get creepy. Probably a bird watcher."

"Maybe," I said.

We left the observation platform and Max drove back to where the crew was loading a utility van. He got out, handed over the truck keys and said he'd see me at the party. He went over to talk to the crew.

Cait came over. "Did you get the job?"

"I've been invited to the cocktail party and got the use of Kirk's pickup, so it looks like I'm joining the crew, thanks to you.'"

"Good. I guess."

"You guess? Is there something I missed?"

"I'm really happy you're on board, but sometimes the whole production seems like *Macbeth*."

"The bad luck play?"

"That's the one. We've had equipment failures and injuries since we started filming."

"You're filming outdoors on location. You're moving equipment around. There are bound to be accidents."

"How many film productions do you know of where one of the crew was eaten by a shark?"

"None that I can remember. Looking on the bright side, how

many film productions are lucky enough to have Ana Roman?"

Cait grinned. "Guess you're right. She's something, isn't she?"

"Yes, she is. Where has she been all this time? Haven't heard about her in years."

"Not surprising. Even the tabloids got sick of rehashing her story."

"Which is?"

"She got sucked down by her husband-director who was addicted to drugs. He made a mess of her investments. Then he died, leaving her to hold the bag. She lost a fortune paying off his debts. Her career slid to a halt, and she was stained by his reputation. She was addicted, as well: prescription painkillers. Thankfully, she kicked the habit. Did some smaller roles, but mostly she's survived by doing voiceovers for television commercials. She's hoping *The Pirate's Daughter* will get her back into the biz."

"Is this the movie that will do it?"

"I think it could be. A lot depends on Jason Kingman, who you'll meet tonight. Jason is the male lead opposite Ana. Just a warning; he's a bit eccentric."

"I know that name. Wasn't Kingman in some big films years ago?"

"*Very* big. He's kinda like James Caan or Robert Duvall. Great actors who never made it to the super-duper star level."

I dug deep into my movie memory. "I remember a western where he played a rancher who took on Quantrill's Raiders

"That was *The Defiant*. Nominated for an Oscar. It should have won, but they gave the Oscar for best film to some screwball comedy."

"How come? I thought *The Defiant* was brilliant."

"The judges said it was too derivative. That it was a rip-off of *Shane*. The real reason, in my opinion? The Academy wasn't ready to award an Oscar to a film that dark, with a hero and villain who were ambiguous. Also, the movie didn't have an ending that had everyone living happily ever after."

"How'd Kingman end up working in *The Pirate's Daughter*?"

"Same way as Ana. Career took a nosedive after the Oscar fiasco. He made a series of bad script choices, played in one turkey after another, and earned the reputation as an unreliable has-been. He never found a script that could revive his career."

"Until now?"

"We'll see. He wouldn't be the first older actor to make a come-back. Working with Ana Roman could give him the juice to make a big splash."

"Speaking of a splash, could you tell me about the guy who had this job before me? I'll understand if you don't want to talk about a friend."

She made a face. "Don't worry about getting me upset, Soc. Kirk Munson didn't *have* any friends. He was known on the set as 'Kirk the Jerk.' He was rude, arrogant and nasty. Mostly because of booze and drugs, but he was just as mean when he was sober. He antagonized everyone on the crew at one time or another."

"If Munson was such a pain, why did Max keep him on?"

"You're not the first to ask. I simply don't know the answer."

A few minutes later, I was in the new pickup, leading the way to the boathouse so Cait would know where I lived. I left the truck and she gave me a ride back to the resort to fetch my boat. As I putt-putted across the bay to my place, I was practically giddy at the turn in my fortunes. I had a job and might be able to pay for the motor repairs and get back into the charter business. I had wheels to get me around. Best of all, I wouldn't have to grovel to my family.

I felt bad that someone had to die for the job to open up, but from what Max had said, Kirk Munson was a train wreck in the making. If it hadn't been a shark it would have been something else. As far as the bad luck Cait had mentioned, I had nothing to worry about as long as I stayed away from great whites. Unfortunately, as I was about be reminded, sharks come in all shapes, colors and sizes. And that the two-legged variety is the deadliest.

CHAPTER 9

After retrieving my boat and running it back across the bay I got into the GMC again and drove to the oyster flats. News of the fire must have been making the rounds of the coffee shop circuit because when I pulled off the King's Highway into the little village near the bay, I ran into a traffic jam.

A line of vehicles was being turned away from the access road by a police officer who stood near the cemetery. He waved me through after I told him I was the owner of the burned-out truck.

Sitting in the center of a big circle of grass and bushes that had been burned to gray ash, the old pickup looked like a crashed UFO. Water run-off from the fire hoses had turned the road nearest the truck to mud. The heat from the morning sun had baked boot prints and tire ruts into the hardened brown muck. The oily stench of burned rubber poisoned the air.

Some people had walked in from the village. They were banging selfie photos into their cell phones with the pickup as the backdrop. I parked the GMC, got out, and stood apart from the crowd, trying to reconstruct the crime scene. I guessed that a look-out had been posted on shore to warn the poachers of anyone approaching over land. They would have been in contact with walkie-talkies. The crew on the mud flats saw me and alerted the look-out, who decided to give my pick-up a hotfoot. The watcher or watchers may have been tucked into the woods when I drove in. I even gave them the means for arson, the newly-filled outboard fuel tank for the skiff I have tied up at the boathouse.

As I pondered the likely scenario, a police SUV came off the access road and pulled up beside me. The driver rolled the window down. Sergeant Nolan, who had interrogated me at the police station, stared at the people taking photos of the burned-out pickup.

"Bad news travels fast," he said, eyeing the crowd.

"Andy Warhol said that everyone gets fifteen minutes of fame, but I didn't know that applied to old trucks."

"Apparently it does." He shook his head. "Someone give you a ride here?"

I pointed to the GMC. "I drove over in my new wheels."

He took off his aviator sunglasses and glanced at the truck. "The insurance company gave you a nice loaner."

"It's on loan, but not from the insurance company. The pickup goes with my new job, working for the film crew that's shooting a movie around the Cape."

"I heard about that. Didn't one of their guys get killed by a shark?"

"That's the rumor. His death created a sudden vacancy and I applied for the job."

"Unlucky for him. Lucky for you. Didn't know you had experience in the movie business."

"I've got lots of movie experience, but it's mostly watching the big screen while munching popcorn. They need someone to help with water transportation. It's temporary, but it'll earn a few bucks while *Thalassa* is down with engine repairs."

He slipped the sunglasses back over his eyes. "That's your charter boat, isn't it?"

"Yup. Thirty-six-foot Grady-White. She's real sweet. Let me know if you'd like to go out fishing."

His mouth turned down at the tips. "Hold on. I thought the *Thalassa* burned to the waterline in Hyannis harbor."

"That was the *Thalassa I*. The new boat is the *Thalassa II*. Can I ask you a question?"

"Sure."

"I don't keep my boat in this town. How'd you know about the fire?"

He chuckled. "You must have been a sharp interrogator in your cop days."

"Easy catch. The *Thalassa I* fire happened more than a year ago. That makes me wonder who's been spreading old news."

"It was kinda accidental. I was talking to a state cop about this fire and mentioned your name. A short while later I got a phone call. Someone you'd pissed off suggested that our department contact the Hyannis fire inspector."

"I've pissed off a lot of people, but the name at the top of the list belongs to our esteemed district attorney."

Nolan's 'Smurfy' smile told me I'd hit the mark.

"How did the DA find out so fast?" I said.

"The Staties have close ties to the DA. They told him that you got shot at and your truck burned up."

"Prepare to be pushed to the sidelines, Officer Nolan. The DA smells blood. He'll move in on this case and hog credit for work others have done. That's his standard MO."

"Yeah, that figures. He wants my department to keep quiet about the shooting. Says this is no longer just about poaching and that it should be handled at the county rather than the town level."

"Bingo! That will put him center stage and give him an opening to tie me into the investigation."

"Looks that way. What did you do to tick him off?"

"I made him look bad on a couple of high-profile murder cases. He almost lost his re-election. The county political machine saved his butt. Talk to ADA Frank Martin and he'll fill you in on

71

the sordid story."

"I already talked to him. He said you're a wise-ass but not an arsonist."

"Frank is too kind. Before the DA screws this up, maybe you can find out who shot at me and torched my truck."

"All I can tell you is that we'll do our best. We checked out the scene this morning, but the tide had come in over the oyster flats. We'll comb the area when the tide gets low again. Maybe the fire inspector will catch a lead when he checks out your truck."

"Thanks, Sergeant. I'm going to look around, if that's okay."

"Sure. You know the drill. Let us know if you find something that may help."

"I'll call you if I find a body in the kelp. Unless the body is me."

He laughed. "Good luck with your new job."

Nolan put the SUV into gear and did a U-turn back onto the access road. I took one more look at the happy crowd enjoying my misfortune and set off on foot along the sand road toward the oyster flats. As I rounded a curve, I saw a shiny black Dodge RAM pickup truck parked on the beach. I recognized the fancy four-by-four that belonged to Guy Rich, the wealthy oyster farmer the other oystermen had nicknamed 'Rich Guy.'

Rich was leaning against the front fender with his back to the hood, peering out toward the bay through binoculars from under the floppy brim of his Tilley hat. I squinted off at where he was looking and saw specks wheeling in the air. Water birds are the fishermen's sentinels. They feed on small bait fish that get chased to the surface by bigger fish.

"Looks like the gulls are working a school of blues," I said.

He lowered the binoculars and jerked his head around at the sound of my voice. He must not have liked being sneaked up on because he gave me a hard stare that lasted a couple of seconds before he spread his lips in his horsey smile.

"You're about the last person I expected to see out here," he said.

"I heard the scuttlebutt about the craziness last night. Unbelievable! Are you okay?"

"I'm fine, thanks. Wish I could say the same for my truck."

"Saw it on the way in. I hope they get the bastards who did that to you." He cocked his head. "I guess rough stuff must go with your investigating job from time to time."

"Who told you I was an investigator?"

"Gill was out here checking his losses and fessed up that he'd hired you to watch his farm. You sure had me fooled with the oyster aficionado impersonation."

"That was easy because it's true." I pointed toward the waterline. "You're a little ahead of low tide."

"Yeah, I know, but I'm anxious to see if there's any loss to my farm."

"From what I saw before the lead started flying, no one was near your grant. Gill was the main target."

"Guess I'm not surprised the poachers would hit him again."

"Why do you say that?"

"Someone must have heard him say he grows the best oysters in the world."

"*Does* he grow the best?"

Rich snorted. "Every farm out here enjoys the benefits of the same tides and the nutrients that flow in from the bay, which means oysters are all premium quality. The only difference is, Gill gets top dollar from the local restaurants."

"How does he do that if there's no difference?"

"He's very effective at marketing his shellfish. He has convinced people that he invented oyster farming. He's created Cap'n Howie, this crusty, salty Cape Cod oysterman who knows the secret method to growing fine oysters."

"You must admit Cap'n Howie *is* crusty and salty."

Rich's lips tightened in a lopsided smile. "There's more than meets the eye when it comes to Gill. Let me ask you something. What would you estimate to be the level of Gill's academic achievement?"

"I think he's probably smarter than a tree stump, but he's no phi beta kappa."

"On the contrary, he *is* phi beta kappa. He holds a doctorate in anthropology from Harvard."

I chortled. "That's hard to believe."

"I had the same incredulous reaction when I heard about his credentials from the security department of my old company."

"Why would your old company snoop into Gill's background?"

"Because I asked. I'm officially retired, but I'm still on the board, so I've got an in with the department that vets new hires. I asked them to investigate Gill after he used a quote from Friedrich Nietzsche that didn't quite fit with his persona as a know-nothing oyster farmer. I was right. His loutish mannerisms, the crude way he speaks—nothing but affectations."

"He had me fooled. He deserves an Oscar."

"Oh, it gets even more interesting. The company investigators turned up another secret Gill is hardly poor. In fact, he's sitting on substantial wealth." He swiveled his body around to face land. "Look at that shoreline and tell me what you see."

"I see a pretty stretch of woods and beach."

"Accurate, as far as it goes. What you can't see is twenty acres of upland bordering the bay. The land alone is worth millions. Even more with houses. And Gill owns every square inch of it."

"I understand the dumb oyster farmer act, if it helps him sell oysters, but why keep his land holdings under wraps?"

"You're probably not aware that my fellow oyster farmers switched my first and last names. To them, I'm Rich Guy."

"I wasn't aware of that," I lied.

"It doesn't bother me. I know that my wealth sets me apart. They think I'm a dilettante, an amateur who has no need to make a living off my oyster farm. But unlike Gill, I'm up front about my wealth. And having money enabled me to post the big reward for the poachers. I believe Gill keeps his holdings a secret for another reason."

"Which is?"

"I think he's been hitting his own farms to cover his tracks. He really wants to drive us all from the flats, so he has to poach his own farm to avoid suspicion."

"Why would he want to wipe everyone out?"

"The first thing that comes to mind is the elimination of competition. It also would increase the value of his land. Buyers aren't going to build a five million dollar house so they can look out their big picture windows at a bunch of trucks and oyster pickers."

"Have you run your theories by the cops?"

"No. I need more evidence. You're the detective, Soc, what do you think?"

"Interesting theory. But why would he hire me to witness one of his poaching operations?"

"What better way to divert suspicion from himself?"

"That would suggest that the poachers came in even though they knew I'd be watching. But from what I saw, the poachers were surprised when I moved in, which is why they may have panicked and started shooting."

"Maybe they were simply cocky, thinking they would get away with it without you noticing."

"So Gill hired me because he thought I couldn't do the job?"

"Sorry. I didn't mean to suggest—"

"Don't worry about it. Maybe Gill was right in thinking I was incompetent. The poachers snuck in right under my nose. I would never have seen them if I hadn't been wearing night vision goggles. I should have called the cops right away, but I didn't know at first that the poachers had night vision, too."

"Thank the Lord you weren't hurt. What do you plan to do next?"

"Haven't given it much thought. I'll keep my eyes and ears open."

"I'd give our uncouth friend a wide berth if I were you. If not, I'd advise you to be very careful in your dealings with *Doctor* Gill." He opened the door to his truck, and said, "Nice chatting with you. We'll have to talk again."

"Let's do that. In the meantime, thanks for filling me in about Gill."

"My pleasure. You seem like a decent person. Hate to see anything happen to you."

"You're not the only one! By the way, what was Gill's quote from Nietzsche?"

He paused in thought, then said, "It's the one about the dangers of looking into the abyss."

He got behind the wheel, started the engine, and drove closer to the water's edge. I stared off across the bay. I had come across the quote while I was studying philosophy at Boston University. Later, the words had come to me in combat when I saw and smelled the effects of napalm on human flesh. Old Freddie N. warned those who fight monsters to take care not to become monsters themselves. Gaze long enough into the abyss, he said, and one thing is certain....

The abyss will always gaze back at you.

CHAPTER 10

On the drive home I made a detour to Town Hall and looked at the property maps in the assessors' office. Gill's name was on a big piece of undeveloped property overlooking the oyster farms. Rich wasn't kidding when he said Gill was sitting on a potential fortune in real estate I brooded over how easily Gill had fooled a smart detective like me. I was still stewing about being played the fool when I walked into the boathouse. Kojak ambushed me with a body slam that jarred me out of my blue funk. He'd shed a few pounds in old age, but Maine Coon cats are as big as the raccoons they're supposedly descended from. I gave him a handful of dry munchies. Then I went out on the deck, flopped into a chair, and stared through half-lidded eyes at the low-lying islands and the distant barrier beach.

The peaceful view calmed my mind and I went back over my conversation with Rich. He had nailed Gill with the info on the land-holdings, which meant what he said about the doctorate might also be true. On the other hand, Gill wasn't the only one pretending to be something he wasn't. Rich wore an eighty-dollar Tilley hat and drove a super-duty RAM pickup. He was playing at oyster farming. Conclusion? Rich was a phony, too.

I glanced at my Swatch. Cait was due come by in fifteen minutes to show me how to get to the Big House. She had said that the party was informal. I'd been hired as a boat skipper and decided I should look the part. I got into my charter boat captain's uniform, tan slacks and blue polo shirt. I tried on a jaunty white admiral's cap I had won at a dockside beer drinking promo. It was loaded with gold braid. Printed on the crown were the words: Keep Calm and Drink Beer. I agreed with the sentiment, but I wanted to project confidence that would justify getting paid two bills an hour. I decided to go bare-headed.

I heard the turbo-charged grumble of a Mini Cooper engine and opened the door for Cait. She had traded her shapeless shorts and faded T-shirt for a jade green, ankle-length, tribal pattern dress with a round collar that showed off her good shoulders.

"Nice," I said. "Green goes with your eyes."

"Thanks. And you look very nautical." She pointed to the logo on my shirt. "What's a *Thalassa*?"

I gave her the condensed explanation and it seemed to satisfy her curiosity. She whispered the word. "You're right. It does sound like the sea. I like it. Ready to go?"

I saluted. "Shipshape and Bristol fashion," I said.

"What's that mean?"

"It means everything is *finestkind*, as my former partner would say."

"I like that too." Her grin got impossibly wide. "You're going to fit in just *finestkind* with this crazy crew."

She got in the Mini, and I followed her out the driveway in the pickup.

Less than fifteen minutes later, she turned off onto a series of back roads that led to a residential neighborhood filled with grand old summer houses. She drove between two square cobblestone pillars, up a long ascending gravel road, and parked in a circular driveway behind the production truck and other vehicles I had seen earlier at the beach. I pulled in behind the Mini and Cait greeted me with a sweep of her arm as I stepped out of the truck.

"Welcome to the Big House, command central for *The Pirate's Daughter* cast and crew," Cait said.

Monster mega-mansions have gobbled up prime shorefront property over the last couple of decades, but this house had an understated architecture, which suggested that it was built back in the day when ostentation was seen as bad taste and seaside mansions were called "cottages" by their owners. The outside was covered in cedar shingles weathered to a velvety silver-gray and the house was trimmed in white. A tower at one end was probably supposed to suggest a lighthouse. The gabled roof was gambrel-style.

"Nice shack," I said. "It looks like it's been around for a while."

"They say it was built in the 1920s by a rum-runner named Louie Mancino. He supposedly ran his rum empire from the house, but he was never caught. The police would surround the place, but when they closed in, Louie would be gone. He was nicknamed, 'the ghost.' "

"That fits. Place looks kinda haunted," I said.

"Maybe. Some of the cast say they've heard weird noises. They think it's Louie, but the current owner is our executive producer, a Wall Street guy who's the main investor in the film. He built a new trophy house at another location for his new trophy wife, so he's letting us use his old place as living quarters for the film crew and a base for production."

We followed a brick walkway around to the back of the house which faced out onto a lawn that looked as if had been clipped with manicure scissors. A porch ran the full length of the house. The lawn flowed to the edge of a bluff, overlooking a great marsh laced with creeks and inlets.

Cait led the way toward a gazebo that floated like an antique boat on a sea of grass so bright green it hurt the eyes. The silvered shingles and white trim on the gazebo matched the house exterior.

People were gathered around the gazebo. Max must have seen us arrive, because he stepped away from the crowd, gave a wave, and strode in our direction.

"This is where you and I part company for a little while," Cait said. "Max wants to do the intros. I'll be around if you need me."

Max came over, gave Cait a quick hug and even quicker kisses on both cheeks, then he pumped my hand. "Thanks for coming, Soc. The crew has been eager to meet you."

With Cait trailing behind, Max led me to the group of people outside the gazebo. I thought back to the Western movie saloon scene where the hero pushes his way through the swinging doors, the bar goes silent, poker play freezes, and all eyes turn toward the stranger. In my case, however, the stares were curious rather than hostile. Ana Roman was standing with the others; she gave me a smile and a wave.

"Gather round folks," Max called out like a carnival barker. "This is the gentleman I've been telling you about. Captain Socarides will be running our boat. He's had lots of experience working in these waters. As you know, we've had some setbacks in our schedule, but with his help, we'll soon get the last of this movie in the can." He turned to me. "Soc, these are the people who are going to make *The Pirate's Daughter* sizzle on the big screen."

Ana came over and stood next to Max. "I couldn't agree more," she said in a ringing stage voice. "As you know, I've been in movies a long time—longer than I'd like to admit." She paused to let the laughter flow. "And I can truthfully say that, while this production crew is small in number, it includes some of the most talented men and women I've ever worked with."

There was applause from the crowd.

A tall, lean man stepped out of the crowd and ambled over to Ana. He walked as if he were bucking a stiff breeze, and I made a wild guess that the drink in his hand wasn't his first. He held the glass high in the air like a boozy version of the Statue of Liberty and started talking in a deep, resonant voice.

"I've probably been around the movie biz longer than Ana, and I wholeheartedly agree with what she just said."

I expected him to slur his words but his diction was crisp and clear.

More applause. Max was beaming. He clamped me on the shoulder.

"I've asked Ana to make the introductions while I tend to some business. After you meet everyone, come over to the Big House. I'll have a treatment for you that will give you an idea of what we're doing."

While Max headed back across the lawn, Ana introduced me to a dozen and a half members of the film crew. Most were young, in their twenties and thirties. They were eager and polite and seemed happy to see me. I worked my way through the introductions in a few minutes. The last person in line was the tall man with the drink. He squeezed my hand in a lobster grip and his gaze took in my gold earring and the shark's tooth pendant.

"You have the air of someone who has sailed under the Jolly Roger," he said, narrowing his eyes.

"Mistaken identity. I'm only a humble fisherman."

"No shame in that, lad. Many of the rascals manning the *Whydah* fished the sea before taking up the skull and crossbones. Welcome, Captain Socarides. My name is Jason Kingman. I play the role of Luke, a half-breed who served under the prince of pirates, Sam Bellamy."

"I know who you are, Mr. Kingman. I saw you single-handedly whup Quantrill's raiders in *The Defiant*."

His bloodshot blue eyes blinked like twin stop lights. "You saw *The Defiant*?"

I nodded. "Beats anything John Ford or Sam Peckinpah ever did. Hands down."

A wide smile came to his craggy face. "Can I get you a drink,

Mr. Socarides?"

"I know better than to refuse a pirate. I'll have what you're having."

"I've been getting into a bottle of Twenty Boat rum if that suits you."

"It does. Rum is the choice of true buccaneers."

"Ana, I think Captain Socarides and I are going to get along very well," he said.

"That's quite evident," she said, arching a perfect eyebrow.

Kingman grinned and stepped up to the bar in the gazebo. Turning to me, Ana said, "Jason will have you singing a duet of 'yo-ho-ho' on a dead man's chest before the night is over." She looked around. "I think you've met everyone on the crew."

"I don't see your assistant. And there was a big guy moving equipment around out on the dunes today."

"You're very observant. That's Tatiana. She serves as make-up person and hairdresser, as well as wardrobe assistant. She's probably in the house getting ready for tomorrow's shoot. The man is her husband, Yergo, who is our assistant gaffer. Maybe they will join us later. Here's Jason with your drink. I'd advise you not to try keeping up with him."

Kingman stepped out of the gazebo with the drinks he'd poured and stuck a tall tinkling tumbler in my hand.

"Heave ho, Captain Socarides!"

"Heave ho to you, Mr. Kingman."

Turning his mouth down in an exaggerated frown, he said, "Please dispense with the formal stuff. I'd be pleased if you called me Jace."

"Be happy to, Jace. And I'd be pleased if you called me Soc."

I studied Kingman over the rim of my glass. He was still handsome but the years, and his bad habits, had taken their toll. His voice had the grittiness that comes from butts and booze, and he carried a very un-pirate-like paunch. His face was gray and pockmarked from repeated use of make-up. He still had a full head of silvery hair, and the best teeth money could buy, which he displayed in the grin that could wow the women or give bad guys the jitters, depending on his acting role.

He flashed his pearly chops. "C'mon, Soc. I'll show you the view." As we walked out toward the edge of the lawn, he dropped his pirate accent, and said, "Tell me, my friend, how'd you get this gig?"

"I'm a charter boat captain. I'm out of work temporarily while my boat has some repairs. I heard about the movie and dropped by to see Cait. She said there was an opening for a boat guy. I lucked out."

We came to the edge of the bluff which dropped down steeply to a creek that flowed into the marshes.

"Not sure how lucky you are."

"Are you talking about the *Macbeth* curse?" I said.

"How did you know about that?"

"Cait mentioned that there had been some accidents even before Munson," I explained.

He snorted like a race horse. "I'm not sure if getting stoned and going for a swim with sharks qualifies as an accident."

"Neither am I. But like I said, I needed the money."

"As an over-the-hill actor, I can appreciate that," he said.

"Cait said that *The Pirate's Daughter* could put you back on the top of the hill."

A weary smile came to his lips. "I love that little gal. Too bad she's—well, she is much too kind. I'll give you some friendly advice, Soc."

I never got the advantage of his sage wisdom because Cait was suddenly calling my name. She was walking toward us, waving her arm.

"Looks like I have to go, Jace. About that advice?"

He must have reconsidered, because he said, "Maybe later."

Cait said, "I'm sorry to interrupt. Just got a call from Max on my cell phone. He's wondering if you can come by the Big House now rather than later."

I nodded. "Nice to meet you, Jace. Guess we'll have an excuse to talk later."

"We'll have ample opportunity over the next few days," he said.

We shook hands and I left Kingman to finish his drink at the overlook. The day had been weird right from the start, with Gill's face framed in my bedroom window. Then came the meeting with Ana, who'd I'd been in love with since I'd seen her on the screen, and the talk with Max, haunted by the legend of an 18th century witch. Not to mention, tossing down shots of rum with one of the most dashing actors of his day. What I didn't know as we walked across the lawn toward the Big House, however, was that my day was about to get a whole lot weirder.

CHAPTER 11

Cait opened an ornate door into the mansion and we entered a foyer bigger than my entire house. She pointed down a hallway. "That's the way to the sunroom. Have fun."

I said I'd see her later, then followed the corridor and stepped into a circular room that must have been the ground level floor of the fake lighthouse I'd seen from the outside. A wrought-iron staircase spiraled down from the second story. Tall windows and French doors wrapped around the perimeter. The cushions on the stark white wicker furnishings were ocean blue. Max sat on a sofa in conversation with a woman who was seated in a chair. I couldn't see her face because she was looking down at the laptop computer resting on her knees. But there was something about her that tickled my brain.

Max waved me over. "Thanks for stopping by, Soc. I was just telling my guest about you."

The woman set the laptop on a side table, rose from her chair and extended her hand.

"Nice to meet you, Captain Socarides," she said. "My name is Sally Carlin."

In the movies, this would have been the moment when invisible violins burst into an upwelling of romantic music as we floated toward each other in slow motion, arms extended for a tender embrace. The orchestra must have been on break. No music. But her lips were stretched in a friendly smile. Intense blue eyes pinned me in a level gaze and she squeezed my fingers to emphasize the silent message.

Play along.

I squeezed back. "Nice to meet you too, Ms. Carlin."

"Please call me Sally. May I call you Soc?"

"I'd be insulted if you didn't, Sally."

Truth is, I would have been *more* than insulted. Sally Carlin and I had once been a couple. We had gazed at each other's faces over glasses of wine and we had held hands in the movies. We had crawled under the sheets, made love and drifted off to sleep with bodies tucked into each other like spoons. Then came the day when she'd decided she had her fill of my bouts of self-pity and mood swings. She got sick of my attempts to drown the demons of my past in alcohol, packed her bags and headed to the nebulous destination the locals call, "off-Cape." The last I knew, she was in Florida working in a marine theme park. I hadn't seen or talked to her in years.

"Well, then," she said, "Sally and Soc it is."

Sally had changed very little since I last saw her. She had a few more smile lines at the corners of her perfect mouth but her dusky skin was as smooth and unblemished as I remembered. Her body had always been athletic without looking hard. The off-white silk halter dress she wore revealed that the few pounds she had gained were all in the right places. Sally's chestnut hair was cut short and woven with strands of silver, but it still sparkled with the red highlights I had noticed the first time we met.

She released my hand, finally, crossed her arms, and brought a forefinger to her lips. I was bursting with questions. Like what brought her to the Big House, for starters.

"Sally researches the behavior of great white sharks," Max said.

"She came by to ask a few questions about Kirk Munson. When I mentioned that you'd been hired to run the boat in his place, she asked to meet with you."

The news about shark studies was another surprise. Sally's expertise had been in marine mammals, not fish. We had met at a marine theme park named Oceanus where she'd trained dolphins. An orca named Rocky was suspected of killing his trainer. I was brought in on the case to find out if Rocky was guilty.

"I'm not sure how much help I can be, Sally. I didn't know Munson."

"That's not a problem. Max mentioned that you were a commercial fisherman and that you now run a charter boat. Your knowledge of local waters could help us unravel this vexing puzzle."

"What puzzle is that, Sally?"

"Why a great white shark would have attacked and killed Mr. Munson."

I shrugged. "All I know about great whites is what I saw in the movie *Jaws*."

"That movie gave me goosebumps," Sally said. "This isn't Amity, the town in that film, we're talking about. The town officials in the movie were trying to hide the shark attacks because the tourists would be scared away. In real life, sharks have been good for the local economy. You can buy a shark baseball cap that has a bite taken out of the visor, cuddly stuffed sharks, T-shirts that have a hungry shark asking to send him another tourist to eat. The local high school calls its athletic teams 'The Sharks.' The Great White Shark Conservancy center is a big tourist draw. Beachgoers love the idea of telling the folks back home how the life guards raised the purple pennant warning of a shark sighting and kicked everyone out of the water. Some people are thrilled at the prospect of seeing a shark kill a seal."

"Munson's death could change that," I said.

She nodded. "A fatal attack on a human isn't going to help the souvenir shops, particularly, if it happens again."

"Is another shark attack a possibility?"

"It's always dangerous when you have people and sharks and seals in the same part of the ocean. I don't want to overstate the danger. The shark's behavior in *Jaws* was completely out of character with what we know about Great Whites. Chomping on everyone in sight and sinking Quint's boat is simply not what I would expect of Emma."

"Emma? I thought we were talking about sharks."

She smiled. "Emma *is* a shark. She's a fourteen-foot female great white we've been tracking since she arrived in Cape Cod waters earlier this year." Sally picked up the laptop and asked me to sit next to her. She clicked the computer and three photos popped up on the screen. "These pictures of Emma were taken with an underwater camera during the tagging encounter. She's easy to identify because of the black splotch on the right side of her face. It's shaped vaguely like the letter M, which was how she got her name."

"Nice teeth," I said, eyeing the rows of triangular-shaped dentures

"And she knows how to use them." Sally turned to Max. "Back to Mr. Munson. You were telling me about his drug problem."

"Having a recreational drug habit isn't unusual in LA," Max said. "I just didn't know he was into hard stuff." He shook his head. "Nor did I know that quaint old Cape Cod has a big heroin and pill epidemic. It wasn't hard for him to find a supplier."

"When did you learn he had major drug issues?" Sally said.

"Not until after we got out here and started shooting. I'd been busy with pre-production. Once we got on location, I knew something was wrong. He would come to work late. He was distracted; sometimes even physically screwed up. Argumentative. Not only with me, but with everyone on the crew. People started to complain. I finally confronted him. He admitted he'd been using, but promised he would stop."

Sally tapped out some notes. "You said earlier that you argued the day of his disappearance."

"Yeah, he really messed up that time. We were filming an important scene, showing the crew jumping off the sinking ship. They were really leaping from the boat. We were going to merge the action with CGI."

"CGI?"

"Computer generated imaging. We were close to shore in relatively shallow water, but with CGI we can splice in an angry sea. Kirk went to move away from a bunch of extras thrashing around in the water, but he hit forward instead of reverse. I pushed him aside and killed the throttle before the prop chopped the actors to pieces. When we got back to the marina I told him he was through. At first he made excuses, saying he'd been up late the night before and didn't get much sleep. I said that he'd put people in danger by his boat handling. When he saw that my decision was firm, his attitude changed."

"In what way?"

"He went into a rage. Raised his fist; he would have hit me if I hadn't grabbed his wrist. You can ask the crew what they thought of the incident. I told him to get off the *Sea Robin*."

"Did he?"

"Yes, but he didn't go very far. He stormed off the boat and stood on the dock. He shook his fist at me, yelling that the movie was finished."

"What did he mean by that?" I asked.

"Maybe he figured we couldn't make the film without him. I told him I was going to call the cops. He walked off. And that was the last I saw of him."

"How did you hear of Mr. Munson's death?"

"I was doing a land shoot the next day. The harbormaster called and said the *Sea Robin* had been found anchored out in the bay beyond the entrance to the harbor, with no one aboard. I went over to the marina and saw Kirk's truck in the parking lot. I tried to call him. No answer, so I called the cops and said I was worried."

"You assumed he had taken the boat," Sally asked.

"It seemed like a reasonable guess. I'd forgotten to ask him to turn over the boat's spare ignition key. The cops were calling in the Coast Guard to widen the search when someone found Kirk's body washed up on shore a few miles from the boat."

"Did the police have any theories about what happened?" Sally said.

"They did after I told them about Kirk's drug habit and how he sometimes took the boat out at night to go fishing. Everyone figured he got stoned, fell off the boat and started swimming, which is when the shark attacked him. Does that sound plausible?"

Sally took her time answering. After a moment of thought, she said, "Maybe. Emma has a radio beacon attached to her fin. The beacon puts her in the vicinity of the boat. They may have crossed paths. Then there's his terrible wound."

"What sort of wound?" I asked.

"His right arm below the elbow was missing. The damage could have been inflicted by a great white."

"You sound like you have doubts," I said.

"Yes, I do. Great whites don't especially like to eat humans. We're not fatty enough. They prefer seal meat. Their usual technique is to take an exploratory bite first. It's called 'groping.' That seems to have happened in this case, because there were non-fatal bite marks on one of the victim's legs."

"So the shark took a test bite and then went for the main meal. The arm."

"Well, with that highly refined sense of taste, and being only interested in blubber, she would have known right after the first bite that she hadn't tasted a seal."

"Why would the shark go for the arm after it found out Munson wasn't a seal, then?"

She sighed. "I simply don't know."

"What did the autopsy show?"

"That the cause of death was from drowning. In addition to the bite mark and the missing arm, he had a bruise on his head that wasn't fatal. If he'd been under the influence of drugs, maybe he fell and hit his head, got up and lost his balance, falling overboard."

I shrugged. "Maybe," I said. "Munson could also have bled out from the bite, gone into shock, weakened and drowned."

"I may not like that conclusion, but it's important that we know what actually happened. Cape Cod has become a world hot spot for great whites and it's a popular recreational area, so there's bound to be interaction between sharks and humans. There have been no fatalities, up to now. We have to find out what was different about this encounter." She shut the cover of her laptop. "Thanks for your time, Max. You too, Soc."

We shook hands, and I said, "Where is Emma spending her time these days?"

"The radio beacon has her tracked back to the far side of the bay, near Plymouth."

"That's a relief," Max said. "The crew has had jitters about the water scenes. I thought I'd have to do future shoots in a motel swimming pool."

Sally gave him a half-smile, handed me a business card, and said she'd find her way out.

"Well, *that* was interesting," Max said after she'd gone. "Don't know what the big mystery is. Kirk went swimming with the sharks and got killed."

I tucked the card in my pocket, thinking that if I left soon, I could catch up with Sally.

"Looks like that's what happened. Well, I've met most of the crew," I said. "I guess I'll head home."

"Are you in a hurry to leave?"

Max would wonder if I seemed eager to catch up with Sally.

"No," I lied. "I'm in no hurry at all."

"Good. Hold on a second and I'll make us drinks." He picked up a bound folder from a side table and handed it over. "This is the treatment I mentioned."

Max went to the bar and put ice cubes and rum into a couple of glasses. I read the words centered on the title page:

Treatment
The Pirate's Daughter
By
Max Corman

I tapped the page with my forefinger. "This must be the lady I've been hearing about."

He returned with the drinks, handed one to me and we clinked glasses. He took a sip from his glass. "That's her. The offspring of the *Prince of Pirates* and the *Wicked Witch of the Devil's Pasture.* This is the story of what happened after Bellamy's ship went down. I used it as the basis for the screenplay, but I'm still making things up as filming goes along."

I riffled the pages. "I'm looking forward to reading it, especially after hearing what you said out at the set about a happy ending."

"I tried to stay away from a schmaltzy Hollywood wrap-up, but I wanted the audience to leave the theater thinking that love conquers all."

"So Mary and Sam live out their days in a beachfront high-rise in Naples, Florida, sipping rum punch and counting their doubloons?"

He shook his head. "Haven't heard that one, but it's not bad."

"You're free to use it."

"Thanks. I'll stick with my story line."

"I don't blame you. From what I hear, Naples is getting crowded. How did you handle it?"

"My screenplay is based on the fact that Bellamy's body was never found. It was presumed that he either drowned or escaped.

The historical record shows that an Indian crewman named John Julian made it safely ashore. He was taken to Boston and disappeared from the record, probably sold into slavery. I thought if there was one Indian, maybe there were two."

"Jason told me he was playing a half-breed Indian named Luke."

"That's right. Luke's mother is the woman who tended to Mary and her baby after she was kicked out of town. Mary gets the chance to repay the favor after the *Whydah* goes down. She helps Luke get to his mother's hut where he recovers. He gets out of town before he's grabbed by the authorities and, like John Julian, disappears from the history books. In my story, he reappears years later. Darken Jason's skin, and with that hawk-like profile, he's almost perfect for the part."

"Who plays the young Indian?"

"Jason is Luke, young and old. Amazing what a wig and quick camera cuts can accomplish when you mix in computer-generated images. But Jason's major job is to play the older Indian who reappears after many years to repay Mary for rescuing him."

"Where is Bellamy in all this?"

"As I said earlier, I didn't want this to be a swashbuckler, which it would be if we portrayed a powerful figure like Black Sam. *The Pirate's Daughter* is about the people who loved him, and how life treated them after he sailed off to make his fortune. It's about relationships. Mary and the ghost of her lover. Mary and her daughter. Mary and the Indian and his mother. Mary and the villagers."

"What about Mary and Satan, who turned her into a witch?"

"All I'll say on that score is that the Indian's mother taught her more than simple weaving."

I got out of my chair. "I'd better get going. Thanks for the drink."

We agreed to meet at the dock in the morning. He escorted me to the front door. I stood out on the porch. The party was over but the gazebo lights were still on. I decided that a walk might blow away some of the craziness that filled my head after my encounter with Sally.

I strolled away from the gazebo to the bluff, stared into the darkness and inhaled the rich, rank smell of marsh and sea. After a minute I turned around and started back across the lawn. At the edge of the circle of light coming from the gazebo I saw someone walking, dressed in a red cloak. I called Ana's name. She froze and stared in my direction. I was still in the shadows and thought I might have startled her, so I called out again.

"Hey Ana. It's me, Soc."

She turned and walked briskly away from me. I started to follow, which is when I heard the light footfalls. Out of the corner of my eye I saw a shadow moving in my direction. The shadow materialized into something solid that slammed into me, like a bowling ball into a pin. I landed hard on my side. My right shoulder took most of the impact. The treatment flew out of my hand.

As I lay on the grass, trying to suck air back into my lungs, a silhouette loomed over me. I brought my right foot up and kicked. The sole of my sneaker hit something soft and yielding. I heard a grunt and the shadow pulled back. I rolled over to my left side, then scrambled to my feet and braced myself for a follow-up assault, but the attacker was nowhere to be seen.

I picked up the treatment and stood there on shaky legs, like a drunk prize fighter, trying to figure out why Ana had run and who had mugged me. But the imaginary canaries tweeting inside my skull drowned out any answers as I staggered back to my truck. This had been a night for the unexpected. First the reunion with Sally. Then this. I should have known that, like many things in life, surprises come in threes.

CHAPTER 12

The drive home seemed to go on forever. Although I used one hand to steer and kept the other one down by my side, every bump in the road set off a hot burst of pain. I turned into my cratered driveway, gritting my teeth for the last round of torture. But I forgot all about my aching shoulder when I saw Gill's multi-colored truck parked outside the boathouse.

I went into the house and put the treatment on the kitchen table. Then, I popped a couple of aspirin and went out on the deck. Gill was lounging in an Adirondack chair, staring out at the darkened bay and sipping on a can of beer. *My* beer.

"Hi Soc," he said. "You really should keep your door locked."

"Yeah, thanks. That's good advice. Otherwise, someone might come in and steal beer from my fridge."

"Guilty as charged. I fed your cat, though. He looked hungry."

"Kojak *always* looks hungry, because he *is* always hungry."

"Uh-oh. You sound mad. Next time I come by I'll bring a six-pack."

"I've got a better idea, *Dr.* Gill. How about bringing me the truth?"

Pause. "How'd you find out?"

"I'm a professional snoop. That's what I do. I snoop."

He grunted. "What do you know?"

"That you're phi beta kappa. That you hold a doctorate in anthropology from Harvard."

"That's good sleuthing. But you left out my undergrad work at Brown University."

"I might have caught that one if I hadn't been busy trying to help an uneducated guy who mucks around in the mud for a living. What's with the masquerade, Howie?"

"Long story, Soc. Mind if I snag another beer from the fridge?"

"Help yourself, as long as you get one for me."

I eased into the other chair. He went inside and came back with two cans of Cape Cod beer. I popped the top of mine and took a gulp. Gill slurped his beer and wiped his mouth with the back of his hand.

"My family goes back a long way in Rhode Island," he said. "Had a mansion in East Providence. Like a lot of the Yankee richie-rich, the Gills made their money through the slave trade. People think of southern plantations, but New Englanders built the ships and provided the financial backing and business acumen for the human commerce."

"Now I get it, Howie. Your ancestors got rich from the triangular trade, which made you so overcome by guilt you felt compelled to hide your identity."

Gill let out a half-growl, half beer belch. "Excuse me. Old habits die hard."

"That's okay. Just as long as they die."

He chuckled quietly. "Nice try at a psychological diagnosis, but you're not even close. You'd have to meet my parents to understand where I'm coming from. They really screwed me up, if you can believe that."

I thought about how my own mother and father had shaped my life for better and for worse and felt a twinge of empathy. "Yeah," I said. "I can understand that very well. Keep going."

"They were both brilliant anthropologists," he said. "I was their only child. They pushed me to study anthropology and drove me to excel. No dinner until I finished my lessons. No time for friends. No *friends*! I figured they'd mellow when I got my doctorate at Harvard. The week before commencement they died in a plane crash in Nepal."

"Sorry to hear that."

"I was sorry too, until the reading of the will. Most of the family fortune went to charities. They left me a pauper, explaining in the will that being penniless would build my character."

"Seems like pretty harsh treatment."

"Not to them. They were hard-assed Yankees. They said the education they had given me was the only tool that I needed to make my way in the world."

"So you went off the deep end to get back at them?"

"Sorta. I wanted to hurt them, but they were dead. All I could do was hurt myself. Booze mostly." He patted his belly. "I blew up like a tick. Became the gross slob you see today. I was a complete failure when it came to dealing with people. Constantly having my nose in a book had left me with no social skills whatsoever."

"Yeah, I noticed. How'd you go from social misfit to the oyster flats?"

"We used to spend summers on the Cape when I was a kid. After wandering around, I drifted back, drawn by the few good memories. I had practically nothing when I arrived."

"Does the waterfront land on the bay count as nothing?"

"Guess you did some homework," Gill said after a pause. "Got me there, Soc. You're a regular Perry Mason."

Gill's voice had dropped to an unfriendly rumble. He didn't like being caught. I didn't care.

"Let me stop you right there, Howie. I'm not a TV lawyer digging a confession from the witness. Try it again, without the attitude. What about the land?"

"Crap," he said. "Whole thing still sticks in my craw. My folks planned to give that land to a conservation trust, but they died before they could sign it over. The trust tried to get me to carry out my parents' wishes. I said, shove it. Politely.

"I saw the oyster farms while I was walking around on the property, and decided to give farming a go. I scraped together some loans to buy seed and did odd jobs until the shellfish crops came ready. Now it's all going down the tubes."

He stared into the night. I could feel the heat of his smoldering anger.

"Maybe it doesn't have to go that way," I said.

"You still willing to help me, knowing I wasn't honest with you?"

"Mostly, I want to help *me*. I want to get the people who shot at me and lit up my truck. But catching them would also keep your oyster operation going."

"I can live with that arrangement," Gill said.

"This won't be a free ride. I'll need your help."

"You've got it. Where do we start?"

"Right here. I'm going to be busy for a few days so I'm turning my junior private eye badge over to you. Are you game?"

"Damn right I am. Can't wait to confront these bastards."

"Too bad, because that's the last thing that's going to happen. We can't go head-to-head with the poachers. These are tough guys with big guns. We're going to find out where the oysters go, then backtrack to the thieves. And when we get close, we'll turn the case over to the cops."

"That's all right. The Glock was all part of the act. I've built up a rapport with the markets and restaurants that carry my stock. I can ask the owners if anyone's ever come to them with an offer to sell oysters at ridiculously low prices. I'll say I want to be sure my price is competitive."

"Good idea. Here's another one. Talk to *former* customers who might now be buying discounted stuff and find out who their new suppliers are."

"Sure, I see. Maybe the poachers undercut my price with oysters they stole from me. I'll talk to the other oyster farmers and see if anyone has taken their customers."

"You're catching on. Contact me immediately if you hear something. Meanwhile, I'll see what's happening with the DA's office."

"Thanks, Soc. I'm feeling good about this. Anything else I can do?"

"Yeah. The next time you come by make sure you bring me that six-pack you promised."

"Deal," he said, extending his hand with his lobster grip.

I sat in the chair and listened as the sound of his truck engine faded down the driveway. I stared off at the lights glittering across the bay and wondered if I had made a good move recruiting Gill to be an assistant gumshoe. I decided I had no choice. The movie was going to take up time that would otherwise be spent tracking down the oyster poachers.

I went to my dock, stripped off the grass-stained clothes, and lowered my body down the ladder until the water was up to my chin. The chill waters of the bay wrapped me in a numbing embrace. After a few minutes I climbed back onto the dock and went into the boathouse to rinse away the salt water with a hot shower.

Wrapping myself in an old terry cloth bathrobe, I sat down at the kitchen table. Kojak jumped up onto my lap and started snoring. I began to read the treatment. I skimmed over the part about Mary and Sam's tryst, her pregnancy and birth of a baby girl, his return in the doomed slave ship *Whydah*, and got right into the main plot of *The Pirate's Daughter*—what happened after the townspeople drove her and her newborn daughter into exile.

Her father, who runs a local tavern, couldn't save her from being driven out to the lonely moors, but he provides a hut and arranges for supplies. Since Bellamy is considered a devil, she must be a witch. So people leave her alone. Even with her father's help she would have died, if not for an Indian woman who saves her and her daughter and teaches Goody the art of weaving. She also instructs her in the dark arts.

The woman's son was on the doomed ship and made it safely to shore. He and Goody had carried Bellamy's body to an island and buried it with the treasure. The Indian is captured and sold into slavery. The treasure is never found.

One day Goody shows up at the village with her exquisite weavings. She hints that whoever buys her work will enjoy good luck. If she uses a plant design, their crops will flourish. A child's face, and their children will be beautiful and healthy. If she weaves a nice house into a tapestry, it will hang on the wall of the luxurious home they will live in one day. On the other hand, if she weaves something bad, the person will have bad luck. People buy her weavings to stay on her good side.

The same group of villagers who drove Goody into exile suspect she has the treasure. For years they have plotted how to find it. They finally get their opportunity when, along with a new batch of weavings to sell, Goody brings her lovely teenage daughter into the village. The villagers divert Goody, allowing the handsome son of one family to strike up a conversation with the daughter. It is part of a plot to seduce the young woman and learn where the treasure is.

The girl has become a skilled weaver and persuades her mother to allow her to bring in some work on her own. She arranges to meet the young man and, in her innocence, falls for him. She lets slip that her mother rows to an island once a month. The villagers tell the girl that her father was a notorious pirate, and that her witch of a mother brought on the winds that killed him. She runs into the woods, falls and hits her head, and ends up in a coma.

The Indian shows up, having escaped from slavery, but his mother has died. He attempts to help Goody, but the villagers kill him. Furious at the state of her daughter and the loss of her friend,

Goody lures the plotters to the island where she exacts her revenge. The other villagers pursue her to Goody Hallett's Meadow where she disappears into the mists. Max knew that Hollywood doesn't like unhappy endings, because as Goody goes to rejoin her dead lover, the pirate's daughter comes out of her coma.

I finished reading the treatment, pushed it aside and headed for bed.

The mugging back at the Big House made me think that the movie job was going to be more complicated than I had first expected. I guess I shouldn't be surprised, I told myself. After all, the last guy who held my job had been eaten by a shark.

CHAPTER 13

Five minutes before the six o'clock alarm was supposed to go off, Kojak stomped across my head to announce that it was time for his breakfast. I got out of bed and swiveled my arm like a pitcher doing a warm-up. Except for a slight soreness around the shoulder joint, I was almost back to normal. I pulled on a pair of shorts, a T-shirt and boat shoes, and fired up the coffee pot.

After I doled out Kojak's breakfast, I poured the coffee into a travel cup, then headed out the driveway in the GMC. A half hour later I arrived at the marina and parked next to the movie company's white utility truck. I was getting out of the pickup when a dark blue Chevy Cruze pulled up alongside. Sally got out of the car wearing white shorts and a blue-green T-shirt printed with a smiling shark.

"Good morning, Captain Socarides," she said. "Nice to see you."

"It's a pleasure to see you again, Ms. Carlin."

She cocked her head. "From the funny look on your face, I'd guess that Max didn't tell you I'd be going out on the boat today."

"Max didn't mention it, but I'm happy to have you aboard. Interested in movie making?"

"That's part of it, but the main reason is to familiarize myself with the general area where Kirk Munson and Emma crossed paths."

"Not a problem. This is an amazing coincidence. You remind

me of a friend I haven't seen in years. Her name was Sally, too, and she was a marine researcher. But she studied mammals, not sharks."

"That's quite the coincidence. She sounds fascinating. I'd like to meet her sometime."

She reached into her car for a knapsack, shut the door and sprinted down the ramp to the boat slips. I hustled to keep up. Max and three members of the crew were standing on the floating dock next to a boat around thirty-five-feet long. The name *Sea Robin* was painted in white letters on the blue hull.

"Good morning, folks," Max said. "Nice to see you again, Sally. This is Eric, my assistant. Joe and Bill are my cameraman and lighting technician. I believe you met them last night, Soc."

We shook hands all around, then Max made a half-bow. "The boat's all yours, Captain. Care to check it out?"

I climbed onto the gunwale and stepped lightly onto the deck. I held out my hand for Sally, who was right behind me, then I waved Max and his crew aboard.

The boat had a center console, a design that allowed the passengers to move around the deck, and was powered by a couple of 150-horsepower Yamaha outboard motors. While Max and the rest of the crew climbed aboard, I did a quick check of the fuel supply, made sure the GPS and the radio were working, inventoried flotation devices, cushions, boat hook, registration, and tested the horn.

A Zodiac inflatable around eight feet long was tied up at the dock. Max asked me to tow it behind the boat. I started the motors, cast off the dock lines, eased the boat out of the slip and cleated the inflatable's bow line to the stern. With the Zodiac bouncing in our wake, we headed past the breakwater into the harbor.

Max pointed toward the low-lying headlands that enclosed the harbor. "We're going to Great Island. Ever been there?"

"A few years ago I hiked onto the island to look for an old whalers' tavern. Turned out the place had closed three-hundred years ago. I didn't even make last call."

"Too bad. The old gin mill was in operation back in Bellamy's day. He may have hoisted a few with some of the local whalers. Did you read the treatment last night?"

I nodded. "It's everything you said it was. Adventure, pirates, witchcraft. A real winner."

"Thanks. I hope you're right, because I've got a lot riding on this movie. Today I want to pin down locales for future scenes. Great Island is where Goody buries Sam's body. There's an air of mystery about the place. It's got dense forests, marshes and misty beaches. Very atmospheric. When we crank up the fog machines, it'll look positively creepy."

I pointed the boat toward the low section of the island, a marshy area flanked by sandy bluffs. Less than five minutes later I slowed the boat speed to a forward idle around a hundred feet or so off the beach. Max squinted toward the cliffs to get his bearings, then gave me the thumbs up. I dropped the hook and killed the outboards.

"The tech guys and I will go to shore in the Zodiac," he said. "We'll hike to the other side of the island and wander around in the woods. We'll be back in about an hour. That should give you and Sally plenty of time to chat."

I glanced at Sally. "I'm sure we'll have plenty to talk about," I said.

"Show is always better than tell," Sally said. "While Max and the others are scouting the island, maybe you could run me out into the bay so I can retrace the route Emma took when she was in the neighborhood."

"Glad to do it, Sally," I said.

"Done deal, then," Max said. "Keep in touch by walkie-talkie in case there's a change in plans."

Max and his crew climbed from the boat into the Zodiac. He started the outboard motor and headed toward shore. When they reached land, they dragged the inflatable up onto the beach and

Max waved.

I started the *Sea Robin*'s outboards, hauled the anchor and headed back out into open water.

Sally came up beside me and put her arm around my waist. It felt nice.

"Sorry about the play-acting," she said. "You must think I'm out of my mind, not letting on to Max that I know you."

"Nothing like that, Sal. I figured you had forgotten what I look like. It has been a while."

"It could have been a thousand years and there's no way on earth I'd ever forget you. I hope the feeling is mutual." She dropped her hand and gave my haunch a friendly pinch.

"Ouch. I just felt a twinge of remembrance. Why all the mystery, Sal?"

"It's not something I intended. When Max first mentioned your name and said you were working on the movie, I almost blurted out that I knew you."

"I don't get it. What difference would that have made?"

"I thought we might have more elbow room if people didn't know we were working together."

"Working together on *what*, Sal?"

"On an investigation of Munson's death."

"Why does it have to be investigated? Seems straightforward. Munson goes for a night swim and gets chewed up by a great white named Emily."

"The shark's name is *Emma*."

"Okay, Emma. Lovely old-fashioned name. Back to the investigation. What's up?"

"Maybe I'm being silly, but something funny is going on with this whole shark attack story."

"Okay, I'll bite."

"Dammit, Soc, this is serious."

"Just trying to lighten things up. How long have you been

chasing great whites? You were studying dolphins and orcas, last I knew."

"The marine theme park business had become too controversial. I decided I didn't like to see marine mammals kept in captivity to perform like clowns. I took some university courses on Great White Sharks and discovered they were intelligent and inquisitive, much more complex creatures than I realized. I went to work for a study group doing research on shark behavior. I knew the area, so I was asked to extend my research to Cape Cod after Munson was killed. A county official had talked about a mitigation program that would use baited drum lines to catch and kill great whites. It was silly talk, but still a worry and the group wanted me here in a hurry to give the sharks backup. I considered the possibility that we might bump into each other but thought, hey...what are the chances of running into an old flame?"

"Surprise," I said.

She laughed. "I should have known, if there was trouble you'd be in the middle of it."

"I'm glad you came back, Sally. And I'm happy we hooked up so soon."

"I'm pleased to hear you say that. After all, we didn't part on the best of terms. I want to hear what's been going on in your life. For instance, how you came to be working on a movie."

"I'll fill you in while we're investigating Munson's death."

"Does that mean you'll help?"

"Like you said. Trouble is my business."

She gave me a kiss on the cheek.

"Thank you, Soc," she said. I could sense the relief in her voice.

She opened her knapsack, pulled out an iPad and turned it on to display a navigational chart of Cape Cod. A blue dot was blinking on the screen.

"Is that Emma?" I was careful to use her correct name.

"Yes. The picture was taken when she was tagged."

She touched the screen and photo of a shark's head appeared. Its wide mouth was partially open so that the rows of triangular teeth were on full display.

"Emma has a nice set of choppers," I said.

"Behind the teeth you see there are rows of hundreds more. If the shark loses a tooth another will pop into place."

"Was the photo taken the same time she was tagged?"

Sally nodded. "There are two main electronic methods for keeping track of sharks. Both involve a harpoon boat tagging a shark in shallow water. One type of tag collects data, like where the shark is swimming, and is pre-programmed to pop off the shark. It floats to the surface and transmits the data through a satellite to the researcher. The other tag is a pinger that sends out a signal to receivers placed near shark habitats. That's what Emma is wearing."

The image showed that the shark had followed the Atlantic shore of the Cape to Provincetown, then she swam back along the Cape peninsula's inner shore into Wellfleet Harbor, where her trail went in circles before she headed across the bay to Plymouth.

"From the looks of it, Emma has been a busy girl." I pointed to the tangled dotted line with my fingertip. "Is this where she crossed Munson's path?"

"That's right. She looks confused, doesn't she?"

"This area is like the Bermuda Triangle," I said. "Time after time, whales have come inside Great Island and followed their directional sense east. They're not aware of the land in the way, and they strand themselves."

"Great whites are a lot smarter than people think they are," Sally said. "Emma found her way out of the trap."

"After her encounter with Munson?"

"That's my guess."

I glanced at the GPS and adjusted the boat's course to take it toward the tangle of dotted lines on the iPad screen. After a few minutes, I cut speed. We were across the harbor from Great Island, about a half mile from the breakwater. I backed up the GPS memory to the date Munson disappeared. A dotted line on the screen showed the course he had followed the night of his death.

"The GPS stores boat routes in its memory," I said. "Here's the record of where Munson went that night. You can see that the boat went right in the middle of Emma's meanderings."

"They were definitely in proximity to each other. Still...."

"You have your doubts."

"Maybe my sympathies are coloring my judgment. You brought up the movie *JAWS*, but in real life sharks have more to fear from humans than humans do from sharks. Last year fewer than a hundred people were bitten by sharks worldwide. In New York City, approximately ten thousand people were bitten by other people. Over the same time span, some researchers say, humans killed more than a hundred million sharks, and that's a conservative estimate. There's a huge market for shark fin soup."

"I see why you feel the way you do, Sally. The odds against a fatal attack were pretty long, but maybe Munson won the shark bite lottery."

"That's possible, but let's talk about what we're dealing with here. Sharks go back more than four hundred million years, making their species older than dinosaurs. *Carcharadon carcharia* can swim up to thirty-five-miles an hour, and their jaws are loaded with up to three hundred teeth in seven rows. Every one of its six senses has evolved for a single purpose: the location and acquisition of prey. They can smell a single drop of blood in ten billion drops of water. They can hear the slightest vibration, and their retinas can adjust to daylight and nighttime conditions. They can even detect electromagnetic signals sent out by prey."

"Very impressive. But from what I've read in the papers, even with all those senses they'll do something dumb, like attack a paddle boat thinking it's a seal."

"You remember what I said last night about taste?"

"Sure. You said sharks are finicky eaters. Humans aren't part of their regular diet because we're not fatty enough. They're looking for seals."

"That's correct. A great white shark has sensory cells in its mouth and throat that send signals to the brain, which decides whether or not to accept a meal. But great whites are opportunistic hunters. They might attack simply because prey is available, not because they're hungry. Most attacks on people aren't fatal because as I said last night, the shark typically takes a bite, finds out that its prey doesn't have the fat content it needs, and swims away."

"Not in this case, apparently, because Munson lost part of his arm."

"That's right. The arm was torn away at the elbow."

"Which indicates Emma took a bite, but instead of going 'phooey' and swimming away, she went 'yum' and took another fatal bite."

"That's a colorful way of putting it. But yes."

"Let's think about the time before the attack. We know Munson was in the water. What we don't know is how he got there." I pointed to the GPS screen. "Maybe Munson comes out of the marina, drops anchor here and starts fishing." I made a cast with an invisible rod. "He hooks a fish." I made believe I was cranking a reel. "He bends over to gaff his catch into the boat, but he's stoned, which makes him unsteady." I leaned over the side. "He falls in and starts to swim and meets up with Emma."

"Why didn't he swim back to the boat? He could have climbed up the ladder off the stern."

"He was probably disoriented."

"Okay, then. You're the detective. Is this something that needs to be investigated?"

"It's sketchy. But the evidence does suggest that Emma was involved, shall we say."

"I know," she said. "But they said that about Rocky, too."

"I remember, Sally. Sounds like you think Emma is getting a bum rap just like Rocky did."

"I don't know. You proved there was more to the charges against Rocky. Maybe you can do something like that again, with Emma."

"I'll do my best. Anything else you want to see while we're out here?"

"Thanks. I'm done for now. Maybe a view from the air would help. Interested in going up in a spotter plane? I can arrange something for tomorrow, if you're free."

"I'll check with Max on the shooting schedule."

I headed the boat back to Great Island. No one was on the beach, so I threw the anchor over the side. Sally asked what I had been doing with my life. I told her about buying Sam's boat after he retired, and why I gave up after being squeezed by the diminishing fish stocks and government regulations. I filled her in on my charter business, and how I came to be working on the movie.

I had to break off our chat when Max and the other men came out of the woods and walked down to the water. They pushed the Zodiac off the beach, got in, and minutes later they were back on board the *Sea Robin*.

"How'd it go?" I asked

Max clapped. "Wow! My head is ready to explode with all the stuff I've got."

"Will we be filming today?" I said.

"Yes, but not here. I've scheduled a big shipwreck scene on the Atlantic shore in a few hours with the extras and Ana. It's at Newcomb's Hollow. How'd you like to play a dead pirate, Soc?"

"Thanks, but my eye patch is at the dry cleaners. I'll come by anyway."

"That's great! Hope your trip out here was productive, Sally."

"Yes. Thanks for having me aboard," Sally said. "I was able to track the shark to her probable intersection with Mr. Munson. I've offered the captain the chance to take a look at the scene from a spotting plane. Maybe seeing it from the air will tell us something."

"Good idea." Max pinched his chin, then said, "Sounds like you're doing a lot of running around, Soc. I've got an idea. Why not stay at the Big House while you're working on the movie? We could move along much faster if you were bunking out with the cast and crew."

"Not sure if I can do that," I said. "I have an old cat at home who has a tight feeding schedule."

"I'd be glad to feed your cat," Sally said. "I think staying at the Big House is a great idea."

I looked at Sally. She had one eyebrow raised.

"Thanks," I said. "That might work out just fine."

We were back at the marina a few minutes later. Before Max left, he gave me the schedule for the shipwreck shoot.

I walked Sally to her car. "I appreciate your offer to feed Kojak. He'll be glad to see you. Where are you staying now?"

"I'm in a motel room. The research project is paying for it, but it's pretty basic."

"Since I'm moving out, why don't you stay at my place while I'm at the Big House? It hasn't changed much since you saw it."

"I'd like that," she said without hesitation. "I can swing by the motel and pick up my things."

I said I would see her at the boathouse after the beach shoot, and then I got back into the GMC. My cell phone chirped, and I answered.

"This is Len, the mechanic at the Hyannis Marina."

"Hi Len. I was going to give you a call. How's it going?"

"I'm not sure. There's a guy here who says he's going to repossess your boat."

"That's impossible. Wait a minute. What's this guy's name?"

"George. That's all he said."

Only one George would make a dumb and empty threat like that.

"Can you pass him the phone, Len?"

"Sure. He's standing right here."

The voice that came on the line a few seconds later said, "Who's this?"

"You know damn well who it is, brother George. Stay away from my property."

"*Thalassa* is not your property, Soc. It belongs to the corporation."

"I'll be there in forty-five minutes. Keep your flour-caked mitts off the boat."

"And if I don't?"

"I'll do what I did when you stole my baseball glove. I'll give you a giant wedgie."

"That really scares me, Soc. I'm really scared." He was putting up a pretty good front, but memories die hard. The fear in his voice made me smile.

CHAPTER 14

Fireworks exploded in my head during the forty-five-minute drive to Hyannis. My fevered imagination pictured the *Thalassa II* being hauled off to *godknowswhere* on a trailer and me swinging the GMC around to block the way. But when I arrived, the boat was still in its slip. No flatbed. No George.

I parked the pickup, got out of the cab and looked around for my brother's car, a white Lincoln Continental with the word PIZZA printed on the vanity plate. Instead, I saw a woman standing near the bulkhead, cell phone glued to her ear. The frown that had pulled my lips down into a Greek mask of anger slowly morphed into a grin. The woman had her back to me but I recognized her immediately.

I strolled over, and said, "Hi Chloe."

My kid sister turned at the sound of my voice and a bright smile lit up her face. She held her forefinger in the air, said something into the phone and clicked off. Then she launched her body at mine, wrapped me in a bear hug, and sealed the deal with a peck on each cheek.

"I've missed you *so* much, big brother."

"I've missed you too, Chloe." I put my hands on her shoulders and gently disengaged from her embrace. "You look great."

Chloe was wearing a honey gold business suit that went well with her olive complexion. Her dark brown hair was tied in a neat braid, and designer sunglasses hid her eyes. Chloe reminded me of a young Irene Papas about the time the Greek actress was starring in *Trojan Women*.

"Thank you. You're as handsome as ever, but not as scruffy as you used to be. And the gray in your hair makes you look distinguished."

"Now you're stretching it," I said. "Hope I didn't interrupt an important call."

"Nothing that can't wait until I get back to Lowell. I was talking to the art person on my staff about a new promotional slogan for our frozen pizza box."

The blue-and-white box with the drawing of the Acropolis, enclosed by the Greek wave border, was the same design Parthenon Pizza used for take-out orders when my parents owned their pizza and sub shop, the genesis of their frozen pizza empire. They had expanded into an impressive line of frozen Greek foods, like spanakopita spinach pie and baklava dessert, but the basic cheese pizza that had launched the family business was their main-stay.

"What happened to the old slogan? 'Parthenon Pizza: A Real Classic.' "

"That line will always be on the box, but people are more health conscious now. You've got to give them a reason to indulge in a carbfest."

"Simple is usually best. What about, 'Parthenon Pizza: Good and Good for You'?"

She groaned. "That is so lame."

"Okay, how about this? Greek yogurt is a big deal now. Capitalize on that. 'Greek Pizza: Sophocles Loved it & So Will You.'? Then add *Kalo Orexi* and the English translation, 'Good appetite.' "

After a pause, she said, "I like it. Not sure about the literary reference. Some people won't know who Sophocles is. But I love the Greek phrase."

"Always glad to help the family business." I looked around the parking lot. "Where's George and his mile-long Lincoln Continental?"

Chloe wrinkled her nose. "He traded that thing in for a big Mercedes to match his over-sized ego. He'll be back after he sees the local distributors. Ma thought it would be a good idea to put some space between you two."

"Ma's here? Why didn't someone tell me we were having a Socarides family reunion?"

"It's not a reunion; it's a corporate meeting. George's idea. He's been insufferable since you called with the bad news about the boat." She folded her arms and, in a disapproving tone of voice, said, "Did you really threaten him?"

"I said I'd give him a sixth grade wedgie if he touched *Thalassa* It wasn't a threat exactly."

She snickered. "It is to George. You know what a namby-pamby he is."

"I'm not sure what a namby-pamby is, but I'm familiar with the Machiavellian machinations of the family matriarch. She left you here to act as peacemaker."

"The United Nations could not make peace between you and George. He's never forgiven you for leaving him to run the business."

"I used to feel guilty about that, but George drives a Mercedes the company probably bought for him. His kids go to top-notch colleges. He's got a beautiful wife who makes him a cocktail when he comes home to his five-bedroom house and cooks him dinner after he's had a hard day. He's got no reason to be grumpy."

"Well, actually, he's got two very good reasons to be grumpy."

"I know the folks can be pains in the butt. Especially the Cretan side. But I left you too, Chloe. You're not bitter at me." I gave her a squint. "Or maybe you are."

"Don't talk like an idiot! I could never be mad at you. It's different for me. I'm a girl. All our parents expected from me was to have a nice Greek husband and a couple of smart kids."

"You tried."

"Yes, I tried, but you're not the only one who disappointed the folks. I screwed up. My big fat Greek wedding was the beginning of the end. My marriage ended in divorce and I moved back into the family house. No kids, thank God. What a mess that would have been."

"Unlike me, though, you stayed with the company and the family. You're doing pretty well, last I heard. Head of marketing is a big deal."

"It's only a big deal because I made it happen. George still wants to run the whole show. He even resents Ma's involvement, which is pretty small. If he had his way I'd be writing news releases about pre-sliced pizza for people who don't own a knife."

"Pre-sliced? Is that Parthenon Pizza's latest technological innovation?"

"Yes. We have it in all our versions now."

"Got me sold. Don't let George put you down, Chloe, you're a natural marketer."

"And you're a natural great big brother, even if I never see you anymore."

"We got together for Easter."

"That was months ago."

"I've been busy with the boat."

"Twelve months a year?"

"All right. I've got no excuse. You said Ma is spending less time with the company. Is it her health?"

"Oh no. She's in amazingly good shape. It's Pop. She goes to see him every day at the assisted living residence."

"Has there been a change since Easter? Last I saw him, he recognized me, so I figured he was doing okay."

"If you call being in La-La Land okay. He's lost ground since you saw him," she said sadly. "The dementia is starting to take its toll physically. Ma's tough as nails, but it's getting to her."

I groaned. "Another reason not to stir up family conflict over the boat."

"Do I dare ask what's going on with the *Thalassa*?"

I said, "Show is better than tell."

I took her over to meet Len, my mechanic pal. Chloe's bubbly nature can lighten up the most doleful personality. They only chatted a few minutes before the sorrowful mechanic changed into a different person, all grins and smiles. But when Len showed her the ailing outboards, his expression reverted to its normal mournfulness. Apparently, even Chloe's happy halo has its limits.

After talking to Len we walked out onto the floating dock and stopped at *Thalassa*'s boat slip. "Okay, let me see if I understand this," Chloe said. "The boat can be back in business, bringing in money, as soon as the motors have been fixed."

"That's right. But paying for the repairs means I miss my payment to the family."

"We can give you time to recover."

"Uh-uh. Like I said, if I get a break, it seems as if I'm getting preferential treatment. Which causes conflict. Which is the last thing the family needs now with Pop getting worse."

"What do you suggest?"

"I can have the money by the end of the week. I'm working with a movie company filming locally. They've hired me to run their boat."

"A movie company? Do they need a marketing person?"

"This is a low budget operation, but they are willing to pay me enough to take care of the loan payment. Will the promise of added interest get it past the family loan sharks?"

"You'll have to ask them. Now's your chance."

A shiny Mercedes sedan the color of a bowling trophy had pulled up to the bulkhead. George got out of the car and walked down the ramp to where we were standing. My younger brother looks a lot like me, if you took a couple of inches off my height, added it to my gut and stuffed the whole package into a pastel green and purple striped Izod golf shirt and turquoise shorts. He shot Chloe an accusatory glance that had 'traitor' written all over it.

Turning to me, he said, "You got here in a hurry, brother. Now I know how to get you to show some interest in the family."

"And I know how to get you off the golf course."

"Who said I was playing golf?"

"Your outfit tells me you were either swinging a nine-iron or you like to dress like a pimp."

George was too shocked to say anything, but Chloe cut in. "Soc!" she said.

I shrugged. "I'm sorry I said that, George. I apologize for the wedgie threat, too. I was just kidding."

He gave me what could have been a smile that looked like the grimace one gets from a gassy stomach, then we shook hands. The pimp comment didn't bother him as much as the reference to how I yanked his pants up to his armpits when we were kids did.

"You shouldn't joke about stuff like that. I was really embarrassed."

"George, it happened when I was in the sixth grade."

"Doesn't matter."

"What about all the times I protected you from other kids?"

"That's even worse."

I tried to lighten his mood. "How are Maria and the kids?"

"Great. She does volunteer work at the church. Jimmy and Ariadne are doing really well in school." He went into detail; his obvious pride must have dampened his anger because he said, "I didn't come down here to harass you, Soc. I just got worried about our investment."

"Don't blame you, George. The company's got a lot of money tied up in this boat."

He nodded in agreement. "Since I didn't hear it directly from you, I drove down to take a look for myself. I talked to the mechanic and he told me you'd given him an on-again, off-again order on the repairs. I blew my top. You should have let me know you had problems."

"You're right, George, I should have. But I thought I could deal with it without disrupting our agreement. Would it have made a difference?"

"You know I didn't want the company to buy the boat in the first place. Ma was the deciding vote." He didn't stamp his foot like an angry little kid. I guess that was something.

"I'm well aware of that. Have you told her what's going on with the boat?"

"Oh yeah. That's why she wanted to come down with me."

"Look, George, we can work this out, but first tell me about Pop. Chloe says he isn't doing well."

"You'd better talk to Ma about that. She's heartbroken but doesn't let on."

I clamped him on the shoulder in a friendly way, then walked up the boat ramp to the Mercedes. My mother was tucked into a corner of the backseat. I got in and gave her a hug, thinking about how skinny she seemed. She wore a black suit that was more stylish than the stark mourning dress she'd worn for years, until the last of her relatives had died off back in Crete.

"How are you, Aristotle?" Although her soft-spoken voice had a slight crackle, it hadn't lost the edge of authority that had served her well as a mother and corporate executive.

"I'm fine, Ma. Sorry you had to drive all the way down here."

"It's no bother if I get to talk to you, Aristotle."

"I'm the one who should have kept in touch. That way I would have known about Pop. Chloe told me he's not doing well."

"He still knows me. He would know you, too, Aristotle."

It was a subtle but well-deserved rebuke.

"I'm coming up to see him next week. Sorry to get everyone

upset over this boat thing when you've got Pop to worry about."

"Don't be sorry, Aristotle. Just think about coming back into the family business."

"You want me to work at the bakery?"

"Oh no," she said with horror in her voice. "You would burn yourself on an oven. You were never made for that kind of work. I want you to know more about the *business of the family*, not Parthenon Pizza, the family business."

"I'll try harder, Ma. You can ask Chloe about the help I gave her with the new box design."

"That makes me happy, Aristotle." It was a verbal pat on the head. "Now what is the problem with *Thalassa*?"

I summed up the situation. Her mind was still quick when it came to business.

She shrugged. "No problem. You fix the boat. You pay us when you get money from your new job."

"What about George?"

"Don't worry about George. I'll deal with your brother."

I gave her another hug, thanked her again, and got out of the car. The window rolled down and she stuck her face out.

"One more thing, Aristotle."

"What's that, Ma?"

She gave me a gold-toothed smile, and in her sweetest voice said, "After this, don't miss any more payments."

CHAPTER 15

After a few more rounds of hugs, goodbyes, and making promises that I'd never keep, I extracted myself from the tender embrace of my family and made my escape. As I pulled out of the parking lot, a black Ford Taurus appeared in the rearview mirror. Dealing with the post-traumatic stress that always followed an encounter with the Socarides clan, I didn't think anything of it at the time.

What looked like the same sedan showed up a few cars back on the Mid-Cape Highway. Still no 'blip' appeared on my mental radar. I was busy sending mind missiles at the slow-motion driver ahead of me. I noticed the car again when I arrived at Newcomb's Hollow beach, but I didn't think anything of it because my mind was on the shoot.

The fleet of support vehicles for *The Pirate's Daughter* was lined up along the edge of a parking lot nestled between high dunes.

I parked near Cait's blue Mini and walked past a gaggle of spectators looking down at the beach from behind the yellow police tape that blocked access to the public. Cait was talking to the park ranger who'd been assigned to the movie production.

I said hello to the ranger, then told Cait that I'd been visiting family and couldn't come sooner.

"No big deal. You didn't miss much. We filmed some establishing shots. Now Max is up on the cliffs coordinating the close-ups with Eric, the assistant director. Let's see how he's doing."

We followed a sandy path to the top of a dune. Max stood on the bluff, barking orders into a walkie-talkie.

"Tell these dead-assed pirates they've gotta remember they were tossed onto the beach by the fury of the storm," he shouted. "See that guy lying there like he's Dracula stretched out in a coffin? Yeah, that's the one, Eric. Turn him over on his side. Make sure his arms and legs are twisted in crazy positions. Rag doll stuff. The guy a couple of stiffs over also looks too damned comfortable."

Around twenty human bodies were scattered on the sand, along with timber, boxes, ragged pieces of canvas and other debris. Eric moved from body to body, stopping to re-arrange arms and legs as Max directed.

Wearing her scarlet cloak, Ana stood with the rest of the film crew near a green-roofed canopy I assumed was the same one that had been set up at Goody Hallett's meadow.

Eric's voice crackled over the hand radio. "How's it look now, Max?"

"Damned good. I'll be right down to get things moving." He saw us watching him and rubbed his palms together like a chef unveiling a new dish. "Good timing, guys. We're about to roll. Glad you could make it, Soc. Did Cait fill you in?"

"She said you're doing close-ups on the beach."

"That's right. This shot follows the scene we filmed at Goody's meadow yesterday."

He framed the scene with his hands. "Ana sees her lover's ship in pieces. She rushes down to look for Bellamy among more than one hundred dead pirates who've washed up on the beach."

"I count less than two dozen."

"This bunch is all the extras our budget allows. Before you arrived we took a wide angle shot of the beach. We'll use it as the place shot to add more bodies with computer imaging."

"You can do that?"

"Sure. The trick is to splice in scenes with live human actors to make it more believable. Gotta make our day. *Hasta la vista.*"

Max loped along the path and minutes later he was trudging on the beach toward Ana, who had moved apart from the group and was now standing alone. Max gave her a quick embrace, then said something to the Steadicam operator and to a man carrying a microphone suspended from a boom anchored to a chest harness. Then Max and his crew stood around as if frozen in place.

"Why isn't anyone moving?" I asked Cait after a couple of minutes had passed.

"They're waiting for the go-ahead from Eric. He runs the set." About thirty seconds later, she said, "Okay, he's just called, 'rolling sound.' No more talking. Once the set is completely quiet, the assistant cameraman yells 'mark!' and claps the clapperboard. There he goes. Now the scene goes to the director."

Max cupped his hands to his mouth. Even with the distance and the rumble of the surf, "Action!" carried up to the cliffs. He ducked under the canopy.

"I thought the director sat in a high chair with a megaphone in his lap," I said.

"Those days are over. Max will watch the shoot on a remote screen connected to the camera."

The set came to life as if a switch had been thrown. Ana ran to the nearest dead pirate, knelt by his side, then went to the next corpse and the next, flitting from body to body like a bee seeking pollen from very dead flowers. The camera operator kept pace with Ana. The sound man walked along behind the cameraman, holding the microphone high above Ana's head.

Halfway through her grim task, Ana knelt by an overturned boat. Next to the boat were two bodies lying face-down. Cait explained that the bodies were those of Sam Bellamy and Luke, the Indian who Jason was playing. The treasure chest was supposedly under the boat.

"Who's playing dead Sam?" I asked.

"One of the extras you saw when you came for your job interview. Only a glimpse of his face will make the final cut."

"I remember seeing the young guy with the beard the day I met you. Not a bad choice."

"I think so. Okay, here's where Ana discovers the Indian is alive."

Jason pushed himself up onto his knees, said something to Ana, and then staggered to his feet. He leaned on her shoulder, looking up and down the beach. They talked again, then they lifted the body of Bellamy, slung his arms around their necks, and dragged him toward the base of the cliffs.

Max popped out from under the canopy and brought his hands to his mouth. "Cut! And print."

Ana and Jason stopped in their tracks. Sam Bellamy straightened up and patted the other actors on their backs. The cameraman followed Max and the assistant director under the canopy. The pirate extras miraculously came to life and got to their feet.

"That's it?" I said.

"Depends on how the take went. Max and his top guys will review the take and decide if the scene needs to be done again. This is nail-biting time." A moment later Max walked out from under the tent followed by the assistants. He began clapping. The assistants joined in.

"Guess the shoot is good?" I said.

"*More* than good," she said with excitement in her voice. "He'll take a closer look at the dailies but that's what happens when you've got a great technical crew and experienced talent like Ana and Jason. Let's go congratulate them."

We walked down the path to the parking lot. The cast was coming up from the beach. Ana led the way, with Jason at her side. The strands from his long, black wig hung down over his nut-brown face. Ana's wardrobe assistant Tatiana was next. In her footsteps was

Yergo, her silent friend with the wide shoulders. The formerly dead pirates straggled behind. The stand-in for Bellamy had his hands in the air giving a double thumbs-up, as if he'd just won an Oscar.

The spectators broke into applause. Ana beamed at the attention. Jason grinned from ear to ear and pumped every hand within reach. It must have been especially sweet for them to be back in the limelight after being banished to Hollywood Purgatory for so long.

Jason wrapped his arm around Cait's shoulder and gave me a high-five with his free hand. "Wonderful to see our *chef de maison* and my fellow rummy," he said. "You saw the shoot?"

"We watched you and Ana from the cliff," Cait said.

"Very exciting," I added.

"You're much too kind. Movie making can be as dull as dishwater. You stand around and drink coffee until someone tells you what to do. You say your lines, so low that only the sound person can hear you." He spit out the sand coating his lips. "I'm as dry as a bone."

"You're *always* as dry as a bone," said Ana, who had come up behind Jason.

He pecked her on the cheek. "True, my dear Goody. But after all the dialogue, I find my throat especially in need of lubrication."

"You didn't have any dialogue. You were half dead. You groaned, grunted, and grunted some more."

"Also true, but it wasn't easy dragging your lover up the sand cliffs."

"You only dragged him ten feet and I helped."

"Nevertheless, grunting is particularly hard on the vocal chords. Enough of this prattle. Will we see you and Cait at the public house up the road, Soc?"

Cait pointed to the pirates who were wandering around the parking lot, demonstrating their *arghs* and posing for pictures with the spectators. "Thanks, Jace, but I've got to get these cutthroats off the set. They get paid by the hour. You go ahead, Soc. I'll see you tonight."

Ana removed her cloak. Under her costume she was dressed for comfort in shorts and a sleeveless blouse. She handed the cloak to her hairdresser. I was more interested in the big guy. He glanced around the crowd like a security guard on the job.

Jason slipped the wig off and handed it to the hairdresser. "Wish these things came with air conditioning. Damned hot under that rug. I'll lead the way to the watering hole, Captain Soc."

He got behind the wheel of a Chrysler van and Ana slid in beside him. I followed in the GMC, driving along a rolling road that ran high above the blue Atlantic. After going about a mile, we turned onto a driveway that sloped down toward the ocean and parked behind a large building sheathed in weather-beaten gray shingles. The former life-saving station used to house the surf men who patrolled the beach night and day on the lookout for ships in trouble. Years before, the old station had been converted into a beachfront bistro called, The Beachcomber.

The deck bar was busy but not yet mobbed with the happy hour crowd. We found a table that came with a good view of the ocean and a tanned young waitress to take our order.

"Yo-ho-ho, Soc," Jason said. "How about rum on the rocks for two?"

"No-no-no," I said, holding my palm up. "Beer will be fine."

Ana poked Jason in the ribs. "Maybe you should lay off the rum. We've got a busy day tomorrow."

"Absolutely right, Ana. No rum. I'll have a Cape Codder. Vodka and cranberry juice."

"You're incorrigible," Ana said.

"And you are persistent," he said with a note of irritation in his voice. "Don't forget, my love, you already came to my rescue back there on the beach. No need to save me from myself."

She stuck her forefinger so close to his face that he went cross-eyed.

"The only thing I care about saving is your liver. It's got to last until filming is done. Then you can pickle every vital organ in your body." She winked at me. "Thank you for coming by the set. It couldn't have been very exciting for you. Movie making is like watching grass grow."

"Jason said the same thing, but watching *you* making a new film was a big thrill."

"Aha," Jason said. "The Greek philosopher pirate exhibits the symptoms of a fan crush."

"Guilty as charged. Can you blame me?"

"Not at all," Jason said. "I've been infatuated with this lovely lady for as long as I can remember. Like you, I've seen every movie she's made."

Ana rolled her eyes. "You sweet-talking lads must have worn the skin off your lips kissing the Blarney stone," she said in a thick brogue.

"Got it." I snapped my fingers. "Erin Mulligan," I said, identifying the familiar line.

"From the movie of the same name," Jason said. "You were magnificent as the Irish girl who defies the British crown to save her doomed lover."

"Bravo, gentlemen. Erin Mulligan it is." Talking again in her natural voice, Ana said, "If you followed the ups and downs of my career, it must have been a roller coaster ride."

"Your career path was as flat as a Kansas interstate compared to mine," Jason said. "Nothing at your nadir compares to *Space Wreck*."

"Oh my, I had forgotten that one. The critics called it 'Space Dreck,' " Ana said.

Jason seemed to shrink into his shoulders. "I suppose I should have been grateful it faded from sight and was so bad it didn't even go to video."

Ana reached out and put her hand on Jason's.

"Sorry to drag up old memories, Jace. And apologies from both of us, Soc, for bringing you to a whine-and-jeez session with a couple of has-beens."

"That's not the way I see it. You two are the best. You must have seen the potential in *The Pirate's Daughter* or you wouldn't be here."

They exchanged glances, and then they broke into laughter.

"You're very flattering, Soc," Ana said. "But our phones weren't exactly ringing off the hook with calls from our agents."

"Speak for yourself, Ana," Jason sniffed. "My phone was ringing."

"Bill collectors."

"That's true. But at least it was ringing," Jason said.

Ana said, "I'll tell you why we're laughing, Soc. When our agents called with this offer, we jumped at the chance to work together."

Jason said, "We needed the work for the benefit of our deflated bank accounts and egos. Spending a couple of weeks by the sea, all expenses paid, and even receiving a small paycheck, were big attractions."

"It was more than that. We were both skeptical about Max because he's had some real flops that didn't help his career," Ana said. "But *The Pirate's Daughter* drew us in. Mary Hallett is such a complex personality. She starts off young and innocent, learns some hard lessons about life and people, and not only survives, but grows stronger."

Jason nodded. "Bellamy is a swashbuckler, and an interesting historical figure, but he's reckless as well. He impregnates Mary. When he does return to make things good, he drowns. The Indian I play is far nobler. Luke is loyal to Bellamy to the end."

The waitress came back to see if we needed a second round. Ana looked around the deck. More young people had arrived and the noise was cranking up.

"We can talk shop later where it's quieter," Ana said. "I understand you're going to join us at the Big House."

"Word travels fast. Yes, I'm moving in. I'll pick up a few things at my place and head over."

Jason said, "Speaking of which, I've got to make a run to the head before we go."

He got up and made his way through the crush of bodies to the restroom.

When he was out of sight, Ana sighed. "I don't know what to do. I was serious about what I said to him."

"About the pickled liver?"

She smiled. "I want his liver to last, but I'm very fond of Jason. I want him to finish this film. For his sake as well as mine. You saw how he reacted when I discouraged him from drinking rum."

"Boozers don't like anything to get in the way of their boozing. Tell you what. I'll keep an eye on him."

"You'd really do that, Soc?"

"I don't know how much I can help, but I'd be glad to give it a try."

"Thank you. I don't know how I can ever repay you for your kindness."

I probably would have gone weak-kneed if I hadn't been sitting down. Then I would have blushed and gushed like a love-sick schoolboy, telling her that simply being in the presence of a great film star like Ana Roman was payment enough. Luckily, I didn't get the chance to embarrass myself.

"Shush," Ana said. "We'll have to talk later. Jason is on his way back to the table."

CHAPTER 16

With a boozer like Jason, the first drink is similar to cocking a pistol. The second is putting the gun to your head. Drink three is squeezing the trigger. It's was a suicidal sequence I knew from experience. Apparently, so did Ana.

Jason had drained his vodka and cranberry juice and raised his finger to signal the waitress for a refill, but Ana cut in. "Thank you for calling for the check, Jason. That's very generous of you to pick up the tab."

Jason slowly lowered his hand and placed it on Ana's, which was resting on the table. In a tough guy voice, he said, "You're killing me, sweetheart. But I'm going to die with a smile on my face." He turned to me and said, "Well, Mr. Movie buff?"

"Sorry. I don't recognize it."

"I do," Ana said. "It's from *The Private Eye*. You were the hard-boiled private detective who falls for the *femme fatale*. You were wonderful."

They gazed affectionately into each other's eyes. This was no act. They might have floated up into the sky in a bubble of love if the waitress hadn't burst it. "Would you like another drink?" she said.

"No thank you," Jason said. "Just the check, please."

A few minutes later, as I stood in the parking lot and watched the van depart, I thought about the fragility of fame. These Hollywood legends had blazed like stars only to burn out and fall back to earth. Now they had another chance at the limelight thanks to *The Pirate's Daughter*. Maybe Max was right about Goody Hallett. Maybe she *had* used her witchy powers to pull Ana and Jason out of obscurity, knowing that two people who were desperate for adulation would tell her and Sam's story better than any of the pretty young faces now decorating the big screen.

I got into my truck and headed home. After the go-around with my family and the voyage into the land of make-believe pirates, all I wanted to do was bask in the mildewed splendor of the boathouse. But that was not to be. When I reached the end of my driveway I saw two vehicles parked side-by-side. The rented Cruze Sally was driving, and the high-lift truck with the goofy camouflage paint job.

I prefer not to mix my personal life with my business, which is why I leaned on the steering wheel and cursed softly in the language of my forefathers. After a minute of this I got out of the pickup and went into the house. A couple of things immediately caught my attention. Kojak didn't ambush my leg. And I could hear the sound of voices from the deck. I pushed open the screen door and stepped outside. Sally and Gill lounged in the Adirondack chairs like passengers on a low-budget luxury liner. Kojak sat on Sally's lap. She was tickling him under the chin. His eyes were shut and he was purring loudly.

Sally gave me the smile that always made my heartbeat quicken.

"Hi Soc," she said. "You never told me your colleague was so fascinating."

I shot Gill a steely-eyed glance. "My colleague?"

"I mentioned that we were collaborating on a case," Gill said. "I didn't exactly say we were colleagues."

"Sorry, Howland," Sally said. "I must have misunderstood when you said you and Soc were like Sherlock and Dr. Watson."

Howland? Somehow, Sally had escaped the certain death that

Gill promised would come to anyone using his proper name. She was having far too much fun jerking my chain.

"I know this is hard to believe," I said with unfeigned weariness in my voice, "but this isn't 221B Baker Street. Howland is a client. He hired me to catch the guys poaching his oysters."

"He told me about that. He also said he may have a lead, although he refused to go into details until he talked to you."

Gill furrowed his brow into a deep V. "As I explained to Sally, I'm not being coy. It would be unprofessional and unethical if I divulged information about the investigation."

"Now that I'm here," I said, "maybe Howland and I should talk about the new developments. Would you excuse us?"

She stroked Kojak's head. The little lap lecher purred even louder.

"Of course," she said. "Does Kojak still like Greenies?"

"Kojak will eat anything you put in front of him, including the plate. You'll find a pack of hairball prevention yummies in the cupboard above his dish."

As soon as Sally went into the house I plunked down in her chair. "You said you'd kill anyone who used your given name. Sally looks pretty healthy. What's up with that?"

"She's very nice, and maybe I was trying to impress her. I still prefer my nickname, if you don't mind."

"Not at all, Howie. And if you don't mind, I'd prefer it if you didn't tell people that you and I are colleagues. Now that's settled, tell me about this supposed lead of yours."

"I think it's the real thing, Soc. I followed your suggestion and went down the list of customers who'd canceled contracts because I couldn't match the low price other suppliers were giving them. I called and said I was thinking of dropping my price. I know what it takes to get an oyster from the flats to market, so I used that as a baseline. Some suppliers shave their profits down to the bone to get business, but I traced only one company that had been selling stock way below cost."

"Which would indicate that the wholesale oyster supplier was paying little or nothing for oysters," I said. "What's the name of this outfit?"

"South by West Seafood. They're out of New Bedford."

"You're telling me these are the guys fencing stolen oysters?"

"It makes sense. Say you were a freelance poacher. An honest dealer would ask questions. A dishonest dealer could take them off your hands, no questions asked."

"I see where you're going. The dealer launders the stolen goods and sells them on the legitimate wholesale market. With control of the supply train, the wholesaler could cook the books to cover the flow of illegal stock from the flats to the consumer."

"That's what I'm thinking," Gill said. "There may even be a double deal in there."

"In what way?"

"The crooks wouldn't have enough stolen oysters to sustain a steady supply. They'd have to supplement them with legal stuff. They could use the poached stock as a sales tool. Give the retailer a taste of the primo stuff, and once they have an agreement, bring in oysters from any place."

"Classic bait and switch. What about the contaminated oysters? No one has gotten sick or worse from eating bad shellfish."

"Poisoned shellfish could be traced back to their source," Gill said. "But the dealer could hold the bad oysters off the market, maybe put them back in the water where they'd be flushed clean, then sold."

"Possible. They'd need a secluded stretch of beachfront."

Gill grinned and reached into the pocket of his work shirt. He pulled out a piece of paper which he carefully unfolded and handed to me. "I researched South by West. This is a Google satellite photo of one of their properties."

The picture showed the roof of a rectangular structure. A long driveway went from the building through some woods to a road. The building was near the shore of an inlet.

"This might fit the bill." I gave the photo back to Gill. "Where is this place?"

"In the Buzzards Bay area. I took a look at it earlier today. I parked out on the road and cut through the woods. People were around so I thought it would be better to come back after dark."

"That was risky. Sure no one saw you?"

"Positive."

I stood up and said, "Okay. Let's do it. I'll meet you at the Route 6 Mid-Cape Burger King at eleven tonight."

Gill heaved his massive body out of his chair. He looked so happy I was afraid he was going to hug me. His diction had improved but he still smelled like the oyster flats.

"Damn, Soc. Thanks for including me in this."

"Before you go," I said, in what I hoped was a subtle hint, "let me ask you about something that's been bugging me. You're sitting on top of all that waterfront property. You could sell it for a few million bucks but you'd rather muck around in the mud. What gives?"

"My parents got the last laugh. The property can't be developed because there's no legal access. The land is cut off from the road by another tract. I hoped to build a little house overlooking the bay, but instead, I live in a trailer park and lease storage space for my oyster gear. Pretty funny, eh?"

I could tell by his doleful voice that Gill didn't consider it funny at all. So all I said was, "See you at eleven."

Sally poked her head out the door. "Kojak's fed. Safe to come out?"

"Come on, Sally. Mr. Gill was just leaving."

We shook hands, then Gill left and I was alone with Sally. We settled into the chairs and sat there without talking.

After a minute, she said, "Things have hardly changed since the last time I sat here looking out at the bay. Such a beautiful spot."

"I've tried to maintain the nautical minimalist décor. But like Barry Manilow says, good things never come easy."

"I wasn't talking about *things*, so much, but I did notice some new rugs and lamps."

"I made a killing at a big yard sale. I had my heart set on the Elvis-on-velvet portrait, but they wanted five bucks for it. Refrigerator is newer. I've got the same old stuff in it. The basic ingredients of the Greek-American bachelor life. Feta cheese, Greek olives and beer. Speaking of which, would you like a cold brew?"

She said that she would. I went inside and came back with two cans of Cape Cod Amber. We popped the tops in unison, toasted each other with a 'clink' of aluminum and both took a sip.

"Nice to be back again," she said.

"Glad to have you back, Sal. I've missed you."

"I've missed you too, Soc. Sorry I left without saying goodbye."

"I don't blame you. I would have left me too. Why waste your time with a dead end?"

She put her hand on my forearm. "You're no dead end and it wasn't always a waste of time, Soc."

"Glad to hear that." I paused. "Wow! We're getting way too serious. How about another beer?"

We were both in a mellow mood when the alarm in Sally's cell phone chirped. She glanced at the caller ID.

"Darn," she said. "I've got a meeting with some of the shark research people."

"And I've got to pack for the move to the Big House."

"Pathetic," she said. "We're just two ships passing in the night, aren't we?"

"Ships can stop and turn, Sal. Let's make a pact. Dinner...come hell or high water."

"You've got a deal."

We shook on it.

"Thanks for the offer to take care of Kojak," I said.

"Glad to do it. After my meeting I'll swing by the motel, pick up my things and come back here. Are we still on for the aerial survey tomorrow?"

"I'll let you know after I get the shooting schedule from Max."

We stood and faced each other, only inches apart in an awkward moment. Past lovers who were no longer lovers. Sally broke the impasse. She put her arms around my shoulders and gave me a light kiss on the lips. It only lasted a second but every pleasure neuron in my brain lit up.

It would have been nice to wrap her in my arms, but we both knew it wasn't time. Maybe it would never be time. We walked side-by-side out to her car and I watched her drive off until the taillights disappeared around a bend. I was sad to see her go. I would have liked to have been here when she got back, but like Robert Frost said, "I had promises to keep."

I went inside, packed a duffel, dug out the bag with the scuba gear, scratched Kojak on the head, told him to have fun with Auntie Sal, then headed to the Big House. I was still giddy from Sally's quick display of affection, but a little voice in my head reminded me that it was not my magnetic personality and rugged good looks that had landed Sally on my doorstep. What brought her back into my life was a dead guy and a great white shark named Emma.

CHAPTER 17

When I got to the Big House I parked next to the shuttle bus used to transport the pirate extras to and from film shoots. I got out of my truck, grabbed my duffle bag, and followed the brick walkway around the house. Raucous laughter was rolling across the lawn. Bellamy's buccaneers had captured the gazebo as if it were a fully-laden merchant ship. They hung over the railings of their prize. Full-throated *arghs* and *ayes* filled the air.

Cait stood near the gazebo, watching the wild scene. I walked up beside her. "Looks like the fake pirates plundered the liquor locker," I said.

Her arms were folded across her chest and her mouth was set in a tight-lipped line. She kept her stony gaze fixed on the gazebo. Nodding slowly, and with great deliberation, she said, "That's exactly what happened."

"The last time I saw these guys they were at the beach signing autographs for their adoring fans. What are they doing here?"

"Max's idea. He invited them over to thank them for their good work today. Everything was going okay before Jason showed up. He was pretty lit. He's the one who led the attack on the gazebo."

As if on cue, someone in the gazebo shouted a *yo-ho-ho* in a baritone voice that could be heard above the background laughter. A hearty cheer went up from the pirate crew. Then Jason stepped out of the gazebo onto the lawn. He drew a cutlass from its scabbard, and even more disturbing, waved it in the air where the setting sun glinted off the metal blade. Encouraged by shouts from his crew, he brought the cutlass around in a long sweeping arc and sank the blade into one of the thick wooden corner posts of the gazebo. When he tried to yank it out, the blade stuck. He lost his balance, staggered backwards and almost fell before catching himself. He raised his arms in victory, triggering an even louder chorus of cheers from his crew.

I bit my lower lip. "Aw crap," I said.

Cait looked at me with narrowed eyes. "Why the, 'aw crap'?"

"After the beach shoot I went out for a drink with Jason and Ana. I told her I'd try to keep him sober. He must have had a few snoot-fulls while I was at my house packing a bag."

"Don't worry, Soc. It's not your fault. Max is going to be furious, though. Uh-oh. Let me correct that. Present tense. Max *is* furious."

I followed her gaze and saw Max trotting across the lawn from the mansion. His hands were balled into tight fists and his arms swung at his sides like train pistons. When he got to the gazebo, he waded into the crowd and came out with Jason in tow.

They stood face-to-face on the lawn. Jason raised his hands in a pleading gesture. Max pointed at the gazebo then jabbed Jason in the chest with his forefinger.

"This is getting physical," Cait said. "I'd better butt in before it gets out of hand."

She strode over to the arguing men. From what I saw, it was already out of hand, which is why I was only a couple of steps behind her.

"Damn you, Jason," Max shouted. "You've screwed up this movie for the last time. Damn you to hell!" Max's face was bright red and spittle dripped from his lips.

Jason grinned like a deranged clown. "I'm not the only pirate scuttling this ship," he said, slurring his words badly.

Max stopped the chest jabbing. Cait saw it as an opening and she stepped in between them. It was a brave but foolish move. She was a hair over five feet tall and both men towered over her.

I muscled in to protect Cait. In doing so, I nudged Max aside. He glared at me as if he couldn't believe his eyes. Then his right hand reached out and his thick fingers gripped the front of my shirt. He tightened his hold until the collar choked my windpipe. His other hand held on to the strap of the bag slung over my shoulder.

Unable to back away, I grabbed his wrist with both hands and gave it a hard twist that persuaded him to let go of my collar. If I had wanted to play rough I would have followed up with an elbow to the face or a knee to the groin. But I didn't want to maul Max; I wanted to get his attention. Pain dampened the hot fire in his eyes. He let go of the shirt and the duffle strap.

Taking a step back, he said, "Sorry, Soc. I didn't mean…"

Max looked as if he was about to cry, and Jason was about to fall on Cait, who held his arm to keep him from toppling over. "Don't worry about it," I said, not meaning a word. "We'll take care of Jason. Looks like the party's over anyway."

The gazebo crowd had gone silent. The extras had figured out that the celebration was over. I took Jason's free arm and Cait and I dragged him to the front porch where we stopped to rest.

Jason gave me a goofy smile and mumbled, "Shiver me timbers." A second later he fell back onto a cushioned wicker settee, passed out cold.

"Good thing he did that," Cait said, catching her breath. "I couldn't take another step." She lifted his legs so that his feet dangled over one arm of the sofa. "Thanks for coming to my rescue. I was out-numbered and out-weighed."

"Is this a regular thing with Jason and Max?"

She let out a deep sigh. "They have their moments. Artistic temperament, I guess."

"Dunno about that, Cait." What I had witnessed was more than a casual argument between a couple of high-strung artistes. Max looked as if he wanted to break Jason in pieces. I wondered what the drunken actor meant with his comment about scuttling the ship and why it had set Max off like a Roman candle.

Cait averted her eyes. She clearly didn't want to talk about it anymore.

"How about showing me where I'm bunking."

She brightened. "Leave your bag inside and I'll give you a VIP tour of the Big House."

We went through the entrance into the spacious foyer where I left my bag, then we climbed a stairway to the second story. A wide hallway ran the length of the house. Paintings of ships and other nautical themes covered the walls. There was a door at one end of the hall; Cait said it led out to the tower room.

"These doors all lead to two-bedroom suites on the second level," she said. She knocked on a door and, when no one answered, opened it. "This is Ana's suite." We went into a spacious room furnished with a canopy bed and rich-looking furniture and rugs.

I looked around, taking in the fine details. "Fit for a queen."

"Even *old* Hollywood royalty gets special treatment. All three of the second-story suites are pretty luxurious. Jason's is only slightly smaller than this one."

"Who gets the third?"

"Tatiana, our make-up artist, and her husband Yergo."

"I've seen them at the beach shoots but we haven't been introduced."

"They're pretty shy because their English isn't great."

"I didn't know make-up artists had royal status."

"You've seen how ageless Ana is. Tatiana keeps her looking that way. She even got her husband a job on the film crew."

"Doesn't a film director qualify as film royalty?"

"Max is pretty egalitarian for a director. He likes to be close to the creative process, so he bunks downstairs in the den which he's turned into the editing room."

We descended the stairs to the first floor to retrieve my duffle. Cait said the rest of the crew shared the four downstairs bedrooms.

"Did Kirk Munson stay at the house?"

"He moved out of the Big House to a room in town." She opened a door and we went into a chamber that had two king-sized beds. "This is my pad."

"I like it."

"Glad to hear you say that, because we're bunking together. That's your bed. Better warn you. I snore like a buzz saw. That's why I got my own room."

I threw my duffle onto the bed. "Then I'll be sure not to sleep like a log."

"Okay, roomie, it's a deal," she said.

We shook hands.

"I've got to pull dinner together."

I volunteered to give her a hand in the kitchen, but on the way we encountered Ana, who'd just arrived.

"I see that Jason decided to take a nap on the porch," she said. "So much for the pledge of sobriety he made when I dropped him off."

Cait knew about my broken promise to keep an eye on Jason, so she excused herself and beat a hasty retreat to the kitchen to make dinner.

"Sorry, Ana," I said. "Jason was well oiled by the time I got here."

"Yes, I know. I spoke to Max on the way in and he told me what happened with Jason and his bloodthirsty gang of pirates."

"From what I saw, blood wasn't what they were thirsting for."

"Now that you have been officially made a part of our movie family, you will quickly learn that this wouldn't be *The Pirate's Daughter* if something didn't go wrong every day."

"Maybe it's the curse of Bellamy and Mary," I joked.

"You must be clairvoyant, Soc. Cait and I have talked about the possibility that the project is haunted. We've both had the feeling that eyes were watching us on Lucifer's Land and in the cedar swamp."

I remembered the shadowy figure I had seen lurking in the pine trees, but I said, "I don't believe in ghosts."

Before starting up the stairs she smiled and said, "You'll believe if you stay in the Big House long enough. See you at dinner."

CHAPTER 18

I was chewing on Ana's cryptic comment about ghosts when Max came through the front door and saw me standing in the foyer. The ogre who looked as if he wanted to have Jason for dinner and me for dessert had vanished, and in its place was the familiar friendly teddy bear.

He flashed a jovial grin. "The situation is under control. The pirates have been clamped in irons and a prison ship is transporting them to their respective home ports so they can mend their ways."

"They'll have to recover from their hangovers before they can mend anything," I said.

"I've taken that into account. I've rescheduled the boat shoot for tomorrow afternoon." He tugged at his beard. "I owe you a big-time apology, Soc. I was a crazy man out there. No excuses."

My head was spinning at how fast he had gone from Mr. Mean to Mr. Happypants, but I said, "None needed. You must be under a lot of pressure."

"Thanks for understanding the situation. It's just that I want the movie to succeed and Jason's antics don't help."

"Will he be able to work tomorrow?"

"He recovers faster than most because the alcohol never leaves his bloodstream. Enough about Jason. Let's see how the dailies look."

As we walked down the hallway to the den, he said, "By the way, where'd you learn that cool arm twist you used to break my grip?"

"Basic unarmed combat training, courtesy of the U.S. Marines."

"You were a Marine? That wasn't in the job application."

"My *Halls of Montezuma* days were a long time ago."

"We'll have to talk when we have a minute. Maybe there's a movie in your story."

"I don't think so, Max."

"Okay, I get it." he said, giving me a brotherly smile. He opened the den door. The cinematographer sat at a table looking at the glowing screen of a laptop.

"When we shoot a scene it's stored on disk," Max said. "We check out the dailies every night. That way we can see how the actors performed and make sure that the scene has been shot from every possible angle. How's it look, Jake?"

The cinematographer shook his head. "Not looking good, Max."

"You're kidding. How could they not be good?"

Jake laughed. "Because they're looking fabulous."

"Bastard." Max cuffed him playfully on the top of his head. "If you're through jerking me around, maybe you could explain to Soc what you've been doing."

"Glad to. This is the scene we shot the day before. Have a seat and enjoy the show."

We pulled up a couple of chairs. Ana's face was looking out from the screen. It was lit by a flickering light from the side, and she was gazing directly into the lens. Her shoulder-length flaxen hair was combed out.

Max said, "This was filmed in an old garage, which we've fitted up to look like the interior of her hut. You've read the script, so you know it presented some real challenges. We had to shoot scenes years apart with the same characters. We have Ana as she looks today. She's a beautiful woman but she's not a young girl as she is at the start of the story."

"You said you hired an actress in Canada to play the younger Ana."

He nodded. "That only works for certain scenes. Ana is the real star. You have to show her face. No amount of make-up or blurred focus or CGI would do her justice. So what I did in this sequence is started with the older Mary telling the story of the shipwreck to the camera, which is the stand-in for her daughter. Run it, Jake."

Jake clicked the computer mouse. Ana's lips moved but no sound came out. Max anticipated my question. "Sound is distracting. We'll just watch the visual for now."

After Ana had talked for a minute or so, her face faded from the screen.

"Well?" Max said.

"That's it?"

"Part of it. The CGI special effects to go with this scene have already been shot in a sound studio and will be added to the live shoot." He framed the screen with his fingers and thumbs. "The next time you see this there will be a sailing ship wallowing in the waves, its sails illuminated by streaks of lightning. Then darkness, gradually turning to light to reveal the ship lying on its side in the water, and back to Ana's face. How's that?"

"Amazing. I almost got seasick imagining the scene."

He gave me a friendly punch in the shoulder. I guessed we were pals again. Jake said that while the rest of the crew was at dinner he would integrate the special effects with the live shoot and set up a full screening for Max to review. Voices could be heard out in the hall. The film crew had returned from the shoot at Newcomb's Hollow. Cait stuck her head through the den doorway and announced that dinner was ready.

A few minutes later I joined the crew around the dining room table. Ana came in and took a seat at the head of the table, a position befitting her film royalty status. She looked smashing in an elegant, off-white pantsuit, a daring choice given that dinner was pasta marinara and the wine was red. Jason straggled in looking like a zombie, only not as lively. He sat and ate his dinner without speaking. More intriguing was who was missing from dinner. The hairdresser and her husband had not made an appearance.

The table chatter centered mostly on the filming. Max laid out the revised schedule for the next day. I was happy to have the morning free to go with Sally on a shark patrol. When dinner was over, we all pitched in to clean up. Then the crew filed into the den to see the dailies.

Jake had connected his computer to a wide screen television monitor. We arranged our chairs in front of the screen. Jake worked the computer mouse, the screen fluttered and Ana's face appeared as I had seen it on the laptop. She was hidden for a few seconds by a clapperboard with the scene information written on it. A banner showing the elapsed time ran along the bottom of the picture.

The slate snapped down and we could hear Ana talking in her low, lush voice. As she narrated her tale, the real Ana—who was sitting beside me—took my hand in hers and gave it a squeeze that sent electricity up my arm. She was silently mouthing the words coming from the screen.

I will never forget the day of the great storm. Never. Not as long as I live.

The woman on the screen talked about going to the cliffs, and how on this day she had to fight against the wind and the cold, blinding rain. When she got to the high bluff she saw a great ship dangerously close to the beach. The vessel was trying to claw away from the shoals that lay just offshore, although its tattered sails offered no power.

Men were climbing into the rigging and scurrying frantically along the decks, except for one figure who stood at the rail, moving a lantern back and forth. She knew without seeing his face that Sam had returned.

As Ana talked, her face faded, and the image on the screen

was that of the dark-hulled ship rolling in towering waves. The computer-generated image grew darker until only the single light remained. Then that, too, blinked out. Ana's voice in the background described how she had stared into the darkness long after the light had vanished before she crawled into her shelter where she fell asleep.

The slate snapped for a second time in front of the camera. The screen showed pale blue sky separated from the dark blue sea by the horizon line.

There was complete silence at first, then the whisper of surf, growing in volume as the camera slowly angled down. The lens took in the ship lying on its side in the rolling seas and the white frills of the foam, finally lingering on the beach and the twisted bodies lying on the sand, like dolls discarded by a careless child.

The hooded figure in the scarlet cloak entered from screen left, ran to the first body, stopped and knelt. Then she was up again, moving to the next body, and the next. The scene ended and the clapperboard announced the new scene, the one shot with the Steadicam on the beach. The camera showed Ana in close-up. The shots were quick, but there was no mistaking the anguish in her face.

She came upon the two bodies next to the overturned boat. As I had seen her do from the cliff top, she threw her body over one. There was only her soft sobbing and the whisper of the surf. Seeing Sam was dead, she moved to the other body—that of the Indian. When she discovered he was still alive, she helped him to his feet. Once he was able to stand, they carried the body of Sam along the beach. Her face reappeared and she ended the narration with the words:

"The sea that had taken my dear Samuel away had returned him to me."

A tear rolled down her cheek. The pain in her eyes was so intense I could feel it in the pit of my stomach. Garbo. Hepburn. Taylor. None of them could hold a candle to the woman sitting by my side.

The reel ended. There was quiet in the room. Then Max began to clap; slowly at first, faster as the rest of us joined in. Even Jason managed to bring his hands together. We all stood and applauded.

Ana rose from her chair and took a bow. "I couldn't have done it without all of you, my friends. I look forward to saying this again on Oscar night."

"Let's watch the dailies again," Max said.

"I'm tired of looking at myself," Ana said. "Let's go to the salon and celebrate with a drink."

There was more applause and the crew followed Ana from the den.

I needed an excuse to leave for my meeting with Gill, so I told Max I had to go back to my house for the scuba gear I'd forgotten. He said he was going to watch the dailies again and would see me later. I left the house and got into the pickup. As I drove away, I looked in the rearview mirror at the silhouette of the mansion and tower room, thinking that the Big House was like a big puzzle box.

The original owner was a rum-runner with a talent for vanishing. The house had dozens of windows and French doors but sunlight failed to penetrate the shadows that hid secrets, like the real story behind Tatiana and the taciturn husband with the wrestler's build and steely eyes. Or the reason for the raw wound that was exposed when the jolly director and the genial drunk of an actor got into a tiff.

Max said Jason was scuttling the project. Ana seemed worried about something too, and I was curious to find out exactly what it was.

I decided to zip my lips, watch, and listen. Otherwise, people could get suspicious about why I was being so nosy. I didn't want to do anything to jeopardize the job I needed to pay off a family debt. Looking back on it, maybe I should have been more inquisitive. Asking questions is not what gets you into trouble. It's not knowing the answers.

CHAPTER 19

Gill blinked his truck headlights to let me know he had arrived at the Burger King, I would have had to be blind not to see the paintball nightmare squatting in the nearly empty lot. I parked next to his pickup, grabbed my knapsack and slid into the cab, which was filled with the cloying smell of fast food. Gill was munching on a triple cheeseburger big enough to feed a family of four.

I rolled down the window to get some fresh air and said, "Didn't your mother ever tell you not to eat anything bigger than your head?"

"I always eat when I'm nervous. Settles my stomach. Want some fries?"

I waved away the ketchup-soaked strips of pure cholesterol.

"Thanks. I've had dinner. Don't worry about tonight. This is not a combat mission, it's simple reconnaissance. We get in, take a quick look around, and get out."

He gave me a thumb's up, demolished the rest of his burger and stuffed the wrapper into a paper bag. Then he wiped the grease off his fingers and started the engine. We headed out of the parking lot onto Route 6.

"How's your movie job going?" he asked.

I could have told Gill that the job was like a living psychiatric textbook. I was infatuated with an older movie star who would always be beyond my reach. The male star was an impossible drunk and the director was passive-aggressive. And that this zany crew of fun-lovers all lived in a haunted house like the Addams Family.

But I didn't tell him any of that. "The job is going fine," I said flatly.

We drove over the Sagamore Bridge to the mainland side of the Cape Cod Canal. We traveled a short distance on the highway alongside the canal and turned off onto a narrow winding road that ran through sparsely-populated scrub forest. After we'd gone a few miles, Gill stopped at a dirt drive marked with a small wooden sign hanging from a post that leaned at a crazy angle. Printed in faded letters on the blistered wood surface were the words: Capeway Cranberries, Wholesale and Retail.

"This is it?" I said.

"Yes. What now?" Gill said.

I snapped on the cab light and looked at the satellite photo.

"Keep going. There's another road ahead that leads into the backside of the property."

Gill drove for about a quarter of a mile and stopped again where tire tracks went into the woods. He checked his rearview mirror to make sure no one was behind us, then drove the truck onto a narrow, overgrown road that made my driveway look like the Mass Turnpike. After we'd gone about a half mile, the woods that had hemmed us in opened up and a cranberry bog appeared in the headlights. The jungle of cranberry vines suggested that the bog had been abandoned. I told Gill to turn the truck around to face the road in case we had to leave in a hurry.

Squadrons of bloodthirsty mosquitoes attacked us the second we stepped out of the truck. Gill and I wore long-sleeved shirts and pants, but the mosquitoes zeroed in on our hands, faces and necks. I dug the insect repellent from the knapsack, covered exposed skin with bug spray, and tossed the can to Gill. While he sprayed,

I slipped night vision goggles over my head and turned them on.

Gill got a fanny pack out of the truck and buckled the straps under his belly.

"You carrying a spare burger in case you get hungry, Howie?" I joked, hoping to relieve the tension.

"No, it's something more practical and less filling. Okay. I'm ready."

"Good. Stay right beside me and keep your mouth shut. I'll tap your shoulder when I want you to stop."

We started off along a wide path that ran around the perimeter of the roughly circular bog. After a few minutes of walking, I saw the roof of a building partially hidden behind a couple of refrigerated trailers.

I tapped Gill on the shoulder, stopped, and cocked my ear, listening for any sound out of the ordinary. The night was quiet except for the insect chorus and the drone of mosquitoes looking for patches of skin we might have missed with the spray.

"Wait here," I whispered. "I'll do a recon of the perimeter and be back in five minutes."

Heading in between the trailers, I pushed the night goggles back on my head, and turned on my halogen flashlight. I played the beam along the weathered shingles of the building. When the bog was being worked, cranberries would have been stored, sorted and packaged here.

Stacked around the warehouse were wooden pallets, plastic boxes, coils of hose, and oyster trays covered with dried seaweed— stacked three deep and ten tall.

I came back to where Gill was standing.

"Anything interesting?" he whispered.

"Yeah. Oyster trays. Lots of them."

I led the way back.

"Wow," he said when he saw the stacks of trays. "You weren't kidding."

"It's going to be tough picking your gear out of that mess."

"Tough, but not impossible. First of all, I'll eliminate the yellow and blue trays. The type I use are black."

"That still leaves hundreds that all look alike."

"To the naked eye, yes. Watch this."

He unzipped his fanny pack, extracted a flashlight with an oversized bulb housing, and flicked it on. He played the deep purple beam over the mountain of black plastic oyster trays, moving it from the top to the bottom of each stack. Some trays glowed with splotches of bright orange.

I chuckled. "The trays were marked with UV paint. Pretty slick, Dr. Gill."

"You're not the only one who believes in simple and uncomplicated. I got the spray paint and black light flashlight off Amazon after the first poaching incident."

"Let's see if we can get inside."

We went between the trailers and up a ramp to the double doors nearest the bog. The latch was secured by a heavy padlock. I studied the set-up for a minute, then reached into my bag and pulled out a foot-long crowbar. Gill held the flashlight while I inserted one end of the bar under the hinge bracket.

I pried the hinge off the door. As I suspected, the wood was as soft as putty. I retrieved my flashlight, slid the door back on its rollers, and stepped through the doorway. The interior of the building smelled of gasoline, oil and fish. More plastic containers and wooden pallets were stacked inside, along with coils of rope and cardboard boxes, but my attention was drawn to a truck. *The* truck. The one I had seen the night the oyster flats became a shooting gallery with me as the target duck.

I opened the truck door and rummaged around; I found nothing, not even registration. Then I got down on my hands and knees and pointed the flashlight beam under the truck. The muffler was wrapped in layers of sound-proofing material.

I got to my feet, took a quick look around and then went back outside. I pushed the hinge bracket back into the door. It looked normal, but the screws would come out if someone breathed on them.

"Still all quiet?" I said to Gill.

"Yeah. But, um…we may have a problem."

He pointed toward a red light blinking on the peak of the roof. "Crap," I said. "Surveillance camera."

"What can we do about it?" he said.

"We'll ask for a set of photos that show our best profile."

"In other words, there's nothing we can do about it."

"Well, yes, we can get the hell out of here in case it's transmitting live."

We hastened back to the truck and bumped along the driveway to the main road. I was pleased that no one was coming the other way. On the drive back to Burger King, Gill said, "Where does the investigation go from here?"

"Before we discuss where it's going, let's talk about where we've just been. We found your stolen gear. From that we can deduce whoever brought the trays there disposed of the oysters that were in them. We found the sound-proofed truck the poachers used to carry off your stock. And all of this stuff is on property owned by South by West."

"Then these are our guys."

"Seems so. But you need more of a connection between evidence and people who moved it there. Are there other properties we could look into?"

"They own some buildings around the New Bedford waterfront."

"Busy place. It might be tougher to break into those buildings than it was to crack the door of an old cranberry house."

"The company also owns a bar in Buzzards Bay. We wouldn't have to break down any doors. What say we check it out? I'll go in posing as a fisherman and see if there's anything I can pick up in conversation."

"Think you'll fool anyone?"

"Hah. I fooled a private detective."

We were pulling into the Burger King parking lot. Gill did pretty well on the recon. He stayed calm and obeyed orders.

"Okay," I said. "We'll meet here tomorrow night at eight."

It was after midnight when I got back to the Big House. As I rounded the corner of the mansion, I saw a figure floating across the lawn. The faint light cast by the porch lanterns fell on the folds of a scarlet cloak. I wondered why Ana was wandering around the property in the dead of night. The last time I interrupted a nocturnal stroll someone dropped a load of bricks on me. So I stayed where I was and watched until she disappeared into the fog shrouding the gazebo.

After a couple of minutes had passed, I made my way to the gazebo. It was empty. I leaned on the damp surface of the bar top wondering if I was going bonkers. A shiver ran down my spine, probably from the wind-blown fog working its way to my bones. Or maybe the talk of the film being haunted by Mary Hallett was getting to me.

I decided to sleep on it. But even that opportunity wasn't available as I learned, when I slipped under the sheets, that Cait didn't snore like a buzz saw. She snored like a whole damn lumber mill.

CHAPTER 20

The next morning I blinked my eyes open in a sunlit and blissfully silent room. I rolled onto my side and saw that Cait's bed was empty. I must have crammed in an entire night's sleep after she got up, because I was feeling pretty chipper. My upcoming meeting with Sally made me feel like a kid on his way to the candy store.

I practically leapt out of bed, showered, shaved and got into a pair of tan cotton cabana pants and a blue chambray work shirt that had been washed so many times it was as light as a spider web. Plunking my faded Red Sox cap on my head, I stepped out of the bedroom into the hall and inhaled the mouth-watering breakfast smells flowing from the kitchen. Voices drifted from the dining room, but I was anxious to be on my way and decided not to have breakfast with the film crew.

I slipped quietly out of the Big House and got on the road, stopping at a gas station quick mart for a cup of coffee and a ham and egg sandwich that was filling and almost edible. More important, it was easy to hold in one hand as I drove along Route 6 to the tip of Cape Cod at Provincetown, where the Grand Army of the Republic Highway ends the transcontinental run that starts in Bishop, California.

A few miles before the highway butts up against the Atlantic

Ocean, I turned off onto the access road to Provincetown Municipal Airport. Built back in the forties, the airport was carved out of the Province Lands, a rolling expanse of grasslands and dunes near the Race Point Coast Guard station. The airport is twenty-five minutes from Boston by Cape Air and ten minutes by taxi from the center of town. In the summer, the planes touching down on the single landing strip bring in people from all over the country. By day, they work on their tans at the beach; by night, these visitors sample the delights of the drag clubs, waterfront restaurants, and enjoy watching or being part of the on-going carnival along Commercial Street.

Sally was waiting for me in the lobby of the one-story terminal.

"Good morning," she said. She gave me a quick hug. "Thanks so much for coming, Soc. I hope it wasn't a problem taking time off from your job."

I couldn't find the words to describe how a rampage by a bunch of fake pirates had wrecked Max's tight schedule and freed me to go shark hunting.

"Technical problems," I said. "We postponed the shoot to this afternoon."

"Sorry about your problems, but I'm delighted that you could be here. Plane's gassed up and ready to go."

She hooked her arm in mine and we walked out of the terminal onto the tarmac. Sally introduced me to the pilot, a stocky man in his fifties named Mike Donnelly. He had a firm handshake and easy smile and wore a baseball cap that had a fake shark bite taken out of the visor. Sally explained that he was a contract pilot who'd been flying spotter runs for the non-profit shark research group that had hired her as a consultant.

Donnelly invited us to get into a blue-and-white high-wing Cessna. Sally suggested I ride in front where I'd have a good view. She got in the back seat. Donnelly started the engine and taxied down the runway. The Cessna gained speed and lifted off over the rolling sand hills. We flew above the sun-dappled Atlantic Ocean before making a turn south along the outer beach. The bluebird sky was cloudless. The Boston skyline was clearly visible in the crystalline air.

Sally explained our flight plan using her curled arm to approximate the shape of the Cape. The first phase of our trip would follow what she described as "the shark highway," flying south along what looks like the wrist and forearm over the Atlantic beaches of the outer Cape to the elbow at Chatham and the main seal colony on Monomoy Island. Then we'd head west over Nantucket Sound, turn north over the biceps, and fly along the inner forearm to the clenched fist at Provincetown.

The plane was over the ocean that bordered the beaches at the Cape's narrow wrist when Donnelly tapped the window and pointed downward. "Got our first hit," he said.

He banked the plane into a wide circle that took us further out over the ocean then curved back to shore above Cape Cod Light, a white spike that sits a few hundred yards from the dune-colored high bluffs. About a dozen seals lounged in the shallow water where the waves began their transformation into white-crested rollers for their final dash toward shore.

A hundred feet from the seals was a grayish outline, sharply tapered at one end.

Sally tapped her iPad screen. "That's Hansel. He was tagged in 2015. The researchers had already logged in a female we named Gretel. He and Gretel were swimming close together, so the spotters named him after her brother."

"Hansel looks like he's been eating a lot of gingerbread."

"He's a big boy. Fourteen feet long. Probably weighs a couple of thousand pounds."

Donnelly pulled the plane out of its circle and pointed the nose southward along the curve of the beach.

"Traffic is picking up on the shark highway," Sally said after a moment.

The iPad app showed two blips on the screen. "We'll be coming up on them shortly. They're probably following seals moving along the coast."

The plane was coming up on a popular public beach. Had this been summer, the strip of sand between dunes and ocean would have been mobbed. Now most of the blankets and umbrellas were clustered close to the parking lot. A few people waded in the shallows. Farther out from shore, figures in shiny black wet suits lay belly down on their boards, paddling to stay in place until the perfect wave arrived. Seals bobbed in the water around the surfers, like spectators watching the show.

My years spent on a fishing boat had given me an eye for what lies under the surface of the ocean. My gaze brushed a dark outline in the sea about fifty feet from the seals and surfers.

"Check out that shadow to the east of the surfer gang," I said.

Donnelly brought the plane around for another pass and Sally peered through her binoculars.

"Good catch, Soc. Definitely a great white." She lowered the binocs and checked the iPad. "This one hasn't been tagged. We'd better call the boat and see if we can get a tag on him, Mike."

Donnelly picked up the microphone. "Spotter plane to tagging boat. Got another customer for you. What's your position?"

A male voice crackled, "We're off Nauset Inlet."

"Head north around a mile or so. Target is east of a bunch of surfers."

"Roger. Be there in five."

"Okay. I'll let the surfers know they've got company."

He flew a tight circle above the shark to warn the surfers. But instead of paddling toward the beach, they waved at the circling plane.

Donnelly groaned. "This has happened before. They think I'm signaling that the area is safe for surfing."

He broke out of the circle and flew low over the tagging boat. People on deck waved at the plane as we passed overhead. We turned and flew north again. The shark had moved.

"Looks like it's closer to the surfers," I said.

"I don't like its aggressive movements," Sally said.

"It's moving its head from side to side. What's that mean?" I asked.

"It means that the shark may be about to attack," she said uneasily.

CHAPTER 21

The seals had sensed the threat and were moving away from the shark, but the maneuver brought them closer to the surfers. The shark followed the pack, still doing its back-and-forth dance; the lazy turns had become quicker and more frenzied.

"Do those surfers have anything to worry about?" I said.

"Maybe," Sally said. "Seals and surfers look alike in the water. Even a highly-developed predator like a great white can make a mistake."

"Crap," Donnelly muttered. "I'll make another pass over the shark. Maybe those guys will catch on this time."

I understood Donnelly's frustration, but trying to warn the surfers seemed like a waste of time. Their brains must have gotten water-logged from all that time in the ocean.

"How low can you fly this thing?" I said.

"I can practically skim the wave-tops. You want me to see if I can spook the shark?"

"Forget the fish. I want you to spook the seals."

"Not a problem."

He pointed the plane's nose down, leveled off a couple of hundred feet above the water, and zeroed in on the bobbing silver-gray heads as if he were a fighter plane strafing the survivors of a sunken troop ship. The seals turned to face the oncoming plane. Seals look like fat old men, but their reflexes are lightning fast. Seconds before the shadow of the plane passed overhead they disappeared from the surface with a snap of their tails, and then scattered in every direction.

Donnelly brought the plane up and circled back. The surfers waved at the plane again. The panicked movement of the seals had drawn the shark away from the surfers. It hung in the water around fifty yards from where we had last seen it.

Sally patted my shoulder. "That was brilliant, using the seals to draw the shark away. Its senses were overloaded by all the moving targets. Now it's listening and watching, trying to figure out where everyone went."

"The fish still has an empty stomach. Any chance it will go after the surfers?"

"I may have overreacted. I don't think it wanted the surfers. It wanted seal meat and got confused."

"I'm worried about what happens when it gets un-confused," I said.

"Boat's coming up," Donnelly said. "Maybe they can chase those idiots away."

The tagging boat had made good time and was closing in on the surfers. Donnelly radioed the boat and said he'd keep circling the shark. The boat slowed to a crawl and stopped within yards of the shark. Someone carrying a harpoon walked out onto the pulpit.

A couple of surfers who'd been sitting on their boards finally figured out that the arrival of the tagging boat meant a great white was in the neighborhood. They started paddling toward shore. Others caught on and followed. The whole surfer fleet was on or near the beach by the time the boat's pulpit was directly over the dark silhouette.

The shark was almost half the length of the boat, which looked to be around thirty feet. We watched the figure on the pulpit jab a harpoon with a detachable tip into the shark's dorsal fin. The tip contained the radio beacon that would keep tabs on the shark. As soon as the fish was tagged, it dove into deeper waters where it was no longer visible.

The crew waved from the deck. Donnelly tilted the plane's wing in reply, then we continued on our planned flight. We saw two more tagged sharks before we got to the main seal colony on the ocean side of Monomoy, a thin strip of dunes and beach that hangs off the elbow of Cape Cod. Thousands of seals crowded the beaches. Three more sharks lurked offshore, attracted by all those ready-to-eat meals.

We flew west a mile or so, then Donnelly put the plane into a turn that would take it north over the Cape and into the bay.

Sally said, "Let's see what Emma is doing." She passed the tablet forward so I could see the track on the screen. Emma had gone across Cape Cod Bay to Plymouth on the far shore of the bay after her encounter with Munson, then retraced her route and was now cruising off Great Island.

"She's looped back to the same general area where Munson's boat was found," I said. "Maybe she's come back for dessert."

"We still haven't made the case that she had Munson for dinner." Sally sighed, "But I'm afraid that her behavior will only serve to convince people she's a criminal returning to the scene of the crime."

"That only happens in the make-believe world. Firebugs are the exception. Arsonists like to watch things burn. Emma isn't an arsonist, last I heard."

"I can say with absolutely certainty that Emma is incapable of being an arsonist. Any other ideas?"

"Yup," I said. "Let's have lunch."

Donnelly flew above the bay side of Great Island and minutes later, he began the approach to the airport. Not long after the plane touched down Sally and I were sitting at the patio table of a beach side bistro that overlooked Provincetown Harbor. It was like a scene from a picture postcard. Gulls wheeled over the fishing draggers anchored in the harbor, and a whale-watch boat was leaving the dock with a load of passengers. But I only had eyes for Sally. I was thinking how the turquoise polo shirt set off her Mediterranean complexion. She looked over the top of her menu and caught me gazing at her.

"Is my hair mussed?"

"No. It looks great. Why would you ask?"

"You're staring at me. Hungrily."

"It's lunchtime and I'm hungry."

"Oh, I get it. You were looking at me because I look like an order of fish and chips."

"Nope. I was thinking that I have really missed you." I was telling the truth, but not all of it. What I was mostly wondering was how I'd let a woman as classy, intelligent and beautiful as Sally slip out of my life.

She parted her lips, paused as if she were deciding what to say, and then said it: "I've missed you too. Staying at the boathouse brings back fond memories."

"Glad to hear that, Sal. How's Kojak doing?"

"He's a dear. He jumps up on the bed like a kitten and sleeps with me."

Lucky Kojak. "If he were human, he'd be in assisted living, but I do my best. Thanks for taking care of the old guy."

The waiter came for our order. Sally smiled and ordered fish and chips. I told him to make that two.

"Now that I've brought you up to date on the boathouse, what's going on at the Big House?" she said.

"Moving in with the movie crew was a good idea. Max told me he fired Munson after Kirk got stoned and almost ran over some of the extras with the *Sea Robin*. Max was furious. Kicked him off the boat when they got back to the marina. Munson then threatened the film project and said the movie was finished. Less than twenty-four hours after stalking off, he was dead."

"You think Munson being fired and his death, are connected?"

"Got to admit it's an odd coincidence."

"Yes, but it could be just that. A coincidence. I wonder what Munson meant when he said the movie was finished?"

"Maybe he planned to sabotage the boat. Loss of the *Sea Robin* would mess up the film schedule. He was seen drinking in a bar earlier. He could have been working up his courage."

"That's possible, but it's still only conjecture. My scientific training tells me to build on what we know, not what we think."

"Okay. Let's work backwards. Munson's body is found dead in the water. The *Sea Robin* is anchored in the harbor. Max said Kirk had a spare ignition key. He could simply have been fishing, but the threats he made suggest that he intended to mess up the engine or sink the boat."

"I don't disagree, except for one thing," Sally said. "How does he plan to get off the boat after he sabotages it?"

"Easy," I said. "He tows the Zodiac behind the boat and runs it back to the marina."

"But Munson's body is found in the harbor. How did the Zodiac come back to the dock?"

"Duh," I said. "Someone else brought the Zodiac back to its slip."

"Which suggests Munson wasn't alone the night he died."

I thought about it. "The medical examiner's report said Munson had a bruise on the left side of his head. Any theories how he got it?"

"It was assumed he stumbled and hit his head on the rail of the boat before he pitched over the side."

"That doesn't fly. If Munson rapped his head against the rail, it's more than likely he would have fallen to the deck."

"Maybe that's what happened. He gets up. He's dizzy and falls overboard."

"What happened to your scientific training, Sal?"

She sighed. "You're saying that an unknown assailant might have been responsible."

"That would be less of a reach than Munson falling overboard after cracking his head. The bruise would be consistent with a blow from a right-handed person facing Munson."

"The assailant could have towed the Zodiac out to the killing grounds, attacked Munson, and taken it back to its slip," she said.

"Maybe we're making this overly complicated," I said. "Munson could have been knocked out when the boat was still at the dock. With Munson sidelined, the bad guy attaches the Zodiac, motors out to where the *Sea Robin* was later found anchored, and tosses his victim into the drink. The bruise was not the cause of death, so he is still alive at this point. Munson comes to and starts swimming. Emma is passing by, thinks he is prey, and takes an exploratory bite, then makes a meal of Munson's arm. He goes into shock and dies."

"Fine as it goes. But we get back to the same problem. It's unlikely Emma would have gone for the arm after the test bite showed that Munson wasn't a seal."

"Unlikely but not impossible," I said.

"No," she said. "Not impossible." Sally's face fell. "So Emma did kill Munson."

"Indirectly. She attacked Munson, but the person who tossed him overboard is the guilty one. No different than pushing someone onto a busy highway in front of an eighteen-wheeler. Who is to blame? The guy who accidentally runs him over? Or the person who put him in harm's way to begin with?"

"Emma wasn't driving a truck. She was conditioned by millions of years of evolution to attack Munson."

"That doesn't change the fact that Munson should never have been in the water at night, pumped up on drugs, dazed and disoriented from the blow to his head. He might have drowned, even if the shark did not bite him. In other words, he was murdered. You said that a shark does what a shark does. Emma was only a means to an end."

"Suppose you're right about all this. Do you have any idea who the killer might be?"

"No, but it all goes back to the movie. Someone wanted Munson removed from the scene, permanently."

Sally pounced on my comment. "In that case, maybe you shouldn't be working as Munson's replacement."

"It's only a few days more. I need the money to pay a boat loan. Maybe I can solve the murder, too. And if I clear Emma's name, that would help your work. You can go back to Florida."

"Is that what you want?"

"I thought that's what you wanted."

"For a smart man, you can be awfully thick. This job isn't the only reason I came north."

Sally has always been full of surprises, but this one floored me. I had been the bad boy for so long I couldn't conceive of her wanting us to get back together. She must have known what I was thinking—she always does—because her eyes were amused.

I said, "Let's talk about it tonight."

"That would be nice. I've got a meeting but I'm free after that. Thanks to the wonders of modern technology I can check on my responsibilities any time."

She put her iPad on the table and tapped the screen. "Damn," she said.

"What's the problem?"

She pushed the tablet across the table. "Emma's tag is no longer broadcasting her whereabouts."

Sally called Mike. I looked at the iPad again.

Sally hung up, and said, "I'm meeting Mike at the airport. We'll see if we can find Emma."

"I hope you do," I said with more than casual interest. The last time Emma had signaled her whereabouts, she was heading toward Great Island, where I'd be filming underwater scenes for

PAUL KEMPRECOS

The Pirate's Daughter.

CHAPTER 22

I drove out of Provincetown, thinking about the lyrics to "Mack the Knife." Especially the part about the scarlet billows that start to spread when the shark bites with its pearly teeth. The right thing would be to tell Max what was going on. But if I told him the shark that may have killed Munson was back in town, he might call off the shoot. And I would lose the day's pay I needed for my boat loan.

If I didn't tell him, someone might get hurt. Sally didn't think Emma had been a bad girl, but she wasn't absolutely sure. I still hadn't decided what to do by the time I pulled into the marina parking lot and saw Max standing near the boat ramp. He waved me over. I pulled the GMC up to the bulkhead, got out and fetched the scuba gear bag from the cab.

As I slung the bag on my shoulder, Max said, "Ahoy, Captain. Ready for an adventure on the bounding main?"

"Aye-aye, Matey," I snarled. "Looking forward to another day in paradise; drinking, pillaging, wenching and flogging."

Max's bushy eyebrows hiked up and down, like a couple of nervous caterpillars. "That's damned good pirate speak, Soc."

"Thanks, but I don't deserve credit. It's something I read on a T-shirt."

"No, no, not the words. Your Long John Silver impression is

terrific. Are you sure you don't want to join the *Whydah* crew?"

"I'd love to take you up on the offer, but termites ate my peg leg."

"Argh," he said. "Hope it wasn't painful."

"Not half as painful as seeing my ship go down under my feet in those computer-generated images of the *Whydah* in the storm."

"As good as this CGI stuff is, you still have to make the scene up close and personal for the audience to relate to. That's what we're doing today. We'll film the pirates jumping off the boat and struggling in the waves. You'll be involved in the second phase of the shoot. The pirates will be seen plunging into the sea from below, with the camera looking up at the surface. I had a Hydroflex unit shipped in by overnight express. Have you ever used an underwater camera?"

"I've shot video for commercial jobs but I'm no cinematographer."

"You'll do fine. The crew will give you enough instruction to get by. The shots will be spliced into the CGI imaging of the ship going down."

"Pretty straightforward. I don't see any problems."

He glanced around. "Don't say that too loudly, Soc. Movie is jinxed, remember?"

Max's sly look told me he was half-joking. He wouldn't have spoken so lightly if he knew that the fourteen-foot great white shark suspected of dining on Munson was back in the 'hood. Maybe it was time to tell him the truth.

I never got the chance. The shuttle van pulled up next to my truck. The door opened and the extras filed out. They were dressed in baggy cut-offs and wore bandannas around their heads, pirate-style, but the pasty-faced and hollow-eyed cutthroats reporting for work didn't look as if they were capable of taking over a gravy boat.

Cait was the last one off the bus. She waved and herded the extras in our direction. Max muttered under his breath when he saw the sorry state of the men. He asked them to line up. He chose the six pirates who looked least likely to toss their cookies and told

Cait to take the others home on the shuttle for further drying out.

As Max blocked out the day's filming for the pirate gang, Cait sidled up. "I'll never forgive Jason for trashing my cast," she seethed.

"Dunno, Cait. These guys are pretty mean looking. Maybe Jason did you a favor, getting them into the role."

She shook her head. "You don't believe that."

"Not really. I was trying to put the best face on it. How's Jason doing this morning?"

"Oh, Jason is doing just fine," she said with a lilt. "While I was setting off to collect this poor excuse for the *Whydah*'s crew he was in the salon, Bloody Mary in hand, going over the script with Ana. I missed your smiling face at breakfast."

"I had an errand in Provincetown."

"I'm relieved. I thought you might be mad because of my snoring."

"Not at all. In fact, it lulled me to sleep."

She scrunched her face. "I appreciate your gallantry, Soc, but if that's really the case you should get your ears checked. See you back at the Big House."

As Cait drove off with her load of rejects, the equipment truck arrived. The photographer and his assistant got out, we exchanged quick hellos, and they began unloading their gear. I carried my dive bag down to the *Sea Robin* and helped load the cases aboard.

The extras filed onto the dock a few minutes later. They and the camera crew would ride in the *Sea Robin*. Max got into the Zodiac. I started the motors, cast off the dock lines, eased the boat out of the slip and followed the inflatable across the harbor at a leisurely speed.

The day was sunny and dry, temperatures in the seventies with a light breeze from the east. Seas were less than one foot. Around a hundred yards off the Great Island beach, Max slowed the Zodiac to a halt. The *Sea Robin*'s depth finder indicated fifteen feet under our hull. Tide was coming in. There were no other boats in the immediate vicinity.

I put the throttle into neutral. Max came over in the inflatable and told me to anchor, then he tied up alongside. The photographer and his assistant got into the inflatable and locked the camera onto a special mount on the Zodiac's prow.

When he was done supervising the camera set-up, Max said, "Here's what will happen, Soc. The extras will jump off the boat and we'll film them flying through the air and flopping around in the water as if they'd just come off the sinking *Whydah*."

He pushed off and maneuvered the Zodiac until it was close to twenty feet off the starboard stern. The photographer squinted into the camera viewfinder and raised his hand to signal he was ready. Max brought the electronic megaphone to his mouth and instructed the extras to take their boots off, so their weight wouldn't drag them men down, and get close to the rail. When he was satisfied with the set he yelled, "Slate!"

The cameraman's assistant clacked the clapperboard in front of the camera. Max called out, "Action!"

The first extra scheduled to jump put one foot onto the rail, pushed off with the other, teetered for a second to get his balance, then launched himself off the boat. Two more jumping pirates followed, then the last three went in all at the same time. The camera lens caught their bodies arcing through the air, then splashing into the water where they disappeared under geysers of foam. They bobbed to the surface and thrashed around like the drowning pirates they were supposed to portray.

Max brought the electronic megaphone to his mouth. "Cut!"

The extras swam to the stern ladder and climbed onto the deck.

Max raised the megaphone to his lips again. "Good job, crew. Almost perfect, but we're gonna do it again. Cool it on the arm flapping this time. You look like turkeys trying to fly. It's okay to move your arms, but just be natural."

He gave the extras a minute to catch their breath, then the

clapperboard clacked and the pirates leaped once more into the sea.

Max reviewed the shot on the camera and raised his arms in a double thumbs up.

"Perfect. Congratulations. Take a break while we get ready for the underwater shots."

The Zodiac was tied up to the *Sea Robin* and the main movie camera removed from the prow. The cameraman gave me instructions on how to operate the Hydroflex. I stripped down to my bathing suit, which I'd worn under my cabana pants. Then I pulled on my weight belt, buoyancy compensator, air tank, and mask. I climbed part way down the ladder, pulled my flippers onto my feet, pushed off into the water and back-kicked a few yards from the boat.

I spit on the mask lens and rinsed it with sea water to prevent fogging, clamped the regulator mouthpiece between my teeth, then released air from the buoyancy compensator— basically a vest that can be inflated and deflated to control ascent and descent. I sank a couple of yards. After taking some breaths to test the regulator I inflated the BC, rose to the surface and yanked out the mouthpiece.

"Visibility's great," I said. "Fifteen to twenty feet."

Max clapped his hands and pushed the Zodiac away from the *Sea Robin*, drifting close to where I floated. The photographer's assistant handed down the Hydroflex.

"Dive down ten feet," Max said. "Keep the camera pointed up at the surface and you'll be fine."

"Give me a minute to set myself up, then have the guys jump."

I bit down on the mouthpiece again and let air out of the vest until I sank below the surface. I brought the view screen up to my mask, pointed the camera toward the shimmering underside of the sun-speckled surface and hit the 'on' button.

The first pirate plunged into the water in an explosion of bubbles and fought his way to the surface. The next pirate jumped and four more followed. I did a sweeping shot of kicking legs, then I headed up.

The pirates were swimming for the boarding ladder. I followed them and handed Max the camera. Using the review function, he checked out the shot, leaned over the rail and gave the camera back.

"Nice job, Soc. Let's do an insurance shot and we'll call it a day."

I had pushed away from the ladder, and was floating on my back, when I heard a plane engine. The blue-and-white spotter plane was coming from Provincetown. The plane flew over Great Island and began to circle. I thought this was curious but when it did a second and third circle, I figured out what was going on. Sally was telling me that Emma was in the neighborhood.

The extras were lining up at the rail for another jump. Maybe it was time to tell Max about the shark. He waved his arm at me in a signal to dive. I did a mental shrug and purged air from the BC. Once I was a few feet below the surface, I spun around and surveyed my surroundings. In my fevered imagination I saw Emma's toothy grin in every shadow.

The first pirate plunged into the water. The others piled in after him. I filmed the bodies and bubbles and rose to the surface. Six heads bobbed in the water. All the extras were present and accounted for. I did some surface shots; the extras swam back to the boat and one of them began to scream and splash his arms. Then he disappeared as if he had been dragged under.

Emma.

My adrenaline spiked, but when I looked at Max I saw that he was laughing. The extra popped to the surface and he was laughing too, so hard that he could hardly stay afloat. Max roared through his bullhorn. "You're over-acting again, pirate guy. Scene's done. Get your ass back onto the boat."

As the pirate swam to the boat, I checked on the plane again. It was still circling, but more to the south of us. I headed to the ladder, handed up the camera and air tank, then I climbed aboard. The pirates were toweling their faces dry. Max praised the dripping extras through his megaphone. "Good work everyone. Calling it a day, Soc," he said. "See you back at the dock."

He goosed the Zodiac's throttle and headed back to the marina.

I slipped out of my scuba gear and brewed a pot of coffee for the crew. Then I started the motors. Before I pointed the bow back to the marina, I glanced up. The plane was a dot floating across the azure sky in the direction of Provincetown. Emma was on the move again.

CHAPTER 23

Although the sun was shining, and the extras had dried their faces and arms, the wind created as the boat cut through the water cooled down their wet clothes. Some took off their shirts and wrung the water out of them. That helped, but I noticed a few of the pirates were shivering, so I opened a hatch and grabbed the bottle of Jack Daniels I had seen my first day on the job. It must have belonged to Munson, but he didn't need it as much as I did.

Holding the bottle above my head, I said, "Avast ye lubbers. The captain meaning me-has ordered a ration of grog for the crew."

Real grog is rum and water. But these weren't real pirates and I wasn't an authentic pirate captain. They held their mugs out and I fortified their coffee with generous shots from the square bottle.

As we approached the slip, I saw a red-haired figure standing on a finger pier. It was Cait and she was waving a skull and crossbones flag. The pirate crew gave a rousing *huzzah*. As soon as we docked, they piled off the boat and followed Cait to the parking lot like kids trailing the Pied Piper.

The Zodiac was tied up in its slip. There was no sign of Max or the film crew. I shouldered my dive bag and tailed after the others. Cait stood by the bus door greeting the extras getting on the shuttle.

I strolled over and said, "Nice move with the Jolly Roger."

Cait had a smug smile on her face. "I found the flag in a souvenir shop. The boys have a tendency to wander off and I thought it might make them focus."

"Speaking of wandering off, what happened to Max and the crew?"

"He was in a hurry to see the dailies. He's slightly crazed over the delay in the shooting schedule. How did things go today?"

"Max seemed pretty pleased with both scenes."

She looked relieved. "I'm so happy to hear that. You have no idea how anxious everyone is to get this film in the can."

A roar of pirate voices from inside the bus almost drowned out her words.

She stared at the grinning faces in the shuttle windows with a puzzled smile. "Wow! This doesn't sound like the gang I dropped off a couple of hours ago. Those guys could barely talk."

Cait wouldn't be happy if she knew I got the extras *likkered* up again. I shrugged nonchalantly. "Fresh air and water can do wonders for a hangover." Another round of shouts came from inside. "Maybe you'd better get on board. Sounds like a mutiny brewing."

Her eyes narrowed. She said she would see me back at the Big House, then got into the shuttle and slid behind the wheel. From the sounds of things, the pirate party was just beginning. I remembered I had left the bottle of Jack Daniels unguarded. Not a good thing to do, even with a bunch of fake pirates.

As I headed toward the GMC a funny thing happened. A black sedan parked in the space next to the truck took off with a screech of tires toward the road. Old cop habits never die. I memorized the license plate number, recalling that I had seen a similar car behind me after meeting up with my family in Hyannis and again at the Newcomb's Hollow film shoot. I shrugged. Maybe my imaginary encounter with Emma was making me jittery. I got into the GMC and headed out of town. I listened to Little Feat playing *Dixie Chicken* on radio station WMVY out of Martha's Vineyard. The sound system was outstanding. The truck cab was big enough to hold the band and its instruments.

It was going to be tough giving up the luxury pickup when the job ended. I still hadn't figured out how I was going to replace my burned-out Jimmy. My thoughts went back to the morning after the old truck went up in flames. In my mind I was standing next to the police car again, the stench of burning oil and gasoline stinging my nostrils. Sergeant Nolan was saying how the DA's office suggested that he talk to the fire inspector about the suspicious fire that consumed my first charter boat.

The sound in my head was my mental gears grinding. Usually, the local cops would look into the incident and file a report that might eventually make its way to the State Police. The locals and the Staties were known to work together, but each had a tendency to guard their own turf. Although Nolan hadn't even completed his report, within hours of the fire, the DA not only knew the details, he was using the Staties to pass down the word that I was a serial arsonist.

My lips clamped together in a frown that didn't fade until I stepped into the boathouse and took a look around. The boathouse would never qualify for a spread in *Good Housekeeping*, and the ramshackle old mold farm had suffered from even more neglect than usual during my busy charter schedule that summer. I inhaled the scent emanating from the bouquet of flowers bunched in a vase on the kitchen table. The counters and kitchen table were uncluttered. The vacuumed rugs no longer matched Kojak's fur. Not a dust bunny or cobweb in sight.

Kojak bounded out to greet me with a double ankle rub and a mighty purr. He was acting almost kittenish.

I scratched the top of his bony head. "Nothing like a pretty lady to put a spring in the step of a couple of old bachelors like us, pal."

I tossed a handful of Greenies into his dish and noticed it no longer resembled a miniature toxic waste dump. Then I grabbed the phone and went out on the deck. The bay looked like rippling molten silver. I closed my eyes and allowed a stream of thoughts to flow through my mind. The water began to flow faster and faster, carrying jetsam and flotsam, dead bodies and drowning pirates, sharks and seals.

My eyelids snapped open. The Zen exercise had brought me no insight, only confusion.

I took a deep breath and let my thoughts drift back to the beautiful late summer day I took the Northeastern University reunion out fishing. All had been normal. Then the outboards had crapped out, I took the job offer from Howie Gill, and my life had spun out of control. If I cleared up the "Great Oyster Heist," maybe my life would spin back into control. I punched out a phone number and counted six rings before Assistant District Attorney Frank Martin answered.

"Hi Soc," he said in a tone that was neither friendly nor unfriendly.

I'd known the garrulous ADA for a long time and had never found him to be a man of few words. Not only was his terse greeting puzzling, it was weird.

"Hi Frank," I said. "Got a minute to chat?"

"Not really, but we can try. I'll let you know if I have to hang up."

Something wasn't right. Martin and I always bantered, gossiped and exchanged corny jokes before getting into serious conversation. Now he sounded as if he were barely moving his lips.

"Oh, I get it. You can't talk because someone is there."

"Nope. Just me. What's up?"

"No big deal. I was wondering whether anyone's figured out who shot at me and set my truck on fire."

"Nothing yet." Pause. "I'll be perfectly honest with you, Soc—"

I cut him off. "Does that mean you have been imperfectly honest with me up to now?"

Martin grunted. It was not a happy grunt.

"Unfortunate figure of speech on my part, Soc. What I'm trying to say is that instead of worrying about the guys who torched your truck, you should simply take the insurance money and get yourself a newer set of wheels."

"You forgot that I got shot at before they burned my truck."

"Forget that too. No one was hurt."

"Yes, of course. That's true, Frank. Let's forget a troublesome detail like assault with intent to murder. I'll be perfectly honest with you. My truck was old. The speedometer had probably gone around a dozen times. There won't be enough in the insurance settlement to buy a pair of fuzzy dice for the rearview mirror."

"Well, yeah, I'm sorry, Soc." He didn't sound sorry.

"Well, yeah, I'm sorry too. But all is not lost, my friend. The Socarides Detective Agency has developed a promising lead in the case. I followed the oyster poachers' trail to the South by West warehouse in Buzzards Bay."

I heard a sharp intake of breath on the other end of the line. "Jeez, Soc. That was a very dangerous thing to do. I told you to stay away from these guys. We're dealing with hard-assed criminals."

"I kinda got the impression they were not boy scouts trying for their merit badges in marksmanship. Here's another newsflash for you, Frank. The truck they drove out on the flats that night is being stored at the warehouse."

"Oh, hell! You went inside?"

"Couldn't resist. The lock fell off."

"I cannot believe this crap! You're going to get your ass burned with this *big time*. Back off!"

"Okay then. I'll leave it up to you. Go get a search warrant and take a look for yourself."

"You were a cop. You know it's not that easy."

"You could try. It wouldn't be the first time a judge allowed a warrant based on information from an anonymous tipster. Gee, Frank, I just remembered. I was the anonymous tipster who made you look good more than once."

"Damn, Soc. This is bigger than oysters. There's a full-scale investigation going on. You spook these guys and you'll not only put yourself in jeopardy, you'll torpedo months of undercover work."

"Why didn't you tell me this before?"

"I couldn't. I have to abide by legal and ethical restraints that private eyes don't worry about."

"You're a lawyer, Frank. That means you have no ethics, by definition."

"Aw, Soc. That's cruel. We've been friends a long time."

"We're still friends. Which is why I didn't expect you to stiff-arm me. What's going on, pal?"

"Okay, I'm sorry. Here's the skinny. The guys who took the oysters are only the tip of the iceberg. We've got heroin and opioid dealing. Big time. Kingpin is a guy named Ricardo. The DA is licking his lips at the prospect of a major bust."

"Too bad he's taken so long going in. Maybe I'd still have a truck instead of a barbecue pit on wheels."

"Will you forget that damned truck?"

"Sure, if you answer this question. Why would *big time* druggies risk getting caught poaching oysters?"

"Money laundering maybe."

"Doesn't fly, Frank. South by West deals in all kinds of fish and shellfish. They've already got the network in place to launder drug money."

"Then I don't know. Who can figure crooks? I answered your question. Now promise me one thing: you'll stay away from the warehouse."

"Okay, Frank. I'll give the warehouse a wide berth."

After a couple of seconds of suspicious silence, he said, "You're not kidding? You'll avoid the warehouse?"

"You've got my word. Now it's your turn." I asked him to run the plate of the black car I'd seen at the marina.

"Glad to do it. Might take a little longer because it's out of state."

"Thanks. One more thing. Promise you will keep me in the loop."

"No problem, Soc. Every step of the way."

Martin wasn't telling the whole truth, but neither was I. I'd keep my promise not to visit the warehouse. But that promise didn't extend to the South by West bar in Buzzards Bay.

CHAPTER 24

There are no actual buzzards in Buzzards Bay, never have been. There is a bay, and the colonists who settled along its shore saw a big bird and called it a 'buzzard.' Times were tough for the first settlers and the bleak observation may have had something to do with their long odds of survival in a strange new land. The bird was actually an osprey, but the mistake was memorialized when the village that sits on the westerly side of the Cape Cod Canal was named.

Buzzards Bay was a bustling business community before a bypass diverted the Cape Cod traffic that used to flow along Route 28, its main thoroughfare. The highway poured Cape-bound day-trippers into the little burg before the stroke of a pen on a highway construction map put an end to that. There are still some shops and restaurants but the village now is only a ghost of its glory days.

The Salty Sou'wester was down a side road about a half mile off the highway, surrounded by falling-down summer cottages that used to offer low-budget family vacations. In a happier day, gangs of sunburned kids would have roamed the narrow alleys. Barbecue smoke from grilling hot dogs would have filled the air instead of the cloud of despair that hung over the abandoned buildings presently.

The one-story brick building looked like a bunker in the Maginot Line. The small windows showcased Bud Lite and Sam

Adams signs. Some of the neon letters had gone bad, so the signs actually touted 'Bud Lit' and 'Sam dams.' Hanging from a wooden post was the carved profile of a bearded man wearing the type of yellow fisherman's cap known as a Sou'wester. I wondered how a rubber hat could be salty, but passed it off as poetic license.

Although a bulb hung over the sign and another light illuminated the bar entrance, the parking lot itself was mostly dark. I told Gill to back the pickup into the shadows under some trees. He killed the engine, leaned on the steering wheel and stared at three low-slung motorcycles lined up in front of the building.

"Is this place a biker bar?"

"Maybe, but don't worry about it. Bikers tend to stick to themselves. Listen to your instincts. If you get a sense that things aren't right, that the place has a bad vibe, go with your gut and get the hell out of there."

"Yeah, no sweat," he said in the gruff tone he used when I first met him.

We shook hands. Then he got out of the truck, sauntered toward the bar—walking with an exaggerated swagger, probably to pump up his courage—and disappeared inside.

Gill and I had hooked up around a half-hour earlier. His truck was parked away from the Burger King instead of right in front of it. When I got in I noticed that the cab didn't reek of fried grease.

"I parked out here to avoid temptation," he said. "It's dangerous being close to cooking smells."

"Are you going on a diet, Howie?"

"You might say that." He turned the key and put the truck in gear. As he drove onto the Mid-Cape Highway, he said, "It's more of an epiphany, my friend. I've been playing a gross, fat lout for so long, I actually turned into a gross, fat lout. Starting today, no more junk food, smoking, or drinking beer."

"Congratulations. What sparked the plunge into this pure and wholesome way of life?"

"I owe it all to you."

"I've never listed Lifestyle Coach on my professional resume. All I did was warn you not to eat anything bigger than your head."

"Even more important, you ripped the cover off my phony identity. I was forced to take a look at the ugly caricature I'd become. Hell, I wasn't even being honest as an oyster farmer. I was masquerading as a colorful denizen of the flats to sell my stock."

"So where is this revelation taking you?"

"Back to academia as soon as I clean up my act."

"I wish you every success, Howie, but I want you to continue your loutish ways, at least for tonight."

"No problem. How's this going down?"

"The first thing I want you to do is stop talking like this is a rerun of *Miami Vice*. As I said before, this is strictly recon. When we get to this joint you'll go inside and sidle up to the bar. Order a beer even though it's not on your new regimen. They'll probably have a couple of TV sets tuned to New England Sports Network. Watch whatever is on NESN as if you're really interested, but be aware of who's in the place. Don't make eye contact. Keep an ear cocked for the conversations around you."

"What if some guy at the bar strikes up a conversation?"

"Play along. Be friendly but not too friendly. Just nod, or grunt."

"I'm good at grunting," he said with a sigh. "What's my cover?"

"If the subject comes up say you're a freelance furniture mover on the way home after a job on the Cape. Speak in generalities. Above all, don't ask questions. You'll come off as nosy."

"I've got it, Soc. Bump on a log. When do you come in?"

"I don't. Not unless I have to. I'm guessing this place attracts regulars. One stranger shows up, it's no big deal. Two strangers and they'll think we're narcs. Take a few sips of beer, then pull the pack of cigarettes out of your pocket, stick one in your mouth and go outside for a smoke. Give me a couple of butts now. I'll come over, light one up and you can tell me what you saw inside."

"What if someone goes out with me for a smoke?"

"I'll stay out of sight unless I see you're alone."

About ten minutes after Gill went into the bar the front door opened. Gill stepped outside. A man followed him and they both lit up and puffed away. The man finished his cigarette, tossed the stub on the ground and walked rather unsteadily to his truck. As soon as he drove away, I walked over to Gill and bummed a light.

I inhaled a puff and, after my coughing fit had come to an end, I said, "Who's your friend?"

"Dunno his name. He was at the bar watching baseball on TV. Red Sox were ahead. Sixth inning."

"That's good news. Now describe what it looks like inside."

"The bar is on your left as you go in, running the length of the room to a hallway with the restrooms and another door that says 'employees only.' A couple of barflies are watching TV. On the opposite side of the room two young guys are playing pool. In between are some tables. They're all empty except for one against the wall where three men are sitting."

"Tell me what they look like."

He blew smoke through his nostrils. "All in their thirties and dressed in black leather. Probably bikers. One seems to be a leader. He's talking and the others are listening, although sometimes he glances toward the back hallway."

"What's he look like?"

"His scalp is shaved and he has a thin mustache that curls down to a razor-cut beard. His pals look like his clones except they've got slightly more hair."

"Can you hear what they're talking about?"

"I'm too far away and they've got their heads together, like a football huddle."

"What are they drinking?"

"Hard stuff in shot glasses."

"Who's paying?"

"No one so far. Bartender keeps bringing rounds over without being asked. Maybe they're running a tab."

"This look like a place where you'd hand the bartender a credit card?"

"I see where you're going. They might be with South by West."

"It's possible."

"That's pretty much it. What do you want me to do?"

I pondered the question.

"How many chairs are at the table?" I asked.

"Three. No, there are actually four. Hey, maybe they're waiting for someone. Like a Mr. Big."

"That's my thought. Go back in. Watch TV. See if Mr. Big shows up over the next fifteen minutes. If not, finish your beer and get out. We'll sit in your truck and stake out the place."

He ground the butt under his heel. "Okay. See you in fifteen."

Gill went back into the bar and I headed for the truck. The high-lift was parked facing into the bushes that lined the lot. I sat in the cab, keeping my eye on the rearview mirror, thinking about what to do if and when Mr. Big arrived. An empty chair at the biker table may have been nothing more than an empty chair. But if Mr. B. did come on the scene, I'd try to get a license plate number.

Ten minutes passed without anything happening. Then a vehicle pulled off the main road and the headlights washed the cab of Gill's pickup. I ducked, expecting the new arrival to park in front of the bar. But the vehicle stopped for at least thirty seconds with its lights on the truck before continuing on to the side of the building and I heard its door shut.

Someone had taken an interest in Gill's pickup. Making sure the dome light switch was on 'off,' I opened the truck door wide enough to crawl out. I pressed it closed behind me, dropped to the broken-up tarmac and crawled into the bushes. Stealthy footsteps approached Gill's truck. Then stopped.

I stood up and peered around a tree. The new arrival was using a cell phone light to check out the truck. After a second he put the phone to his ear and the light illuminated the wide floppy brim of his hat. Alarms went off in my head. The last time I had seen a hat like that was during a conversation on the oyster flats.

The man turned and walked away, veering off from the front door and around a corner of the building. He was going in through the back door. I pictured the place through Gill's eyes. The man would emerge from the restroom hallway with a clear view of the bar. And he would see Gill. I popped out of the bushes and raced past the motorcycles for the entrance. My gut was warning me that I had only seconds to spare.

CHAPTER 25

The dingy interior of the Salty Sou'wester was like a bat cave, only not as nice. I did a quick visual sweep of the badly-lit room, taking in the sad tableau, trying not to breathe in the yeasty atmosphere that reeked of disinfectant, cigarette smoke and hopelessness. Gill was sitting next to a gray-haired barfly who had his head bent over a beer like a wilted flower. The bartender was watching the baseball game on TV.

Off to the right, a couple of men in their twenties were racking up the balls at a pool table. Three tough-faced guys in black leather occupied a table in the back. The skinhead sitting between the other two was taking a drag on a cigarette. I guess he didn't see the *No Smoking* sign on the mustard-colored wall above his head. The boozy tranquility of the scene was interrupted by chirping. The skinhead dropped his cigarette to the floor and picked up the cell phone on the table. He listened, scowled, and then stared at Gill. His unibrow furrowed to a V. I knew what just happened. Howie had been ID'd.

Like they used to say on *Miami Vice*, this was about to "go down."

I strolled over to the bar, slapped Gill lightly on the back and put my mouth close to his ear as if I were telling him a joke.

"Say nighty-night to your friend, then head for the door, slowly," I said. "I'll be right behind you."

I reached for my wallet and slapped a twenty on the bar to cover the bill. Gill slid off the stool and unhurriedly made his way toward the exit with me a couple of paces behind him. We stepped out into the night and I pointed to the pickup. "Run!"

I dashed for the pickup, key in hand, and had started the engine by the time Gill climbed onto the passenger seat, puffing like a steam engine.

The three men in leather spilled out of the bar into the parking lot, saw the truck moving out and ran to the driveway entrance where they stood in a line to block our escape. Skinhead was reaching under his jacket. I guessed he wasn't scratching an itch.

Gill barely got his door shut when I dropped the gear shift into drive and nailed the gas pedal. The tires spun in the gravel and the truck lurched forward. I aimed it directly at Skinhead. The men scattered like dry leaves hit with a blast from a leaf blower. The high-lift fishtailed out of the parking lot onto the road. There was no other traffic. I pressed down on the gas pedal, swore to myself, then lifted my foot, put the truck into a screeching U-turn and drove back to the bar.

"What the hell are you doing?" Gill shouted.

"Bikes. I forgot about the damn bikes."

We roared back into the parking lot. The headlight beams caught Skinhead and his pals straddling their motorcycles. I gritted my teeth, gripped the steering wheel even tighter, and aimed for the motorcycles and riders. They hopped off the bikes seconds before the truck's heavy front bumper crashed into the first of the choppers.

Metal crunched metal as the bike I'd hit slammed into the other motorcycle, then they both crashed into the third. I threw the shift lever into reverse, then snapped it into drive and headed out of the parking lot for the second time.

Gill looked through the back window. "That's really going to make them mad."

"Couldn't be helped. Those rice rockets would have caught us quicker than you can say Kawasaki."

"What happened back there? Last time I looked those guys were quietly drinking. Something stirred them up like a hornet's nest."

"Not something. Some*one*. Mr. Big arrived."

"Wow! You saw him?"

"Not his face. He was headed around to the back door of the bar."

"I don't understand. How'd you figure I was in trouble?"

I could have told him that the wide-brimmed Tilley hat was a giveaway. And that Mr. Big and Guy Rich were one and the same. Gill was trying to be calm and civilized, but he had a lot of anger building inside. I didn't want him to head back to the flats to confront Rich. The drama at the Salty Sou'wester had suggested that Rich was in a position to order someone killed.

"This is getting a lot more complicated," I said. "I've got to ask you for a favor."

"What sort of favor?" he said in a wary voice.

"Trust me."

"I don't know who to trust anymore, Soc."

"Trust. Me. I need time to poke around. Deal?"

"All right. We've got a deal. Anything I can do to help in the meantime?"

"Yeah. Make yourself scarce. Stay away from the flats. Work on your resume for college."

"That's not a bad suggestion. Promise you'll call when you've got it figured out?"

"I promise. What I'm trying to figure out now is the best way to get home."

I looked in the rearview mirror. There were headlights far behind, and they didn't seem to be getting closer, as they would if someone were chasing us.

We crossed the Bourne Bridge, but rather than take the road that bordered the canal, I cut across the Cape, following a convoluted route along back roads to the Burger King. I told Gill I would see him the next day. He thanked me for all I was doing, which only made me feel guilty, because I didn't seem to be doing much at all.

On the drive along the Mid-Cape Highway, I considered my limited options. I could go to ADA Martin, and have him tell me once more to butt out of the case. I could try to dig up more evidence, but that would take time I didn't have. Or I could do what I seemed to do best. Stir things up.

Whatever I decided would have to wait. The second I stepped into the Big House the first breath I took triggered a series of stomach gurgles. With all the fun I was having at the Salty Sou'wester, I'd forgotten to eat. I followed the delectable aroma of food to its source. Cait was in the kitchen.

She gave me a smile and said, "Hi, Soc. I cooked a roast for dinner. Have a seat and I'll make a sandwich for you."

"Thanks, Cait. I'd like that."

While she assembled the sandwich, I plunked down at the kitchen table and asked how her day went after she left the pier in the shuttle bus. She said she had safely delivered the movie pirates after stopping at a Dunkin' Donuts to sober them up with lots of coffee.

She arched an eyebrow. "Somehow they got hold of whiskey, but you probably don't know anything about that."

I played innocent. "You know how pirates are, always thirsty. Where's the film crew?"

"In the salon playing Texas Hold'em. Ana and Azra are up in their rooms."

"What's tomorrow's schedule?" I asked.

"Max can tell you about it. He's in the editing room making sure every scene has been shot to perfection."

I dug into the sandwich, which was piled high with wafer-thin roast beef layered between thick slabs of whole grain bread. It was done just right, between rare and medium rare, and flavored with tangy horseradish. I washed the sandwich down with a cold Cape Cod beer from the refrigerator.

When I was through chowing down, I thanked Cait. She said it was a small thing in return for putting up with her snoring.

I was still amazed at how much sound could come from someone as slightly built as Cait. It was too late to pick up ear plugs. On the way out of the kitchen I plucked some tissues from a holder, tucked them into my pocket, then grabbed my beer and strolled down the hallway. I poked my head through the open door of the editing room and Max waved me in. He was sitting in front of the screen.

"Hi, Soc. Missed you at dinner."

"Not to worry. Cait fed me. How did the dailies come out?"

"Have a seat and see for yourself."

I settled into a chair next to Max. He clicked the remote and the screen filled with bodies hurtling through the air and splashing into the water. Then there were quick shots of legs and arms flailing underwater in clouds of bubbles.

"Is that the effect you were looking for?" I said.

"Perfect. Panic and confusion."

I asked about the shooting schedule.

"Tomorrow Ana rows out to Great Island. The villagers who hatched the plot that messed up her daughter will follow her through the mists. We'll start the filming from the boat. The crew will assemble after breakfast."

I left Max gazing into the screen and I headed to the salon to watch the card game. On the way, I encountered Ana who was descending the stairs that led up to the second level. She put her finger to her lips and beckoned me to follow her outside to the gazebo. We sat knee-to-knee in a wicker sofa, and in a hushed voice, she said, "You're a policeman."

The reference to my distant past caught me by surprise. After a pause, I said, "I was a police detective in Boston, but I retired a long time ago. How did you know?"

"Cait told me."

I remembered mentioning my cop work to Cait when I filled out the job application. "Is it a problem?"

"Quite the contrary. *I'm* the one with the problem. And I need your help."

"I can't help until I know what this is all about, Ana."

She closed her eyes and opened them, then said, "Tatiana's companion is missing."

"You mean Yergo, the big guy; her husband?"

"He is not her husband. He is her bodyguard."

"Why would a hairdresser need a bodyguard?"

"All I can say is…he went into town on an errand and never came back. For security reasons, Tatiana doesn't have a phone, but Yergo has my number. I got a call that displayed his phone ID, but the person at the other end of the line hung up when I answered. Someone is trying to track her down."

"Who would want to find Tatiana?"

"I can't go into that right now, except to say is that her real name is not Tatiana. It is Azra."

"Okay. Who would want to find Azra?"

"I must ask you to believe me when I say that Azra is in danger. That's all you have to know at this point."

A long time ago I learned the folly of sticking my nose into situations that smelled of trouble, but this was Ana Roman, the movie star I'd fantasized over, who was asking me to throw caution to the wind. So, naturally, I threw caution to the wind.

"Okay," I said. "How can I help?"

"We've made plans for her to leave tomorrow night. In the meantime I need you to keep a close eye on her when we're away from the Big House working on location."

"I'll do my best."

She leaned closer and planted a warm kiss on my lips. Then she stood up and strode across the lawn. I watched her go into the Big House and then I stared at the closed door. Even a short time in the movie biz had shown me that it was all magic and sleight of hand, but there was nothing fake about Ana's fear. She must have been desperate to ask for my help. After all, I was no dashing screen hero who would drop down from the skies to rescue her from the jaws of death. I was an over-the-hill PI who was better at getting into trouble than out of it, but I guess I would have to do.

CHAPTER 26

The card game was still going on in the sunroom. I played a few hands of penny poker with the photographer, the sound man and their assistants, staying just long enough to knock down a beer and lighten my wallet by a dollar and sixteen cents.

I said goodnight and headed for bed. Cait rose with the sun, so she was already sawing up a storm. Before slipping under the covers I tore off a couple wads of tissue and tucked them in my ears. The makeshift plugs didn't cut down on the vibration but helped dampen the sound level.

I was feeling pretty good the next morning when I woke up, got dressed, and joined the crew in the dining room. Ana smiled as if we had never had that serious talk in the gazebo and waved me to a chair on her right.

Jason arrived and took a seat on my left. His handsome face still had the alcoholic blush that was visible when he didn't have his Indian make-up on, but at least his eyes didn't look like they were bleeding. He nudged my ribs with his elbow.

"Glad to see you haven't bailed out of this rum production."

"I wouldn't dream of it. But I need a clear head, so I've been laying off demon rum."

"Me too. I've been persuaded that detox is in my best interest," he said, tilting his head in Ana's direction. Lowering his voice, he said, "I'm not talking about rum in a bottle, my friend. I'm using the word as an adjective; as in rum fellow or rum business. It's a British affectation. Means peculiar or odd."

"Not sure I get you, Jason."

"We'll talk about it after breakfast. Lady Cait has served up a feast fit for a king's court."

With the end of the filming in sight, Cait was trying to clean out the larder. She had whipped up cheesy scrambled eggs with ham, and home fries smothered under layers of onions, peppers, and Hollandaise sauce. Conversation was suspended as the crew wolfed down the breakfast until, finally, Max pushed his empty plate away, tapped his coffee mug with a knife, and got to his feet.

"Thanks, Cait, for that amazing meal. Don't know what we're going to do without you when production wraps up but I'm happy to say that time is fast approaching, especially after the good day we had yesterday. I'm hoping we can build on that momentum. Today we film the scene where the bad guys get what's coming to them." He rubbed his palms together. "The villagers who despoiled Mary's daughter follow her to the island. But Mary has prepared some nasty surprises for them. Proving you don't mess with a witch, right Ana?"

"I don't consider myself a witch. A witch would cackle and cackle and she'd have a big wart right here." Ana put her finger on the tip of her perfect nose. "I prefer to think of myself as a practitioner of the dark arts."

Max let out a whooping laugh. "As you wish, my fair practitioner." He was cranked with excitement. "I'm sure the difference will be lost on the villagers. Any questions?"

I waved a half-eaten slice of toast in the air. "Could you sketch out the day's plans for the boat?"

"I'd be glad to, Soc. You read the script so you know there's a scene where the villagers learn that Ana rows out to the island on a regular basis."

"Sure. She goes out there to visit the grave of her lover."

"Right. The villagers learn about these trips. They think she's going for Bellamy's treasure, and follow in another boat. They don't know that she has set a trap for them."

"What will you need from me?"

"This scene has a bunch of moving parts. We'll use the Zodiac for shots of both rowboats from every angle. You will transport the cast and fog machines and tow the rowing boats out to the set. After we wrap up the rowing scene we move onto the island for the chase."

"No problem from my end. Things should go smoothly."

Every pair of eyes at the table turned in my direction. Ana put her hand lightly on my arm.

"I know this is silly, but we've become very superstitious during this production. Saying something is 'no problem' may invite bad luck, as we tend to talk in elliptical terms."

"Sorry about that, folks. As a Red Sox fan I should know about jinxes. Forget what I said about things going smoothly. We'll be damn lucky if the boat doesn't sink."

"Thanks, Soc," Ana said. "That should do the trick. Sorry to interrupt your presentation, Max."

"Not a problem, Ana. If we're through exorcising demons, maybe we can get back to the shoot," Max said. "We'll assemble at the marina in two hours."

He clapped his hands and the crew rose from the table. Cait asked them to help clean up because she had to fetch the extras for the day's shooting and order sandwiches from the caterer. She put some breakfast in a covered dish for Ana to take up to Azra. I walked with Ana to the bottom of the stairs where she paused, and said, "I told Azra that you are going to help. She said she can't thank you enough."

"Maybe she'd like to thank me in person."

Ana shook her head. "That's impossible. I was serious when I told you that knowing too much could be dangerous."

"The way I see it, knowing not enough could be even more dangerous. Why don't we ask Azra if she wants to talk to me?"

Ana answered with an impatient sigh but didn't resist when I took the dish from her hands, and said, "Her breakfast is getting cold. I'll only ask her one question. Deal?"

"Okay," she said. "One question." She didn't sound happy.

We climbed the stairs to the second floor. Ana knocked lightly and opened the door. Azra was at a desk pecking away at a laptop. She turned, saw me standing next to Ana, holding the breakfast tray, and stopped typing.

"Mr. Socarides asked if he could talk with you," Ana said. "I tried to dissuade him. We agreed to leave it up to you."

Azra pinned me with a level gaze. There was no fear or anger in her eyes. Only curiosity.

"Of course. I'd be happy to talk to Mr. Socarides," she said. She rose from her chair, took the dish and set it on a table. We shook hands. She had a firm grip. A slight smile came to her lips. She was probably amused at the way my jaw was resting on my Adam's apple. Standing in front of me was a younger version of Ana Roman.

I said, "That was you I saw walking in the fog the night I came over to meet the crew."

She nodded.

"Now I know why you didn't answer when I called you Ana."

"I'm sorry about what happened. Some evenings after the house quiets down I wander around the property. Yergo follows at a distance so I can have some privacy, but he keeps an eye out. The night was foggy. He thought you might be a threat and tried to protect me."

Ana stepped forward. "We don't have much time, Azra. I said Mr. Socarides could ask you one question."

"That was the deal," I said. "I'll make it simple. Who are you?"

She glanced at Ana. "That's not as simple as it sounds."

Ana said, "Azra is my younger sister. Since I answered your

question, you can ask another."

"Fair enough. Why do you need a bodyguard, Azra?"

Ana gave her a nod.

"Someone wants to kill me. Yergo was supposed to prevent that from happening."

Ana cut me off before I could sneak in a follow-up.

"That will be all for now," she said. "Max is expecting us on the set."

She went to the door and held it open. I thanked Azra, expressed my hope that we could talk again, and went downstairs to my room for the keys to the pickup. On my way out the door I got a call from my pal, Sergeant Nolan.

"The DPW is going to clear away what's left of your truck this afternoon. People have been complaining that it's unsightly. Thought I'd let you know in case you wanted to be there when they haul it."

"Thanks, Sergeant. I'll be out on the water today so I don't think I can make it. Guess I'll see it next time I'm at the town dump."

A few minutes later I was sitting in the GMC when Ana and her sister came out with Jason and got into their van. Azra was wearing the straw hat, wig and sunglasses that hid her identity.

The van pulled out of the parking lot with me right behind it. Since I didn't know who I was guarding against, I kept a sharp eye peeled for anything out of the ordinary. Although I wasn't sure what I would do if someone made a move. The drive was uneventful and we got to the marina without being ambushed. The fleet of movie vehicles had arrived ahead of us. Members of the crew were unloading gear.

A truck hauling a trailer that carried two double-ended dories was backing down the boat ramp. I parked near the movie trucks and helped the driver move the rowboats from the truck and into the water. We got in the dories and rowed them to the finger pier where the *Sea Robin* had its slip.

Cait arrived in the shuttle with four extras dressed as villagers in baggy pants and shirts that weren't half as gaudy as their pirate outfits. She dropped off a cooler full of sandwiches she'd picked up from the caterer. She had to tend to paperwork back at the Big House and would return to pick up the extras after the shoot. Max said the park ranger would meet us on the island, then he got into the Zodiac with the cameraman and his assistant. Ana and Azra came on board the *Sea Robin* with Jason and the villagers. I moved the boat out of its slip; the dories were attached to the stern. With the Zodiac leading the way, we towed the rowboats across the harbor.

The Zodiac continued onto the beach where the park ranger was waiting. I tossed the *Sea Robin's* anchor over the side and killed the engine.

Max called Jason on the walkie-talkie. "We're going to run a test as soon as the fog machines are in place," Max said. "Stand by."

Max and the crew unloaded two black boxes from the Zodiac and placed them at the water's edge around fifty feet apart. Max took up a position about halfway between, pointed something at the boxes, and after a minute or so the machines began to belch twin streams of gray mist that enveloped Max and merged into a low-lying cloud that rolled across the water toward the *Sea Robin*.

"He's activated the boxes with a remote control," Jason said. "Otherwise, you're seeing the same old-fashioned Hollywood high tech used in the first *Dracula* film. The machines pump out a mixture of water, glycerin and mineral oil. The mix makes the fog heavy and keeps it low."

The mists soon obscured the machines producing them. Max and the others on the beach were ghostly silhouettes behind the moving curtain of fog. The cloud expanded along its edges until a big section of beach was no longer visible.

Max's voice came over the walkie-talkie. "The machines are

working fine. I've shut them down so we can see what we're doing. Time for the cast to get into the boats."

Azra handed a red cloak to Ana, who slipped it onto her shoulders and pulled the hood over her head. I helped Ana climb down into her rowboat and offered to give her some rowing hints.

She settled onto a seat. "Thanks, Soc, but I'll be fine. Max is like a chess player. He thinks several steps ahead. He made sure the extras and I practiced rowing. We've spent hours in these boats."

I gave her boat a shove. As soon as she was in the clear, Ana grabbed the oar handles and rowed a short distance. The extras piled into their boat and rowed over to Ana. The fog had thinned and the beach was visible again. Max and his crew attached the camera to its mount, pushed the Zodiac away from the beach and motored out so they were between the rowboats and the island.

When everyone was ready, the cameraman snapped the clapperboard. Max called out through his electronic megaphone. "Action!" He clicked the remote. Fog poured out of the machines. The billows blanketed the water with a thick slow-moving layer of ghostly mist.

Ana pulled on the oars, putting her back into each stroke. The boat picked up speed, cutting through the layer of fog as if it were floating on a cloud.

Max maneuvered the Zodiac so the cameraman could get shots of the rowboat from the front, both sides, close-ups of the paddles going into the water, and of Ana's hooded face from every direction, until she disappeared in the rising mists.

Max yelled, "Cut!"

He called for the villagers to start rowing. The clapperboard announced the new scene and Max yelled for action again. The boat with the villagers followed Ana into the fog. Max turned off the fog machines. The mists dissipated, leaving only a thin layer that hung over the water. Max reviewed the shots on the camera view-screen. Then he ran the Zodiac alongside the *Sea Robin*.

"The shots are all perfect. We'll move the rowboats onto the beach and I'll give Tatiana and Jason a ride to shore."

"Will you need me for anything?" I said.

"Not until the shoot is over. It's going to take a while to set things up. Come back in about four hours, Soc. Don't worry about getting paid. You're still on the clock. Enjoy your time off. Going back to the Big House?"

I thought about it, then said, "Naw. Got to say goodbye to an old friend."

CHAPTER 27

The Slow-Poke Society must have been in town because every car I got behind was going five miles under the speed limit. By the time I turned off Route 6A and arrived at the arson scene, the cremated remains of my truck had been cleared away. The air still stunk of burned oil and gasoline, but all that was left of my pickup was a greasy circle of burned grass.

I stared at the crater that had been scooped out along with the burned up wreckage. Sergeant Nolan didn't get it. I wasn't being sentimental about an old bucket of bolts that started on the first try less than half the time. It was more than that. Losing the truck on top of my boat problems had messed up a family situation that was already overly-complicated, especially with my father's descent into dementia. And my family issues had put me squarely in the sights of my mother's guilt projector.

I needed some fresh air, so I walked down the sand road and then through the dunes. With the tide in, the flats were inaccessible for oyster picking. I was surprised to see Guy Rich's truck parked on the beach facing the bay.

My mind flashed back to the Tilley hat I glimpsed outside the Salty Sou'wester. I thought of the crap I'd gone through since I was first introduced to Rich and I went into a slow burn. If I was right in my thinking, Rich was in this thing up to the lobes of his long ears. I continued on toward the truck.

Rich was in the cab talking on his phone. He didn't notice me until I was a few yards away. He said a few words into his phone, then hung up and got out of the truck. The unnaturally white smile flashed on as if someone had flipped a light switch, and he gave me a knuckle-grinding handshake.

"Good to see you again, Soc."

"Nice to see you too, Guy. Enjoying the view?"

"Yes, as a matter of fact. I rarely get to savor my surroundings when I'm tromping around in the mud." He tucked the phone in a shirt pocket. "But business waits for no man. I was talking to a buyer about an oyster delivery. How are things going?"

"Okay, I guess." I shrugged. "Thanks for telling me about Gill. I checked him out after we talked. Like you said, he's not the poor, dumb oyster farmer he pretends to be. Damn embarrassing to admit it, but he had me fooled. And I'm a professional investigator."

"He had us all fooled. Now you see why I'm suspicious about his grant being hit again and again. I'm convinced he poached his own oysters and used his so-called losses to cover the fact that he was stealing shellfish from the other farmers."

"That would explain a lot. But do you think he'd actually do something that sleazy?"

"We both know for a fact that Gill can't be trusted."

"No argument there," I said, putting a hint of anger in my voice. "I'm done with that guy."

"It's none of my business, of course, but cutting him loose would be a smart move on your part."

"Absolutely!" I said. "I'll tell him I'm through, as soon as I clear up a few loose ends in the case."

Rich looked as if he'd been hit with a sudden case of indigestion. "Loose ends, you say?"

I gave a perplexed shake of the head, a move I had picked up from the old *Columbo* TV series. "The question that's nagged me from the start is, what happened to the stolen oysters? I figured that if we could track down the people buying the stolen shellfish that would break the whole case."

"Seems like a logical conclusion. Too bad you can't follow up on your interesting premise."

"That's not exactly true."

I lowered my voice, although we were the only ones on the beach. "I was talking to a contact at the State Police. He let slip that the stolen oysters might be going to an outfit named South by West Seafood. Ever heard of them?"

I had to hand it to Rich. He didn't even blink. "I sell my stock locally so I don't know anything about them. Did the State Police say anything else?"

I shook my head. "The Statie clamped his mouth shut after he mentioned them. But it fits in with what you said about Gill stealing his own stock. He also robs you and the other farmers and sells it to these same guys. We could nail Gill to the wall with this info."

"Too bad you don't have any evidence backing it up."

"True, but I may know where I can find evidence," I said. "South by West has a warehouse in Buzzards Bay and I'm going to check it out tonight."

"Is that wise?" Rich said. "These may be the same people who shot at you."

"I'll be carrying a gun this time. If these are the scumbuckets who torched my truck, maybe I'll get a chance to even the score. Cops might never catch this crew."

"You said the poachers used automatic weapons. You'd be heavily outgunned if they see you."

"I don't intend to be seen." I put a snarl in my voice like a fictional PI.

Rich shook his head. "You apparently won't be deterred. All I can say is, be careful. Please let me know how your investigation turns out."

"You'll be the first to know."

"Good luck," he said. We shook hands. "Now if you'll excuse me, I'll be on my way."

I watched him drive off the beach and I smiled as I imagined him on the phone spreading the word about my visit that night to the warehouse. I got back in my truck, and on the drive out to the main road, I passed the *No Trespassing* sign marking the dirt track that led toward Gill's property.

I stopped, backed up, and turned off. The track ended after a few hundred feet in a cleared turn-around spot. A road had been bulldozed from the clearing into the woods. I left the truck and followed the strip of disturbed earth. On both sides, the scrub pine and oak trees and the bushes were festooned with neon pink ribbons, suggesting that the land was marked for development.

The bulldozed lane ended and I followed a path until I was out of the pink-ribbon area. Something glittered like diamonds through the trees up ahead. I kept walking to where the woods ended on a low bluff that overlooked the sun-sparkled waters of the bay. I tried to picture the property map I had seen in the town assessors 'office.

In the quiet setting the snap of a branch cracking was like a gunshot. I turned at the sound. Gill was coming out of the woods.

"Hey, Soc," he said. "I saw your truck. What's going on?"

"I was poking around your high-priced bird sanctuary."

A beatific smile came to his lips. "Pretty place, isn't it? We're standing about where I wanted to build my house."

"Million-dollar view, if you could get to it without passing through pink-ribbon land."

He wrinkled his pug nose. "Yeah, they bulldozed the road a couple of months ago. Been doing drainage tests and marking roads. I guess they're getting close to developing the land. Their tract doesn't have the great water view you mentioned, but it borders the road which means it blocks access to my land-locked property."

"Anything info on who the developers are?"

"Nope. I've dug around a little bit. It's hard to get past the corporate layering."

"If you've finished your resume, why don't you use your research skills to find out who owns the land and who's financing the development. It could be important."

"I'll start digging again. Have you turned up anything new since we last talked?"

"I've started shaking the trees. Fruit should soon start plummeting to the ground."

"Just remember not to be under the tree when the fruit falls."

"Good advice." I glanced at my watch. "I've got to move along. Maybe I'll have something tomorrow when we talk."

We parted ways, and I walked back to the truck. About twenty minutes later I was on the Mid-Cape Highway, and a short while after that, I was on the winding road through cranberry bog country on the mainland side of the Cape Cod Canal. I slowed and hooked a U-turn, made another pass, then turned onto a dirt road across from the driveway that led to the warehouse.

I tucked the GMC out of sight behind a strip of trees and walked back toward the road. I came across the remnant of a stone wall in the woods where I could sit and watch the warehouse driveway without being seen.

A half hour later a South by West delivery truck trundled by my observation post and turned off onto the driveway. Faster action than I'd expected. Rich must have been burning up the phone lines. Even more interesting were the three men on motorcycles who followed the truck off the road. The bikes were scratched and dented from their encounter with the bumper of Gill's high lift truck back at the bar in Buzzards Bay. The guttural exhaust from one of motorcycles indicated that it had lost its muffler. Fifteen minutes later the three bikers came out. Instead of the delivery truck, they followed the pickup that matched the vehicle on the flats the night of the big shoot-out.

I dashed to the Jimmy; within minutes I'd caught up with the poacher vehicle. I stayed a half mile back, following the caravan as it made its way to the main highway leading to the Cape Cod Canal.

Our little caravan crossed the Bourne Bridge, then followed the road along the Cape Cod Canal, connecting with the Mid-Cape Highway. We got off the exit ramp using a reverse of the route I had been on earlier. We passed through the bay-side village that bordered the oyster farms and the truck turned onto a drive that had an entrance flanked by two square pillars constructed of large stones. I waited until the motorcycle escorts followed the truck down the driveway and stopped to stare at the left-hand column.

The thick, block, capital letters emblazoned on the big bronze plaque spelled out a familiar name:

R-I-C-H

I stared at the letters until they began to blur. I visualized how the cops would react to a nosy PI telling them that a wealthy taxpayer was involved with an oyster poaching operation, and maybe worse. I'd be slapped down like a fly. But even if I did nothing, Rich and his pals might decide that I had to be eliminated.

Gill had been spot-on when he advised me not to stand under the tree when I shook the branches, but from the looks of things, his warning had come too late. The fruit had already started to fall.

CHAPTER 28

When I brought the boat back to Great Island I learned that the land shoot had gone off mostly without a hitch, except for an actor who got lost in the woods for a short time. Everyone was now accounted for, though, and all were in high spirits when they climbed back onto the *Sea Robin*. Max and the film crew pulled up beside the bigger boat so they could unload the fog machines, then we tied the dories to the boat and set off across the harbor behind the Zodiac.

Max and the others were eager to celebrate the day's work. I wish I could have shared their exuberance. But on the drive back to the Big House I tried to sketch out where things stood, and it wasn't a pretty picture. When I told Rich I was going to visit the warehouse that night, I wanted to see what would happen. I thought the clean-up crew would move the truck to another hidey-hole. I never figured they'd go directly to his house. Maybe he wouldn't suspect that I'd already been to the warehouse. But Rich seemed like the kind of careful guy who would tell the biker boys to bring him the surveillance camera tapes.

By now, Rich could have seen the video of Gill and me breaking into the old cranberry warehouse in Buzzards Bay. He would know I was onto him; he might even send his gun-slinging poachers to finish the job they attempted when they turned the oyster flats into a shooting gallery. I pondered calling ADA Martin for help, but after our telephone sparring match I didn't know if I could trust him.

I made a side trip to my boathouse to check on Kojak and give him a snack. After he finished, I carried him out onto the deck, sat in a chair with him on my lap, and told him about the predicament I had put myself in with Guy Rich and his merry band of bikers. He fell asleep, so I carried him back inside.

Not long after tucking him into his bed, I pulled into the driveway of the Big House and saw that the place looked like command central for the Policemen's Ball. I parked behind the trio of cruisers in the driveway and walked around to the lawn side of the mansion. Uniformed police officers were talking to members of the film crew on the porch.

Cait broke away from the pack to come over and greet me. Her usual sunny smile was missing.

"What's all the fuss about?" I said.

"Better talk to Max. He's in the salon with Ana and Jason."

I said I would see her later and went into the house. I walked into the sunroom and saw Max sitting on the sofa next to Ana. They were talking to a policeman and a policewoman seated across from them. Everyone looked very serious, including Jason, who stood nearby—his hands clasped behind his back.

Max gave me a quick flick of his fingers that would have been insulting, if I let myself be insulted. "Can't talk to you now, Soc. I'll fill the crew in as soon as we're done with this interview."

Ana put a hand on Max's arm. "Soc used to be a policeman. It might be valuable to get his take on the situation."

Max's eyebrows did a little hop. "I didn't know—well, in that case, if the officers don't mind."

"I was a homicide detective with the Boston Police Department," I said to the police officers. "I can give you a number to call if you want to check it out."

Before either cop could reply, I stepped next to Jason to show the police I knew my place. The young woman officer gave me a look, but she must have decided she didn't have to call the BPD because she went back to her questioning.

"When did you first hear that your hairdresser's husband was missing?" she asked Ana.

Ana said, "Yergo's wife, Tatiana, knocked on my door around two in the morning. She said Yergo had gone into town around eleven o'clock to buy cigarettes. She had awakened and Yergo wasn't there. We searched the house and grounds, then called the police to report him missing, with the description of the car he was driving. The police called around five to say that his car had been found at a convenience store. We didn't hear anything more until this afternoon when we got a second call saying his body had washed up on a beach."

"What exactly was the deceased's job?"

"He was a production assistant," Max said. "He mostly moved equipment around."

The policewoman consulted her notebook. "As I understand it, he was in this country on a work visa."

"That's right. He's Croatian."

"Lots of Eastern European kids work here in the summer," the male cop said. "Most have jobs in restaurants or retail. How did this gentleman get hooked up with a movie production?"

Ana said, "I'm also of Croatian ancestry, as is Tatiana, my hairdresser. She and Yergo have been living in Los Angeles. She didn't want to be away from her husband and wondered if he could work on the movie. I asked Max to hire him."

"We're going to have to talk to his wife."

"Yes, of course," Ana said. "She's quite distraught. If you could give her a little time to compose herself, I'll make her available. Would tomorrow morning work for you?"

"Sure. We'll finish taking statements from the rest of the crew and drop by first thing."

"Thank you for your understanding. I'd be happy to relay any questions you have for her to think about."

"The main question would be whether she knew if he had any enemies or knows of anyone who might want to harm him."

Ending my short vow of silence, I said, "Why do you ask if he had enemies?"

The policewoman looked over at the male cop, who nodded, then she said, "The victim's found on the beach, so our first conclusion was that he drowned. But his body was covered with wounds."

"What kind of wounds?" I asked. She glanced at Max and Ana, probably thinking back to cop school, where she learned no one, even an actress and a movie director, should be excluded as a suspect, then she pinned me with a none-of-your-business stare.

I shrugged. "Sorry. Once a cop, always a cop."

The hard-eyed expression didn't change. "Cuts and burns over most of the body."

"Injuries consistent with torture?"

"That will be up to the medical examiner." She closed her notebook, deciding she had said enough. "We'll go over what we've got and come back in the morning to talk to your hairdresser. Hope you folks aren't planning to go anywhere soon."

"We'll be filming locally for another few days," Max said. "You have my cell phone number. Please call me any time."

The officers stood and thanked everyone, then headed for the exit. Max said he had better talk to the crew and asked Jason to go with him.

"This is terrible," Ana said after they'd left. "I'd better tend to Azra."

"Do the police know she's your sister?" I said.

"No. Even Max doesn't know we're related."

"Cops are cops. They'll find out eventually."

"I know. But it would have been too complicated to explain. You won't tell them, will you?"

"No. I'll keep quiet to see where all this goes. For now. "I plunked down on the sofa beside her. "Maybe you should uncomplicate it for me," I said. "When you asked me to babysit Azra you told me all I had to know was that she was in danger. I didn't pursue getting more information, even though my gut was warning me not to take a bodyguard job without knowing what I'd be guarding against."

"Soc, I—"

"That was dumb on my part," I interrupted. "But I went along because I like you and wanted to lend a hand. Tell me why I should keep walking blindfolded into something that involves murder and torture."

Ana wiped away a brimming tear with the back of her hand. "I suppose it's time you knew the whole story."

"It may be past time, but give it a try."

"It's very complicated." She pursed her lips, collecting her thoughts, then said, "My real name is Ivana Klavic. I changed it to Ana Roman to advance my career. When I was born, Croatia was part of Yugoslavia, a collection of Balkan countries bound together by the iron hand of a dictator named Tito. After he died, Yugoslavia disintegrated into bloody civil wars during the 1990s. Azra had become a journalist, and was assigned to cover the Balkan wars. An international tribunal indicted some Serbian army officers for war crimes, based in part on her reporting. Azra also reported on a Croatian paramilitary figure named Drazik who massacred hundreds of civilians. As a Croatian herself, she was incensed. But he disappeared rather than be brought up on charges. A corpse with his ID was later found."

"And Azra?"

"She always harbored suspicions about Drazik's death. About a year ago she uncovered a network of human traffickers. She is a skilled reporter, and produced proof that the head trafficker was Drazik, still very much alive. He was arrested and she offered to be a witness at his trial on charges of war crimes."

"That was very brave of her."

"Some would say it was foolhardy. Drazik was in prison but he smuggled out orders to his brothers to kill her. After a particularly close call, she realized she had to go into hiding."

"How did she end up as your hairdresser?"

"Max had already asked if I'd do the movie. Azra had always done my hair when we were kids. We used to take turns making each other up. When she called looking for help, I decided a movie hairdresser would be an ideal cover for her until Drazik was brought to trial."

"Looks like you were wrong."

"I underestimated Drazik's reach."

"How do you figure they tracked her down?"

"Yergo had been her bodyguard during the wars, so she asked him to come with her to the U.S. and pose as her husband. They slept in different rooms in her suite. He doesn't speak English and grew lonely. She caught him talking to people back home about his movie job. His general whereabouts may have been traced through phone taps."

I thought back to the shadow I had seen lurking in the woods near Goody Hallett's meadow. "Do you think they've been watching the film shoots?"

"I've seen no sign of it. I think they would have made their move earlier if they knew exactly where to find Azra. My guess is that they were aware of Yergo's general location. Perhaps they pinpointed him on his cell phone when he went to town. Now they're trying to track Azra down."

"Which could happen soon," I said. "Yergo might have cracked under torture. Azra should get off Cape Cod."

"Drazik's trial will be held within days. Arrangements are being made to get her away safely, but her escorts don't arrive until tomorrow. She will have to stay here tonight, and she'll need your protection."

"You're asking me for something I can't give. I'm not armed and there's only one of me. What about talking to the police?"

"They would have to verify everything. Azra would be exposed in the meantime. Can't you do something? It's just for tonight."

"The best I can do is keep watch. If I see something funny, I'll call the police."

"Thank you! I'll stay with Azra. She's very agitated and I don't want her to do anything unwise. She can't be allowed to leave this house."

I pictured a band of killers sneaking up on the Big House and me facing them with the only weapons at hand—a rubber pirate's cutlass and a plastic flintlock pistol.

But I said, "I'll do my best, Ana."

She leaned over, put her arms around me and kissed my cheek. "I know you will." With those words, she rose from the sofa and breezed out of the room, leaving her wonderful scent floating in the air, and my head spinning.

I twisted my lips into what was supposed to be a rueful grin. I remembered how I had grumbled about being so hard up for cash I had to take a job guarding an oyster patch, thinking that it was too trivial a case for a tough private eye and former street-smart city cop like me.

And now I was supposed to protect a maiden in distress from international thugs, like a cut-rate James Bond, reaffirming a lesson I had learned long ago:

Be careful what you wish for.

CHAPTER 29

Dinner that night was like a wake. Except that the deceased couldn't make it because he had an appointment with the medical examiner. Cait had whipped together a meal of pesto chicken thighs, garlic mashed potatoes and green beans. But no one was in the mood for creative cuisine. The film crew sat around the table, heads bent over their plates, picking at their food. Except for Jason, who filled his plate as fast as he cleaned it.

No one had known Yergo very well. But his death was one more bucketful of bad luck poured into a production that had already seen misfortune. If anyone had reason to put on a long face, though, it should have been me. Taking over as Azra's bodyguard was the second time I had stepped into the shoes of a man who had died a nasty death.

Max did his best to blow away the funeral parlor atmosphere. He proposed a toast to Yergo, then quickly changed the subject. The filming that day had been spectacular, he said. He couldn't wait to see the dailies. He pried a few smiles out of the solemn crew with his story about the actor who got temporarily lost in the woods. The cameraman had caught the actor coming out of the trees in total confusion, clothes torn to tatters by thorns.

"It was absolutely amazing," Max crowed. "The wild-eyed look on his face was exactly what I was looking for." He clapped his hands. "If everyone is done with dinner, let's go to the movies."

We all pitched in with the clean-up. Max shouted up the stairs to the second level, calling Ana, who'd eaten her dinner in Azra's room. She came down a couple of minutes later and settled next to Jason in the front-row chair reserved for her in the editing room.

Max stood in front of the screen. "You all know the basic premise," he said. "The four villagers follow Goody to the island, thinking she will lead them to pirate treasure. What they don't know is that she is luring them to their doom."

Pacing back and forth and waving his hands in the air to add drama, Max explained the scene. After the villagers make landfall, Goody sneaks around and hides both boats, marooning the villagers on her turf. They try to stick together but she picks them off one at a time. She lures one villager over a staked pitfall. Another is caught in a spring snare that hoists him feet-first in the air where he slowly asphyxiates. The third villager gets stuck in the muddy bottom of a marsh creek and drowns trying to escape. She takes pity on the young man who enticed her daughter and merely drives him crazy with fear.

"The last guy is the extra who got lost in the woods. The ghost of Goody Hallett must have been in a good mood, because he came out of the woods with tattered clothes that gave him the perfect look for the part."

"Goody was a busy girl," Jason intoned in his voice from the grave. His vow of sobriety must have expired because his words were slurred.

The room filled with laughter, suggesting that Yergo's wake was officially over.

"Yes, she was, but the threat she poses in these scenes is implied with shadows and quick cuts, rather than shown," Max said. "The imagination is scarier than any blood spatter on film. It's also cheaper to fool the viewer with phantoms, very important for a low budget operation."

"You should know about fooling people with phantoms," Jason said.

There was more laughter. It was directed at Jason's drunken manner, because the puzzling comment wasn't particularly funny. Still, the only one in the room not laughing was Max. His lips were frozen in a grin that didn't match his hostile stare aimed at Jason's flushed face. He abruptly told the cameraman to roll the dailies.

The screen flickered, the clapperboard clacked, and we were looking at the four villagers dashing through the woods in pursuit of a fleeting figure in a scarlet cape. The fog machines must have been at full blast because rolling mists hid the lower parts of their bodies. The villagers followed Ana to a low hill that rose from the mists. She pushed back her hood and the camera moved in on her face. With the wild tendrils of hair framing her stony gaze, Ana looked like a marble statue of the Medusa.

The villagers hesitated, but their leader urged them on. Ana bent down, picked up something at her feet and held it above her head. She smiled. Not a nice smile. The villagers stopped and stared at the skull in her hands.

"You want Sam's treasure," she hissed. "Ask *him* where it is."

She bowled the skull down the hill into the villagers. The men tried to dodge the rolling skull. When she spread her cloak like a giant scarlet bird and seemed to float down the hill, they turned and ran. The scene ended.

Max stood and began to clap and everyone in the room followed his lead. When the applause finally died, he glanced around at the happy faces.

"We are all saddened by today's bad news," he said. "We didn't know Yergo well, but he was a hard-working member of our crew. We'll be done with shooting in a few days and the film editors will take over and turn our work into an amazing movie. It's a damn shame Yergo won't be able to see it."

He asked the cameraman to show the rest of the dailies. The camera followed the villagers as they ran blindly through the foggy woods. Sometimes the lens caught them in flight. At other times, it showed the scene from the villagers' point of view. In between, Ana seemed to glide through the mists, taking her time as she drove them to their doom. As each man is about to meet his fate, the camera zooms in for a close-up of Ana's face.

Ana was a wonderful witch; evil, cold, taunting each man with a cackle.

"You make a lovely pin cushion," she says to the pitfall victim. "Swept you off your feet, lad," to the man who will die dangling upside down. "Say hello to the devil on the way down to hell," she taunts the villager doomed to drown in the marsh creek. She kisses the last young man and says she wants him as a lover. His hair will turn white and, for as long as he lives, he will remind the village just what happens when you annoy a witch.

Max explained that the special effects will be filmed with stunt doubles at a sound studio and then spliced in later. He invited everyone into the salon to celebrate with shots of brandy. After making a couple of toasts, Max suggested that the crew get a good night's sleep. It had been a long day, so most people followed his advice. Ana whispered a 'thank you' in my ear, then she, too, was gone and I was left alone. I poured myself a stiff shot of brandy and shoved thoughts of everything else aside while I concentrated on keeping Azra safe until the morning.

I did what I usually do when I don't want to face facts. I rationalized. Maybe Yergo had defied his tormentors and there was no reason to be worried. I quickly tossed that theory in the wishful thinking bin. Torture can loosen the tongue, even with a big guy like Yergo.

I tossed down the last of my brandy and headed for my room. Cait was sound asleep, and her snoring was down to a soft purr. I grabbed the blankets off my bed and on the way out I stopped in the kitchen. Someone had made coffee after dinner. I poured what was left into a thermos, went out the front door and walked across the lawn to the gazebo. I moved a chair around to face the house. I settled into the chair, wrapped myself in blankets, made sure the cell phone was fully charged and set it on a side table.

When you do stakeouts, you learn to put your mind into a neutral zone while staying alert to anything out of the ordinary. It's the mental equivalent of a cat nap. You sleep with your ears cocked for any odd sound.

A little after midnight tendrils of fog began to move in, obscuring the house behind a thin gray curtain and covering my blankets with drops of moisture. Around 1 A.M. I pushed the damp blankets aside, got out of my chair, and walked across the wet grass, around the house and back to the gazebo. I repeated the patrol every half hour. On the 2:30 A.M. loop, I was on my way across the lawn when I saw a light in the gazebo. It flashed on, then off, barely visible in the haze of fog that Mother Nature had supplied. I had left my chair only minutes before. I would have seen anyone coming out the front door of the Big House.

The light came on again, producing the reddish glow that occurs when someone shields the beam with a hand, then it moved across the lawn toward the parking lot. I followed and saw a car dome's light go on and off. In the quick burst, I saw Azra get behind the wheel. The car engine started. My truck keys were in the pocket of my windbreaker. It was a stroke of luck. Otherwise, I would have had to run back into the house and Azra would have driven off in one of the film company's cars.

I loped over to the GMC and got it started. By the time I was out of the parking area, she was already a half dozen car lengths down the road. I kept the headlights doused so she wouldn't know I was following. I pressed the accelerator to keep up, but eased off when red taillights flicked on ahead and off to the side of the road. The lights belonged to a black Cadillac SUV, parked on the berm that pulled out between us and sped up. It tried to pass Azra's car but she must have seen the maneuver in her mirror, and hit the gas.

The driver accelerated, caught up with her car and began to pass. I expected an attempt to cut Azra off, but what I saw next was far worse. Someone was holding what looked like a flickering torch out the passenger window of the SUV. I could smell the stench of burning gasoline. Then, the Molotov cocktail arced through the air and hit the side of Azra's car in a blinding explosion of liquid flame.

CHAPTER 30

My foot mashed the brake pedal like a sledgehammer. The pickup fishtailed to a skidding halt behind Azra's car. I flipped the transmission lever into park and stumbled out of the cab with more speed than grace. Catching my balance, I buried my nose in the crook of my raised arm and advanced on the burning automobile, like Dracula moving in on a bloody meal.

Greasy black billows stung my eyes to tears. The heat blasted my exposed skin. I side-stepped into the street to get away from the flying sparks. Through a rift in the smoke I saw fire enveloping the rear half of the car. The thrower had probably aimed for the front seat. Maybe the fire bomb was getting too hot to hold and was tossed an instant too soon, sparing Azra from being incinerated. That situation would change if the fire crept forward much further. The door was open a couple of inches. Fingers groped around the edge.

I yanked my sleeve cuff down to protect my fingers, grabbed the hot handle and pulled the door open. With my free hand, I took Azra by the wrist and pulled. She wouldn't budge. I yelled at her to get out of the car. No response. I reached in and undid her seat belt buckle. Then I wrapped my arm around her waist and dragged her into the street seconds before the whole interior of the car became an inferno. I hustled her toward the GMC, intending to get us both far away before the fire reached the gas tank.

The bomb-tossers had stopped a short distance ahead of the burning car. We had only taken a few steps before the SUV pulled out into the road, made a tight U-turn, raced in our direction and screeched to a halt on the opposite side of the street. The doors flew open. Four men dressed in black running suits spilled out into the street. The dancing light from the fire reflected off the pistols clutched in their hands. Balaclavas hid their faces. The foursome spread out and moved toward us. Without a miracle we'd be starting our trip to the morgue within seconds.

Miracles come in all shapes and sizes, I guess. A car horn blared and stayed on, drowning out the crackling roar of the fire. Headlights blinked to life, and from our right a black Ford Taurus sped down the road. The gunmen scrambled out of the path of the oncoming vehicle like clowns at a circus. The car swept past, did an expert, skidding U-turn and came to a stop. Motor purring, it sat there like a tiger tightening its muscles for an attack.

The gunslingers stepped back into the road and started to raise their guns. The SUV's driver had anticipated the move. The vehicle sprang forward as if launched from a catapult. With no time to get off a shot or dodge the motorized missile, the gunmen plastered their backs against the SUV. The Taurus swerved toward the gunmen and missed their toes by inches before making an even quicker U-turn, putting it in position to launch a third attack.

The attackers piled into the Cadillac and it took off on smoking tires. The sedan started toward us, moving slowly. The driver was invisible behind the dark tinted windows. As the car went past, the horn beeped a playful rhythm.

Beep-beep, beep-beep-beep. Beep-beep.

Leaving an inch of tire rubber on the road, the car accelerated and disappeared into the night.

The gunmen could return at any second. With the mysterious Good Samaritan out of the picture, we'd be toast. I helped Azra climb into the GMC's cab. Then I got behind the steering wheel, backed away from the raging bonfire, snapped the gear shift into drive and nailed the accelerator. The truck was pushing sixty miles an hour before I realized that I didn't know where I was going. I slowed down to figure out what to do next, just as a couple of police cars and a fire truck passed me going in the opposite direction.

The bad guys might be watching for us to return to the Big House. Only one place I could think of offered a modicum of safety.

I must have glanced in the rearview mirror a hundred times before I turned the truck onto the potholed driveway to my boathouse. The windows were in darkness. Azra hadn't spoken a word since we'd left the flaming car. When I helped her out of the truck her legs turned to rubber. I picked her up in my arms, staggered to the front door and called out Sally's name.

The outside light came on and Sally opened the door. Her sleep-filled eyes blinked, then snapped up like window shades.

"*Migod*, Soc. Is she dead?"

"She's alive. She's had a rough night but she'll be okay."

"Who is she?"

"Someone who needs help."

Sally opened the door wide and stepped aside. "Come in," she said. "Put her on the sofa."

Azra was a slim woman, but I'm not the muscled Greek god of my youth. I was glad to plunk her on the couch. Kojak, who was snoozing at one end of the sofa, gave me a dirty look. Sally gently picked him up and hustled him into the bedroom. She returned with a blanket and spread it over Azra, who looked around and murmured, "Where am I?"

"This is my house and this is my friend Sally," I said. "You're safe here."

"Safe from what?" Sally silently mouthed the words.

Sally's inquisitive mind can drive me crazy. I said, "Let me get Azra some water, then we'll talk."

Sally nodded.

I told Azra to call if she needed anything. She pulled the blanket under her chin and closed her eyes. We went into the kitchen and Sally leaned into my ear.

"Please tell me what's going on with your friend."

"She's in trouble."

"Dammit, Soc. Any idiot can see that. What kind of trouble?"

"Big trouble. She was nearly killed in a car fire."

Sally glanced toward the living room, an expression of horror on her face. "That's terrifying! She's probably still in shock. Why isn't she on her way to the hospital?"

"It wouldn't be safe."

"You're telling me a hospital wouldn't be safe? What's going on?"

I shrugged. "Stuff. I'll explain after we get her settled in."

She shook her head, then poured a glass of water and shoved it in my hand. "Give this to your friend while I make tea."

I carried the glass out to Azra and a few sips seemed to revive her. She perked up even more when Sally brought her a cup of tea and a facecloth soaked with cold water that she placed on Azra's brow.

"Thank you," Azra said. "Both of you."

Her almond-shaped green eyes seemed more alert than they had been a few minutes earlier. I asked if she felt like answering questions.

She nodded slowly.

"Good," I said. "Do you remember what happened after you left the Big House?"

In a whispery voice, she said, "I remember driving away from the house, then someone coming up fast behind me. Bright light and heat. Trying to get out of the car." She rubbed her eyes. "What happened?"

"Someone threw a Molotov cocktail at your car," I said.

Her jaw hardened. "Drazik's men."

"Whoever they were followed you from the Big House."

She frowned. "It was stupid of me to leave. I snuck off while Ana was sleeping. I was afraid I would make trouble for the movie people. Thought maybe I could find a hotel." She looked around the room. "I've got to get out of here."

"That wouldn't be a good idea. Drazik's thugs don't know where I live but they might be prowling the roads. We'll wait until morning to make a move. I'll let Ana know where you are."

Her eyelids drooped. "Yes. Thank you. That will be fine." A second later she was asleep.

I called Ana's cell phone. As soon as she answered, I said, "Azra's with me. She's fine."

"Dear God. I've been frantic. I want to talk to her."

"Not now. She's sleeping."

"Why did she run off?"

"She was worried she'd put the movie crew in danger. Drazik's men tried to stop her but she got away."

I heard a sharp intake of breath. "Tell me where you live. I'll come right over."

"Bad idea. I want you to stay where you are for now. You could lead Drazik's thugs to my place. She'll be safe here. I'll call you in the morning."

"I can't thank you enough. Please call me as soon as she wakes up."

I clicked off and saw Sally sitting with her arms crossed, her intelligent eyes bore into mine with the probing expression I had come to know as *The Look*.

"How about going onto the deck and getting some fresh air," I said.

"Good idea," Sally said. "But we need something stronger than tea."

I grabbed a couple of beers from the refrigerator. We plunked ourselves into the Adirondack chairs and clinked bottles.

"Here's to full disclosure," she said. "Why don't you start by telling me who the lady is?"

I slugged down the cold liquid and stared out at the pinpoints of light across the dark bay. It was hard to reconcile the peaceful night with the brutal attack on Azra.

"Her full name is Azra Klavic. She's the younger sister of Ana Roman, the actress I've been working with. Ana asked me to keep an eye on her sister tonight. She didn't want to tell me why, but I finally got it out of her. Azra is a journalist. She's supposed to testify as a witness against a human trafficker being charged with war crimes."

"Would that be the Drazik you mentioned?"

"That's the one. He's in prison but he's got a long reach. In fact, he reached all the way to Cape Cod with a Molotov cocktail."

Sally heaved a deep sigh. "I've known you a long time, and you constantly find yourself in these crazy situations. This could be the craziest one ever. How do you do it?"

I downed the rest of the beer. "Just lucky, I guess."

"I guess," she said. "What's your plan, Mr. Lucky?"

"Keep her here until morning. I think she's safe, but there's a slim chance Drazik's men could track us down. You might want to think about spending the night someplace else."

"And leave you alone with an attractive woman? Not on your life, Socarides."

"Thanks, Sal. We'll have to take shifts. I'll block the driveway with my truck. Maybe that will help a little."

While Sally went to check on Azra, I moved the pickup almost to the end of the winding driveway and left it there. The truck wouldn't prevent someone from moving close to the house on foot, but it would stop an SUV full of thugs from driving up to the front door with guns blazing.

I walked back to the boathouse and stepped through the front door. The phone was ringing. I picked it up and said hello.

"Nice work tonight, Sir Galahad," the man on the line said.

It had been months since I had heard the resonant voice, but I recognized it immediately. It seemed out of place, though, to hear from my old comrade-in-arms from my Viet Nam days, which is why I put a question in my tone when I said "Flagg?"

He chuckled. "Naw, it's the Hero of the Year Society calling about the medal we're giving you for getting your ass singed pulling that lady out of the burning car. How's she doing?"

"Little shaken up, but she'll be okay."

"Good. I want her to stay that way. I've got someone at the end of your driveway keeping watch. I'll call you in the morning."

He hung up and I said to Sally, "That was John Flagg."

"So I surmised. How did John get into this mix?"

"I'll ask him when we get together in the morning. He says not to worry because he's got someone watching the house. We won't have to do shifts."

"That's a relief." She yawned, and said, "I'm exhausted. Let's go to bed."

I took a deep breath and inhaled the greasy odor of gasoline that permeated my hair and skin. "I'll take a shower first."

"That would be nice. Then come to bed."

I lathered my body from head to toe under the outside shower. After drying myself I went back into the house and put on clean skivvies and a T-shirt. As I slipped under the covers, disturbing Kojak's sleep for the second time, I heard Sally laughing.

"What's so funny, Sal?"

"I was just thinking about sharks. Two thousand pounds of muscle, more than a dozen feet long, and a mouth filled with rows of razor-sharp teeth; yet, compared to some of your acquaintances, the average great white is nothing but a lovable old pussy cat like Kojak."

She kissed me goodnight and rolled over on her side, an invitation to spoon. I hesitated a few seconds, staring at the ceiling, before I wrapped my arm around her slim waist and buried my nose in her hair. Sally couldn't have been more right about sharks and humans. On the question of which species was more deadly, the ones with the dorsal fin or the two-legged version it wasn't even a contest.

CHAPTER 31

Sleep didn't come easily. I kept seeing the ugly splash of flames that had nearly turned Azra into a pile of cinders. In time, the warmth of Sally's body and the rhythm of her soft breathing lulled me into a light slumber. I woke up as the first rays of dawn streamed in the window and painted the ceiling and walls of the bedroom in a rosy golden light. Sally was gone from the bed. I slipped out from under the covers and got into well-worn jeans and a polo shirt with the *Thalassa II* logo.

Sally was in the kitchen brewing a pot of coffee.

"Good morning," she said with a smile. "Sleep okay?"

"I've had better nights. How's Azra doing?"

"She's in the bathroom washing up. I loaned her some clothes, since hers got all smoky. It makes me shiver when I think of how close she came to...."

Sally looked relieved when the phone rang and she didn't have to finish her sentence with all its nasty implications. I reached for the phone and said hello.

"Powwow time," said Flagg, who hoards words like a miser counting pennies.

"I'm ready. Come by the boathouse. Sally's brewing a pot of coffee."

"Tell her thanks, but we need privacy. Someone will watch your house. Preferably off-site."

I thought about it a few seconds and suggested a rendezvous point.

He grunted and said, "See you in fifteen. Bring coffee."

I told Sally I was meeting Flagg, estimated I'd be back in an hour and told her someone was keeping an eye on the boathouse. She sent me on my way with a hug, a thermos of coffee and two mugs in a bag. I went out on the deck and down the stairs to the dock. The outboard motor roared to life after a couple of pulls on the cord. I cast off the lines, pushed away from the dock and headed out into the bay. There wasn't a whisper of a breeze and the water was flat calm. I had the sensation of gliding across liquid glass.

I headed for the resort where Cait had signed me up for the movie job. Flagg was standing on the dock, dressed in a gray suit and a white shirt, He looked like a guest at a wedding rather than a trouble-shooter for the obscure government intelligence agency he joined after his army service. I killed the motor and drifted up to the dock. Flagg looks like someone whose creator had made a mistake when he was assembled. His wide shoulders and a barrel chest sit on thick legs that are too short for his upper body. Although he looks and sometimes acts like a human battering ram, he can move like a cat.

He heaved himself into the boat with an agility that seemed impossible for someone of his build and plunked down in the bow seat, hands like sledgehammers resting on his knees. Silver reflecting aviator glasses covered eyes I knew to be as dark as anthracite. The lower jaw and unsmiling mouth looked as if they had been carved out of hard oak.

I started the motor, put it into reverse, then spun the boat around and pointed the bow away from the dock. Minutes later I killed the motor and we floated a few hundred feet off-shore.

"How's this for privacy?" I said.

SHARK BAIT

He grunted his approval. "Where's that coffee?" he said.

I got the thermos out of the bag and poured two mugs full. He took a sip. The coffee was hot but the heat didn't seem to burn his lips, or if it did, he ignored it. He looked off across the azure waters of the bay, and said, "Too bad we can't toss a line over the side. Catch us some fish to fry up."

Reaching down, I pulled a tackle box out from under my seat and popped the lid. "Got a couple of hand lines. Be my guest."

He took the box and looked inside. "No lures."

"You only need lures if you want to catch fish. I come out here to get away from it all. Catching a fish distracts from that goal."

He clamped the lid down and handed the box back. "Rain check. After you pour more coffee maybe you can tell me how you got into this mess."

"Which mess is that, Flagg?"

"The one where you're pulling a woman out of a burning car and bad guys would've shot you full of holes if an old pal hadn't stepped in."

"Thanks for the assist. I should have known who was at the wheel from the way the driver weaponized the big sedan. How'd you happen to get involved in last night's craziness?"

"I asked you first."

"So you did." I collected my thoughts, took a deep breath, and said, "It all started when my charter boat broke down. I needed a quick cash infusion for the outboard repairs. The movie crew had a vacancy for a boat captain. I applied and got the job."

"Lucky break. What happened to the captain who had the job before you?"

"A shark probably ate him."

Flagg slowly removed his glasses and stared at me with his dark, flat eyes. "This is serious business we're dealing with here, Soc."

"I know damn well it's serious business, Flagg. As you'll recall, I'm getting a medal because I got my ass toasted last night. No joke this time. The guy was killed by a great white shark."

"Shark," he said in a monotone as if hearing the word for the first time. The corners of his thin lips turned up slightly. "Go on."

"The star of the film is an actress named Ana Roman. She brought along her personal hairdresser and makeup artist, a woman named Tatiana, and a guy named Yergo who was posing as her husband. He worked as an assistant with the film crew until a couple of days ago, when he disappeared and his body later floated ashore. He'd been tortured and murdered. Ana came to me and said Tatiana was her sister and Yergo was her bodyguard. She asked me to fill in for Yergo."

Flagg chuckled. "*Now* you're being funny. First guy was eaten by a shark; second one murdered. You sure know how to pick your jobs, Soc."

"Hah. You don't have to tell me that bad things happen in threes."

"What else did Ana tell you about her sister?"

"That she's in hiding and in big trouble."

"You have no idea how much trouble, Soc."

"*Au contraire, mon ami.* I know that her name is Azra Klavic. That she's a journalist who's agreed to be a witness in a war crimes trial involving a lowlife named Drazik. That he's out to stop her. And it's probably his goon squad who torched her car last night."

"Covers most of it," he said. "Anything you don't know?"

"Lots. For starters, I don't know how you got into this mess. Ball's in your court."

"Fair enough. Azra and I go back around twenty years. She was covering the Serbian-Croatian wars. I was on loan to NATO. She's gutsy as hell. Got in close to the bad stuff. Atrocities, ethnic cleansing, and citizen massacres. Her reports gave us a baseline to send cruise missiles into Belgrade."

"Impressive. How'd she end up making a movie on ol' Cape Cod?"

"Someone tried to kill her. A real close call. Drazik was pulling the strings from his jail cell. Trying to stop her testimony. Ana Roman suggested she hide out with the movie crew. Not a lot of people know they're sisters. Azra kept the connection secret because she didn't want to build a journalism career by riding on her sister's name. Yergo had been Azra's bodyguard on reporting assignments. She asked him to come over and do the same job here. She got Ana to get him hired."

"When did you come into the picture?"

"Azra asked me to help slip her and Yergo into the U.S. without going through the usual channels. Only a handful of people in Washington knew she was in the country. We figured her cover was solid and giving her extra protection might attract attention. Few weeks ago we heard that Drazik had been recorded talking to a hit squad, made up of family members, that had tracked her to Cape Cod."

"Ana said that Yergo got lonely and called home a couple of times."

"He signed his own death warrant with those calls. Bad guys were intercepting his messages, but they still didn't know exactly where Azra was hiding. I'm familiar with this area, so I got sent here to assess the situation. I figured she'd be most vulnerable during the movie shoots. It was easy duty, watching a movie get made."

Flagg's comment triggered a memory of the ghostly figure at the edge of Goody Hallett's meadow after Ana had been filmed gazing out to sea.

"Was that you I saw in the woods on the cliff a few days ago?"

"That was me. Got sloppy from hanging 'round. Couldn't believe it when you showed up. You've had a busy week."

"I'm not the only one who's been busy, Flagg. That was you at the marina parking lot. And in Hyannis. And you're right about being sloppy. I got your license plate number."

"Good luck with that. Car's registered in Spookville. I was just playing with you."

"Yeah, but the fun ended when Drazik's guys murdered Yergo."

"Azra got real nervous after that happened and wanted to get out of Dodge. I told her it was too dangerous to move until I had assets in place. I suggested she stay put and get you to keep watch until morning."

"She ignored the part about staying put."

"Like I said, she's gutsy. Lucky you followed her. Back-up is on its way. All I've got now is a guy I pulled in from the Boston office. We've still got a big problem once we take her off your hands. They'll go after Ana and try to use her to persuade her sister not to testify. She's got to drop out of sight, too."

"I doubt that will happen. Ana is determined to finish the movie."

"How much more is there to film?"

"A couple of scenes, and if they go well, it'll wrap up."

"Maybe we can convince her it's too risky. Say that Azra's not out of the woods until Drazik is tossed down a well. Hold on a sec."

He slipped his hand into his jacket, pulled out a chirping cell phone and put it to his ear. His expression darkened.

"I'll be back in a few minutes. Keep a sharp eye out for others." He slipped the phone back in his pocket. "Get this thing started. We've got to get back pronto."

I reached for the engine cord and gave it a yank. The motor started on the first pull. "What's going on?"

"That was my guy who's been watching your driveway. Says a bad-ass with a bomb just tried to bust through to your boathouse and there may be more."

CHAPTER 32

Flagg weighs more than two hundred pounds, most of it muscle. The outboard motor sounded like a popcorn popper on steroids as it tried to cope with the added ballast. While the skiff crawled through the water I kept my gaze fixed on the boathouse, thinking I'd get there sooner if I swam home.

While I fretted and fumed, Flagg sat in the bow, a stony expression etched onto his wide face. He stayed calm and collected, arms crossed, slowly wagging his head from time to time to signify his impatience. A switch seemed to go off when the skiff got within a few yards of the dock and I killed the motor. He unfolded his body, looped the bow line over a cleat and scrambled out of the boat. I snagged the stern line, then raced up the stairs on his heels.

Sally opened the back door and stepped out onto the deck. I yelled at her to get back inside. I caught a glimpse of the startled look on her face before Flagg and I were around the corner of the house, pounding down the rutted driveway.

As Flagg plodded along, his hand reached for the holster at his waist. I outdistanced him, rounded a bend in the driveway and saw a camouflage-painted high-lift pickup sandwiched between the GMC and a black Tahoe SUV.

Gill was big, but he was a long way from being bad-ass. He stood in the driveway, holding a cardboard box high above his head. The worried expression on his face may have had something to do with the fact that two men wearing dark suits and mirrored sunglasses had pistols raised in two-hand grips, aimed in his direction.

He saw me and yelled, "Soc!"

The pistols swung around and pointed at me. I stopped short and raised my hands in the air. The men must have realized that they'd left Gill unguarded. After some back and forth they figured out they could keep one pistol aimed at me, the other at Gill.

Flagg huffed up beside me. "You know this guy?" he said.

"Yeah. His name is Howie Gill. He's my only client, so please don't shoot him."

"That's right," Gill said with a vigorous nod.

"What's in the box?" Flagg said.

"Documents," was Gill's quick answer "I was dropping them off for Soc. They're getting very heavy."

"Put the box down. Slowly," Flagg said. He holstered his pistol and ordered his men to put their guns away. "Azra inside the boathouse?" he said to me.

"That's right. She's with Sally."

"I'll be right back. Tell your client it's okay to blink."

He headed toward the house, knocked on the door and went inside. His men followed and took up positions flanking the doorway. Gill hadn't moved after he'd put the box down. I asked if he was all right.

He rubbed his arms. "I'll be fine if I can restore my circulation. Who are these guys?"

"The real *Men in Black*. Flagg and the suits work for the government. You'll like them once you get to know them."

Gill's frown told me he wasn't buying it. We walked back to the house and waited outside. After a few minutes Flagg came out with Azra and Sally. The reunion must have gone well because they were all smiling.

Azra gave Sally a hug and a couple of cheek kisses, then she turned to me. "Thank you so much for last night. Sorry to cause so much trouble."

"Glad I could help. I'll call your sister and tell her you're okay."

"No need. On the way to the airport Mr. Flagg is taking me to see Ana at the Big House so we can say goodbye. By this time tomorrow I'll be in The Hague preparing to testify against Drazik."

"Good luck flushing Drazik down the sewer he crawled out of. Before you go, Azra, I have a quick question about something that's been bothering me. How did you sneak out of the Big House without me seeing you?"

"It wasn't difficult," she said with a smile.

"Then maybe you'd share the secret of invisibility with me."

"It has nothing to do with invisibility. When we first moved into the house I was in the library and came across a history of the Big House. I'm interested in history, and I needed something to read. The mansion was built during Prohibition by a rum-runner, according to the history"

"Cait told me about him. He's the guy who was never caught."

"That's because while the police were at the door, he would walk from the master bedroom suite, the one I'm using, down the hall to the turret room where he would disappear."

"So the stories were true?"

"Oh yes. The author of the history was vague on details. I have a journalist's curiosity, so of course I went into the turret and descended the staircase to ground level. I found a trap door, opened it and saw a ladder. Naturally I got a flashlight and went exploring."

"Naturally." Flagg said Azra was gutsy.

"At the bottom of the ladder was the entrance to a tunnel. I flashed my light inside and saw that the tunnel was lined with concrete, wide and high enough to allow someone as tall as you to pass through without stooping."

"And even easier for someone of your height."

"Oh yes. It only took a minute or so to go through the tunnel which ended at another ladder. Up I went, then through a trap door into what seemed like a big wooden box. I unlatched a section of the box, slid it aside and poked my head out. I was in the gazebo."

"Let me guess. The box was actually the inside of the bar."

She nodded. "The opening was big enough to crawl through. No one saw me emerge. I sat on a bar stool for a while, then went back through the tunnel to the turret room."

"Much like the rum-runner must have done after the cops were through ransacking his house."

"I used it a number of times, mostly at night. I must have made noise going through the house, because people joked at breakfast that they'd heard ghosts. Even Yergo didn't know, except for one time. He woke up and came out onto the lawn looking for me, which is when he encountered you. When everyone was asleep, I'd walk around the lawn and gaze at the stars. Sometimes I'd dance on the grass."

"Except for last night when you danced yourself off the property."

"I almost got stuck in the tunnel. The dampness from the fog must have warped the trap door and I couldn't move it. Thank goodness I had the sword to pry it open."

I was chewing over Azra's confession, how she had made a dolt of me, and was only half-listening. When it finally sank in, I said, "What was that you said about a sword?"

"Like the ones the pirates use in the movie." She drew an arc with her finger to show the curved blade. "Only it was real, not plastic. It was lying in the tunnel near the ladder."

"Had you seen it there before?"

"No. I see what you're getting at. I wasn't the only one who'd discovered the secret tunnel."

Just then, Flagg pulled me aside. "Sorry to interrupt. The guys I had guarding the road stopped three sleazy-looking bikers. They said they were lost, but they're carrying some high-powered military-style hardware."

"Crap," I said. "Is one of them a skinhead?"

Flagg talked into the phone, then turned back to me. "Yeah, one guy's got a shaved noggin."

Guy Rich's hoods had tracked me down. "They're not lost. They're bad boys from another case, looking to settle a score."

"Figured as much. What do you want me to do with them?"

"Any way to keep them on ice?"

"Sure. I can say they were interfering with a federal operation. We can only hold them a couple of nights."

"That's all the time I'll need."

"Anyone ever tell you you're a piece of work, Soc?"

"Lots of people, including you."

He gave me his quick smile. "Can't wait to hear about this one." Then he tapped his wristwatch. "Got to get on the road with Azra. You and I can talk later, Soc."

Azra and I said our final goodbyes and Flagg led her to the waiting SUV, which headed out of the driveway.

Sally, who had been standing nearby talking to Gill, came over.

She had a half-smile on her lips. "I'd forgotten until last night what an interesting life you lead. If you'll excuse me, I've got to get to a boring old shark meeting."

"Are we still on for dinner tonight?" I said. "I think we said we'd honor our pact come hell or high water."

"I hope it doesn't come to either of those things," she said. "I'll call you after my meeting."

Sally drove off, leaving me with Gill, who was still standing where he'd set the documents down.

I walked over and picked up the box at his feet. "Mind if I take this inside for a look?"

"Be my guest. Damned thing almost got me shot."

I led the way into the boathouse, plunked the box on the kitchen table, and told him to take a seat while I rustled up some coffee.

A few minutes later, when I carried a couple of mugs over to the table, he had removed the documents from the box and arranged them in a neat stack six inches high.

"You asked me a simple question. Who owns the land that borders my property? The answer wasn't as simple as the question."

"I didn't think it would be."

He nodded. "The ownership was hidden under layers of shell corporations. It was like sifting through layers of soil at an archaeological dig. Instead of searching for clues in shards of pottery, I used a forensic computer program to look for keywords. I focused on a few areas until I found one loose strand of yarn and pulled it."

"From the looks of that pile of paper, you unraveled the whole sweater."

A triumphant grin wreathed his jack o' lantern face. "I did. And wearing the sweater was our friend Guy Rich." He turned the stack over so that the bottom document was on top. "No need to go through all the paperwork. This is the smoking gun." He slid the top sheet off and handed it to me. "You're holding the corporate document that shows Guy Rich is the majority stockholder in the real estate trust that offered to buy my land."

I read over the document and handed it back. "With your land and his access he'd have a nice little piece of waterfront property that would be ripe for development."

"Correct. The poaching wasn't done to steal oysters. Rich wanted to ruin my business so I'd have to sell."

"And *Rich Guy* would be first in line with a check."

"Right. What a con man! He was always so sympathetic. He completely gained my trust when he set up the reward."

"He conned me too, Howie. I never suspected a respectable businessman to be connected with a sketchy wholesale fish outfit."

He tapped the pile of papers. "A court document shows that he changed his last name from Ricardo."

"According to ADA Martin, that's the same last name as the guy who owns the fish company."

"Quite the coincidence. Now what do we do with this evidence?"

"I'm up to my eyeballs in the movie business for another day or more. Put together a summary and take it with copies of these documents to ADA Martin. Make sure it gets into his hands only."

"I'll get right on it."

He stuffed the papers back into their box and snapped down the cover. We shook hands across the table. He rose from his seat and tucked the box under one arm. "You know something, Soc? Your friends in black weren't far off the mark in thinking that I had a bomb. This could be more explosive than TNT."

"Here's hoping," I said.

I went back inside and gave Kojak a kitty snack as an apology for disrupting his daily routine. I was feeling warm and fuzzy. Azra was safely on her way and, with just a little shove, we'd push Guy Rich over a cliff. The silly smile on my lips lasted only a few seconds, fading as I remembered that Ana was still in danger. I hurried out to my truck and headed to the Big House.

CHAPTER 33

The entire fleet of movie vehicles was in the parking lot, which made me think that the crew was still at breakfast. But when I went into the Big House no one was in the dining room. I found Cait in the kitchen emptying the dishwasher. She yelped in pleasure and threw her arms around me.

"Hi roomie. I was worried about you. Your bed was empty. Then you didn't show up at breakfast."

"Sorry. I had errands to get out of the way."

"I've cleared away breakfast but there are a few sausage patties left in the fridge."

I realized I hadn't had anything to eat and accepted her offer. I sat at the table and took a bite of sausage that was tucked into a toasted English muffin. "Sheer heaven," I said. "Where is everybody?"

"Max and the gang are shooting a scene on the premises."

"I read the script. I don't remember a scene at the Big House."

"It wasn't in the original script. Max added the scene. I'll block it out for you. After the ship is wrecked, Mary and the Indian Jason plays retrieve the treasure and bury it on the island. Sam Bellamy's body is placed on top of the treasure chest so that his ghost will guard the treasure for eternity."

"Or until Mary uses his skull for a bowling ball."

"Ana was simply amazing, wasn't she? Anyhow, after she dispatches the villagers she and the Indian decide to move the treasure in case people come out from the village to look for their missing pals. While she scouts out a new burial ground, Jason digs up the chest, which is what we're filming this morning. Max hired a couple of local guys to dig the treasure hole."

"I'm confused. Those earlier scenes were shot on Great Island."

She nodded. "The National Park Service didn't mind us tromping around the island under the supervision of a park ranger, but it drew the line at tearing up the turf. Max suggested we film the scene here in a nearby patch of woods that's similar to the island terrain. Why don't you head over and I'll meet you after I'm done here?"

I said that would be fine. She told me to follow a path into the forest that bordered a section of the lawn. I went through the woods for a few hundred feet and broke out of the trees into an irregularly-shaped clearing around ten yards across. At the center of the open space was a rectangular pit about four feet square. Next to it was a pile of dirt. Lying on the pile were bones and the skull that had mowed down the villagers like bowling pins.

Lights and microphone stands had been set up around the pit. The thick branch of an oak tree extended directly over the hole. Hanging from the limb was a rope and pulley set-up. Max was talking to his assistant and the cameraman. He saw me and broke off his conversation.

"Hi, Soc. Guess you didn't hear that we won't need you today."

Max's mouth was set in its usual grin but his voice had the slight edge that I had detected since he found out I was a cop.

"The movie bug must have bitten me. I'll hang out and watch, if that's okay."

Max raised his palms as if he were about to push me away. "This is just a transition scene that shows the treasure being lifted out of the ground. You'd find it boring."

A disembodied voice issued from the pit. "What the hell are

you talking about, Max? If you think it's boring get down in this hell hole with me."

Max slowly lowered his hands to his sides. I stepped around him and went to the edge of the pit. A ladder went down to the bottom of a hole about eight feet deep. Jason stood next to a copper-bound iron chest. His clothes were caked with dirt. He had his Indian makeup on. He saw me looking down and a grin came to his face.

"Fifteen men on a dead man's chest," I said.

"Drink and the devil have taken all the rest. I'll be out as soon as they get a shot of me lifting this chest full of stones out of this hole."

"Need any help?" I said.

"You forget that this is low-budget. It's set up for me to do single-handedly. After I lock the pulling rope in place, I climb the ladder and use the additional line to swing the chest away from the pit."

I studied the set-up. A rope went from the chest to a pair of blocks that could be used to secure the line between two metal jaws. A second line ran from the chest up and over the edge of the hole and lay coiled on the ground.

Max called my name. "We're clearing the set," he said.

I stepped back to the edge of the clearing. Seconds later the clapperboard snapped. Max shouted, "Action."

The hauling rope went taut. The camera followed the chest as it rose out of the pit and came to a stop a few feet below the pulleys.

"Cut," Max said. "We'll move in for the close-ups of Jason in the pit."

The cameraman lowered his camera. Max told his assistant to hold off on the slate. He slowly circled the pit, framing the scene with his fingers, stopping to rearrange the skull and bones. He looked up at the chest hanging from the end of the rope, then stepped back and called out, "Action."

I would have turned my attention back down to ground level but a movement in the tree caught my eye. A gray squirrel jumped from one branch to another. As I lowered my gaze, I noticed a strange fuzziness in a section of rope below the pulleys. Strands were parting. The rope was about to snap.

It's been a long time since anyone has mistaken me for the Incredible Hulk, so I wasn't about to catch the falling chest before it mashed Jason's classically handsome features into a bloody mess. Or worse. But he might have a chance if I could get the chest to fall outside the hole. The end of the rope attached to the top of the chest was a few feet away. I snatched up the coils, wrapped the line around my hand, dug my heels in and leaned backwards.

The chest swung slowly toward my side of the pit. When the chest was at its apogee, I slipped the rope off my hand and pushed. The chest swung back like a pendulum and reached the far end of its oscillation. The rope snapped.

The chest thumped onto the ground, teetered, and might have toppled into the opening if it hadn't been for the lighting man who was closest to the edge of the pit. He grabbed the handles on the side of the box and kept it from falling in.

Jason climbed partway up the ladder and his head popped out of the hole. "What's going on with the damned chest, Max?" he said. "Wasn't that thing supposed to hang there until I climbed out?"

Max said, "Equipment failure."

Jason looked up at the frayed end of the rope swaying high above his head. "Holy crap!"

He was up the ladder and out of the hole in an instant. The crew crowded around him offering shoulder squeezes and back pats. I walked around to the other side of the pit, knelt next to the chest and touched the frayed end of the rope. The fibers were brittle. A white powdery substance came off on my fingers and burned my skin.

I was brushing my fingers off in the dirt and happened to glance up. Max stood on the other side of the pit staring at me, his brow furrowed. He saw me look in his direction and quickly turned to the film crew.

"Okay, folks. I think we'll all agree that we've had enough

excitement for today. Thanks for your hard work. Tomorrow we wrap it. Let's go back to the screen room and check out the dailies."

A cheer went up from the crew. Max led the boisterous group back through the woods to the Big House. Jason stayed behind. He walked around to my side of the pit and gazed at the chest. "This is what Max calls an equipment failure?"

"That's one way to put it."

"I may be an over-the-hill drunken actor, Soc, but I'm no fool. And I've done enough action films to know that you can't rely on the crew to do a safety check. Especially on a low-budget project like this one. Before I put myself into a hole and sat squarely under a hundred pounds of rocks, I inspected the rope and the way it was fastened. The knots were tight. The nylon line was brand new."

"Did you actually touch the line?"

"No. I could tell it was sound by its appearance. There was no reason to touch it."

I pointed to the broken rope. "Well, I did touch this part and something burned my fingers. The line may have looked good, but nylon doesn't do well when it's been doused with acid."

Jason drilled me with his flinty blue-gray eyes. "Acid. What are you saying?"

"That the section of line that snapped had been exposed to a corrosive."

Jason gave the muscles in his jaw a workout. "We have to talk. But first I need a drink."

We made our way out of the woods and walked across the lawn toward the gazebo.

"Thank you for saving me from being squashed like a fly," Jason said. "I always figured I'd go like Errol Flynn, who ended his life of dissipation in scandal after cavorting with his under-aged girlfriend."

"Cavorting with under-aged girls will get you in trouble with the law, Jace."

"True. It's not my style, in any event. Besides, I'm smitten with a mature lady of unparalleled grace and beauty."

I raised an eyebrow. "Would Ana be that mature lady?"

"None other, if she'll have me."

"You're not the first one to fall for her, as you know."

"But I hope I will be the last she falls for. Once this project is over I intend to ask her to marry me."

"My heart is broken, but I wish you the best of luck. I'll even buy you a drink to toast your success."

We stepped into the gazebo, poured a couple of glasses of locally-made Twenty Boat rum on ice with a squeeze of lime, and bellied up to the bar. We clinked glasses. Jason guzzled half the rum, then set the glass down hard on the bar top.

"Max did it," he said. "Max sabotaged the rope."

"Maybe nobody sabotaged it, Jason. The line could have come in contact with acid during transit, or when it was being stored."

He poured himself another shot. "You're reaching, Soc."

"Could be. But why would Max kill the male lead in a movie he's desperate to finish?"

"Hell, Soc. He was thinking of writing me out of the script anyhow because of my drinking."

"Doesn't he need you to finish the film?"

"He'd simply rewrite the screenplay and use the existing scenes. Like when Bela Lugosi died during a filming and the director brought in a stand-in who crept around with a cloak covering his face."

"You still haven't told me why he'd want to kill you."

"Because I know what's going on behind the scenes." He only drained the glass. "Ana said you're a cop."

"I was a Boston police detective a long time ago. I've got my private investigator's license and take a case now and then, but that's it."

"Good enough. I'd like you to take a case for me. I want you to prevent Max from doing me harm."

"I said I was a detective, not hired muscle."

"I don't want to hire you as a bodyguard. I want you to get him locked up."

"That only works if he's done something wrong. We're talking about accusing Max of attempted murder on the basis of a broken rope. Think back to the private eye you played in that great movie, *Death Walks the Streets*. Investigations always start with method, motive and opportunity. We've got method, *maybe*, and opportunity, but no motive."

"Wrong on two counts, Soc. First, that movie was a stinker and should have been named *Turkey Walks the Streets*. It was filled with every PI cliché possible. And second, there is a motive."

"Now that I think back on it, the dialogue was kinda cheesy and you were always talking out of the side of your mouth about your gat or your heater. So what was the motive?"

"Let me tell you a little story. One day after I had too much bubbly with lunch I went into the salon to take a nap. I was scrunched up in a big corner sofa when Max and Munson came in. They were arguing. Max was trying to calm him down, keeping his voice low, but Munson got loud. He wanted a raise. I thought I heard something about Texas."

"You've lost me. How does the Lone Star State fit into it?"

"It doesn't. I wasn't wearing my hearing aids."

"Didn't know you wore them."

"I hide them under my wig. But at one point, Munson got even louder. He was talking about *taxes*."

"What was he saying?"

"Couldn't catch it. I was curious, so later that day I rummaged through Max's office. He hates computers, and keeps papers in manila files. I couldn't locate a tax folder, but I found a payroll record. The salary listed for me was astronomically higher than what I am actually paid. I assumed it was the same for the others."

"Proving what? That Max is a terrible bookkeeper?"

"Proving that he was inflating the salaries on paper."

"Why would he do that?"

"The state gives tax credits as an incentive to shoot movies in Massachusetts. It pumps money into the local economy. Max submits a report saying he's paying these famous actors huge salaries, when he's not. The state cuts him a big fat check. Munson somehow got his hooks on this information and used it as blackmail to pry more money out of Max."

"So Max is scamming the Commonwealth. Why does that give Max a reason to want *you* dead?"

"Max didn't have a reason until he and I had a blowout about my drinking. He was going to let me go. I told him that before he died, Munson had confided in me over drinks. Told me about the tax scam. Max got defensive. Said he was doing it for the good of the film. Expenses were higher than expected. He pleaded with me to keep my mouth shut. I suggested that I'd be too busy to talk to the authorities if I was given a bigger part in the film."

"And if he overlooked your drinking problem."

"That was part of the deal. You saw how he backed down after I got the extras drunk out here at the gazebo. Even *I* would have fired me after a stunt like that."

"You argued with Max that day. Accused him of wrecking the film. What was that all about?"

"I didn't like the way he was shooting some scenes. Normally, I would never argue with a director over artistic differences, but the rum loosened by tongue. I felt I could say anything to him and he couldn't fire me because I'd expose him."

"Let me see if I got this right. Now that the filming is almost over, he no longer has an incentive to keep you alive. And an even greater incentive to drop a treasure chest on your head."

"*Voila*. Motive. Time to cut Jason out of the screenplay. Permanently."

He waved an invisible sword over his head, reminding me of the first time I saw Jason, when he was in full pirate mode, slicing the air with a cutlass. I remembered how the sunlight glinted off the sharp blade.

"Speaking of the day you and your crew captured the gazebo, what happened to the cutlass you were waving around?"

"Last time I saw it the cutlass was stuck in the gazebo post. I guess Max took it away."

I reached out and touched the notch the sword had inflicted in one of the wooden posts that held the roof up. The gash was deep. The cutlass was a low-tech weapon designed for cutting a swath through a wall of living flesh. In the hands of someone with a powerful arm, it could inflict terrible damage.

"The swords the extras used were of plastic. Was that the only steel blade cutlass?"

"That's right. We call it the *Real McCoy*. The weapon was brought out for scenes where a sharp edge was needed to provide verisimilitude, like chopping trees away to dig for the treasure chest. It was never used for fight scenes. Too dangerous."

"How did you come to have it?"

"I was rummaging around in the props and found it in with the plastic swords. I don't know where it went after Max took it. Maybe it found its way back to the prop shed."

Talk of the missing cutlass had planted a seed in my mind. And it was fast growing into a full-blown scenario that was too awful to contemplate.

"Let's go take a look," I said.

CHAPTER 34

The prop department was stashed in a nondescript, silver-shingled garden shed trimmed in white that had fallen into disrepair when a landscaping company started to care for the Big House grounds. Jason said Max wanted the props kept in the shed so that the extras wouldn't have to go tromping in and out of the Big House, which he regarded as the creative center of *The Pirate's Daughter*. As a lead actor Jason had a key to the padlock. He opened the door and we went inside the musty old building.

Light streamed through the windows on some well-worn rakes and shovels leaning up against an old wheelbarrow that had a flat tire. But most of the space was taken up by the costumes hanging from metal poles that stretched along two walls.

Jason ran his hand over the clothes hanging from one pole. "These are the pirate outfits on this rack," he said. "Breeches and puffy-sleeve shirts. Standard uniform for Bellamy's crew back in the day, but I think it's a bit *frou-frou* for bloodthirsty pirates, don't you?"

"The way I figure it, a guy with pistols and daggers tucked in his belt can wear anything he wants to."

"Good point." He pointed to a big plastic storage box. "Be my guest."

I pushed the lid back. Lying on the green felt at the bottom of the box were a dozen flintlock pistols and a couple of muskets. I picked up one of the pistols, examined the mechanism, and then aimed the weapon at a windowpane.

"Pretty authentic look and feel," I said, squinting down the barrel.

"Max is a stickler for accuracy when it comes to props."

With a dramatic flourish Jason pushed aside the pirate costumes to expose the interior wall behind the rack. Hanging from hooks were a dozen cutlasses and a handful of wicked-looking daggers. I returned the pistol to the box and took a cutlass off the wall. The blade was around thirty inches long but the weapon only weighed a couple of pounds because it was plastic.

"Except for its light weight this could pass for the real thing," I said.

I passed it to Jason who drew his thumb along the edge.

"Another big difference," he said. "The *Real McCoy* would draw blood if I did that."

"Is the metal cutlass here?"

"No. The pommel on the metal sword is engraved with the figure of a woman. As you can see, these all have plain hand guards."

He passed the cutlass back. I held the sword in both hands. "Could I borrow this?"

"Why not? You're technically still a member of the crew. And all the swordplay scenes have been shot."

Walking around in public with even a fake cutlass didn't seem like a good idea. I found a beat-up leather duffle bag in the shed that was big enough to hold the cutlass. We stepped outside. While he was locking up, I got a call from Sally.

"Hi, Soc," she said. "Just got back to the boathouse. Are we still on for dinner?"

"Wouldn't miss it for the world. Wondered if you could do me a favor." I told her what I wanted. "I know it isn't the kind of thing you'd bring to dinner."

"That's what I'd call an understatement."

"I wouldn't ask if it weren't important. And it might help resolve Emma's case."

"That would be wonderful, Soc. See you in an hour."

I hung up. Jason said, "What now?"

Hefting the duffle on my shoulder, I said, "First, I put this in my truck. Then we go to the Big House. When you see Max, you will put on a happy face."

"Dammit, Soc. I'm not sure even an actor of my vast experience and talent can pull that one off, but I'll give it a try. I'll deserve an Oscar if it works out."

"I'm glad to hear that, Jason, because your life may depend on it."

If anyone deserved an Oscar, it was Max. He didn't come across like a guy who'd set up another human being to be mashed like a fly. He was in the salon pouring drinks from a cocktail shaker into the martini glasses clutched in the outstretched hands of the crew members. They milled around him, smiling and laughing. His free arm was wrapped around Ana.

When we walked into the salon Max raised the shaker over his head and gave it a waggle. Jason pasted a vapid smile on his dark-stained face and waved back. At the same time his sonorous voice murmured, "That cold-blooded bastard has balls of brass. Pardon me while I rip Ana from the grasp his slimy tentacles."

I stretched my lips in a ventriloquist's grin. "While you're ripping tentacles don't forget our strategy."

"Not to worry. I haven't forgotten your advice. Don't be alone with Max. Don't give him any cause to suspect I know he's out to get me. Don't leave my bedroom door unlocked. And the hardest of all: Don't get drunk."

"Especially the last one. You'll need your wits about you if you want to live long enough to marry the woman of *our* dreams. Please tell the bride-to-be that I'll talk to her later."

Jason bumped my shoulder with his fist, then made his way toward Max. He waved away the offer of a drink and whispered in Ana's ear. She pursed her lips, nodded, and blew me a kiss. Cait was talking to one of the crew, but she broke off the conversation and caught me at the door.

"Please don't tell me my favorite roommate is leaving the party," she said.

"Duty calls. I'll be back in a few hours."

"I'll consider that a promise," she said. She gave me a peck on the cheek and sauntered back to her conversation.

I went to meet Sally at a restaurant overlooking the marina where the *Sea Robin* had its slip. I got there a few minutes early and found a table on the second-floor deck. Only one other table was occupied. I set the duffle bag on a chair and strolled to the railing. The low silhouette of Great Island was visible, dark and mysterious against the deepening blue sky.

I felt a gentle poke in the small of my back, turned and saw Sally. She had traded her shark motif T-shirt and shorts for a pearl-colored silk pantsuit that set off her dusky complexion. Her eyes were curious.

"A penny for your thoughts," she said.

"They're not worth that much. I was just thinking that I detect a hint of fall in the air."

"Which means winter won't be far behind. Do you ever think of flying south with the geese?"

"My arms would get tired before I made it to the Cape Cod Canal."

She rolled her eyes. "I think I've heard that one before, Soc."

"Probably, but it always wows them at the Rotary Club breakfasts. Yeah, I think about warmth maybe a hundred times a day in the winter when there's nothing to see here except gray skies, gray ocean and gray faces. Maybe we can get together in Florida this winter. We'll go out for an Early Bird Special with Sam and Millie."

"That would be nice," she said. "How did the filming go off Great Island?"

"Wet but successful. I saw the spotter plane circling near. What was going on?"

"Emma was in the neighborhood, heading north. But she was a good half-mile from where you were filming. You weren't worried, were you?"

"The last time Emma came through, someone died. I didn't know until today that I had nothing to worry about."

"What changed your mind?"

"I'll tell you after I see the photos from the medical examiner."

She handed me a large, brown envelope. "Here you go."

"Thanks," I said. "Let's get it over with."

We went back to the table and ordered a couple of glasses of sauvignon blanc wine made from the vineyard in Truro a few miles from where we were sitting. I slipped the photos out of the envelope and held them on my knee where they'd be invisible to anyone at another table. The light was dim, but good enough to make out more of Munson's truncated arm than I needed to see before dinner.

After a quick shuffle through the photos, I stuffed them back in the envelope and placed it on an empty chair just as our wine arrived. We toasted each other, and Sally said, "Please explain how these awful photos might help Emma."

"Do you remember the first time we talked about the case? You said Munson's fatal injury was inconsistent with what we know about great whites."

"That's right. It was almost surgical. Judging from the size of the teeth marks on the leg, I'd expect the arm bite to be ragged."

"What if Munson's injuries came from different sources? Let's say Emma leaves her mark on the leg, but she didn't bite off the arm. It was already gone when she arrived. Paint me a likely shark scenario."

"But—"

I raised my hand. "Bear with me a little while longer. What would Emma have done if she happened to be in the neighborhood and picked up a blood trail?"

"Sharks have an incredible sense of smell. She would have swum back and forth in the blood slick until she found the source of the bleeding. Which in this case would have been a dead or dying man."

"According to the autopsy, Munson died from drowning. Would the shark still go for him if he'd been dead?"

"Sharks are designed to eat living prey but they will scavenge as well. It's quite common for a shark to eat the carcass of a dead whale."

"Then it's possible that Emma took an exploratory leg bite, decided Munson wasn't what's for dinner that night, and swam away without going in for another attack."

"Yes, that's a possibility. But if Emma isn't responsible, what else could have amputated the arm like that?"

A young couple was seated a few tables away. A quick glance told me that they only had eyes for each other. I pulled the cutlass from the duffle and held it out of their line of sight.

"Not what. *Who.* Using something like this."

"A sword?"

"A pirate's cutlass. This one is plastic, but an authentic version, with a steel blade, could have done the trick."

"But how?"

"I'm more interested in who. And when I find out, I'll let you know. But I think there's enough here to lay out a circumstantial case that would clear the reputation of our favorite great white shark."

She shook her head. "I'm having a hard time processing this. When will you know for sure?"

"After tonight, maybe. I'll call you if I learn something, either way."

She gazed across the table. "You're amazing. Simply amazing. I can't wait to spring this on the research committee."

"Glad I could help." I handed her a menu. "Now to more important things. Dinner."

"I'm starved. What are you thinking of getting?"

I thought of the photos I had just seen, so steak didn't appeal. And even if Emma didn't remove Munson's arm, talking again about great white shark dining habits had diminished my appetite for seafood. I flipped over to the salad section of the menu.

"Tonight I think I'll go vegetarian."

CHAPTER 35

The party at the Big House had ended. The mansion was eerily quiet. Nothing like a few brain-numbing martinis to pave the way to an early bedtime. Tip-toeing like a thief, I made my way to the kitchen and rummaged in a drawer until I found a LED flashlight I had seen while on clean-up duty.

On the way back from the kitchen I glanced into the combo den and editing room, but it was dark. Continuing on, I climbed the stairs to the second floor and followed the corridor past the master suites to the turret room. Starlight filtered in through the tall windows. Wicker chairs facing out ringed most of the octagon room's perimeter.

In the center of the room, a metal railing encircled a spiral staircase. I descended the cast-iron stairs to the ground floor. Again, chairs ringed the room, and at the base of the stairs was a sofa. My boathouse offers stark evidence of my lack of interior decorating talents, but the sofa seemed out of place.

Under the sofa was a fringed Persian carpet. I reached down, picked up one end of the sofa and lifted it off to the side. Like the chairs, the sofa was wicker and easy to move. The rug was tacked down onto the shiny oak floor along all four sides. I got my fingers under a fold and lifted. After slight resistance, the rug came off the floor with multiple snapping sounds.

The tacks were actually brass fasteners that snapped into sockets carved in the floor. I reattached the rug with the press of a finger, then unsnapped it again. Then I rolled back the rug and the rubber pad and played the flashlight beam on the floor enclosed by the rectangle of sockets. The oak squares were about six inches across. Each one had a complicated light and dark design of smaller rectangles. Combined with the swirls in the wood, the pattern confused the eye.

I rapped my knuckles on the floor and again outside the area framed by the fasteners. The second sound was definitely hollower. One-by-one, I pressed the heel of my palm on the tiles directly under the rug. After a few tries I heard a soft *click*. Three sides of a rectangular section rose up at an angle. I lifted the raised edge of a trap door.

I poked my flashlight into the opening and the beam revealed a wooden ladder. I sat on the floor with my feet dangling through the trap door opening and gradually put weight on the first step. It had a solid feel to it, so I lowered myself through the hatchway. The ladder went down a shaft. The walls were reinforced with wooden planks; held in place by vertical and horizontal timbers.

After descending around fifteen feet, I stepped off the last rung onto the concrete floor. A tunnel led off from the bottom of the shaft. The tunnel was roughly a yard wide and the ceiling near six feet high. Like the ladder shaft, the tunnel was as well-engineered as a copper mine. The walls were fashioned of wide planks strengthened with two by fours. The air was damp but not as musty as I would have expected. Whoever built the tunnel did a good job ventilating it.

I only had to hunch over a little as I stepped into the tunnel. It ran in a straight line for what I estimated was a couple of hundred feet, about the same distance between the Big House and the gazebo. I kept the flashlight beam pointed at the floor, which is how I saw the circular cover of a metal grate that probably hid a cistern for drainage. Beyond the bull's-eye of light was inky darkness, but that changed when the tunnel suddenly flooded with light.

I looked up and discovered that I wasn't alone. Holding the handle of a camp lantern in his left hand, Max stood ten feet away, in front of a ladder like the one I had climbed down. His right hand clutched a pistol and I was close enough to see his forefinger wrapped around the trigger. The muzzle was like a malevolent eye staring at a point on my chest where a bullet would transform my sternum into splinters.

"Hello, Soc," he said in a quiet voice that still managed to echo off the walls of the tunnel. "What a nice surprise."

"You're not the only one who's surprised, Max." It wasn't much of a comeback, but it was the best I could do under the circumstances.

He chuckled and said, "That's understandable. Please drop your flashlight to the floor and raise your hands behind your head. Slowly."

I did as I was told.

"Thank you. Now tell me how you knew about this tunnel."

"Azra read about it in a history of the Big House. She must have mentioned it to you, too."

"Indirectly. Azra told Ana, who commented on it in passing. I couldn't resist taking a look for myself. I thought I was the only other person who knew about it until I saw you skulk by the editing room with a flashlight. I was curious, and followed you to the turret."

"I didn't see anyone watching the dailies. The editing room was dark."

"I do my best thinking in the dark. I was going through the movie in my mind. Scene by scene, to make sure I had filmed *The Pirate's Daughter* as Goody would have wanted the story told."

"Sounds like Goody is your muse."

"In a way. It's more complicated. Remember what I told you

when we first met on the set at Lucifer Land? How I could feel Goody's presence watching over the production?"

"I remember. You said she was telling you she wanted her story told."

He smiled. "It took me a while to figure out what she wanted. Every time I deviated from her wishes she corrected me like a mother guides a child, with punishment and reward."

"So when things went wrong, it was Goody giving you a rap on the knuckles."

"Not a bad way to put it. For instance, I was going with the version of her story where she sells her soul to the devil and uses her power to raise the storm that killed Bellamy. When I tried to film it, she sent a gust of wind that almost blew Ana off the cliff. She wanted me to know that she didn't hate Bellamy; she loved him."

"You based that on a gust of wind?"

"As you've learned, people in the film business are superstitious. You trust your instincts. My gut picked up on bad vibes. So I rewrote the script. Seemed crazy at the time."

"You'll have to admit, Max, it's unusual to have a ghost as a film consultant."

"I was skeptical at first, but when I tried to film her wandering the moors as a crazy old crone, we experienced three straight days of pouring rain that washed out our schedule. During that time, I again rewrote the script. There's the scene where she explains that she is learning witchcraft to protect her daughter, who is her only link to Sam. She hints that she has sold her soul to the devil in exchange for the promise to be reunited with Sam. She throws herself over the cliff because she realizes that the devil's promise is a sham. That the only way she will be reunited with her lover is to join him in his world of the dead. Mehitabel will carry on for her."

"I thought Mehitabel was in a coma."

"She comes out of her coma as her mother flings herself into the sea. The implication is that this is part of a renegotiated deal with the devil. She goes out and burns the hut. Later she boards a sailing ship that will take her away from all this. The captain is a young, handsome man who says he saw smoke when he was sailing into port. She smiles, and it is clear that they will become lovers."

"I like it." I said, then changing the subject. "You didn't say anything about the scene back at the Big House. The one where Jason almost gets squashed under a treasure chest."

He smiled. A nasty smile. "I've taken that scene out of the script. It's too dangerous and unnecessary to the story anyhow."

"Maybe that's why it wasn't in my copy of the screenplay."

"Making a film is organic. The people who filmed *Casablanca* changed and added to the screenplay as production moved along. We've done the same thing with *The Pirate's Daughter*. We add action and we take it out to improve the final product."

"Is that what happened to Munson? He was taken out to improve the product?"

"Yes. In a way. Munson was a junkie and a drunk. He was endangering the success of the movie. If he hadn't died, I would have fired him."

"Jason says you kept Munson on the job because he knew you were skimming money from the state."

"Jason has a big mouth."

"It's true, though."

"Unfortunately, it is. I had to keep Munson on the crew, give him a raise, and look the other way during his binges. Even when Munson wanted more money, I tried to reason with him. I set up a meeting on the boat to say that I could give him a little more."

"That's when you decided to kill him?"

"It was never a real decision. He upped the ante. He knew how much money I was getting in tax reimbursements. I said I'd cut him in for more when the film made some money. He said it was a crappy film, and that I couldn't direct a porn video."

"Maybe he was right. I heard that was the word around

Hollywood. And the reason you never made it to the big time was that you didn't have the talent."

"You're pushing what little luck you have left," he snarled.

"Just saying what I heard."

It was risky to rile up guy who had two choices on how to kill you. I thought maybe if I got him angry enough he'd make a mistake. It was all I had.

"What you heard was wrong. *The Pirate's Daughter* is going to get an Academy Award nomination. It's an amazing story. You saw the performance I got out of Ana and even that fool Jason."

"Yes, I did, Max, which is why I can't understand where it went wrong. What happened on the boat?"

"Munson had a gun, but he put it down to open a compartment for more booze. I picked up his empty bottle and, when he turned back, brought it down on his head. I thought I killed him. The first thing I had to do was dispose of the body. I took the *Sea Robin* and the Zodiac out into the bay, intending to dump him over the side. People would think he got drunk, hit his head and fell off the boat."

"But that's not what happened."

"Munson was tougher than I figured. While I was running the boat, he regained consciousness and got his gun, which had fallen to the deck. He was still in a daze, staggering about, almost falling, but he would have shot me if I hadn't stopped him."

"With the cutlass."

"Yes. The cutlass. It was on the boat from a previous shoot. When he came at me, I brought it down and severed his arm below the elbow. I picked up the gun, but I didn't need it. He collapsed. He was bleeding all over the deck, so I threw him over the side. I tossed his arm over too."

"Of course. You wouldn't want a messy deck."

"You're a detective, so you can appreciate what a lousy murderer I am. This was far from the perfect crime. Someone would find the body washed up, missing an arm, and know right away that this was not an accident. I thought maybe I should throw the cutlass over, but I needed it for the production and could never explain how it just happened to disappear. I washed down the deck, got in the Zodiac, went back to the slip, and left the marina. I sweated for days. It was even worse when the body washed ashore. I was waiting to be found out."

"Which would have happened if a great white shark hadn't been blamed."

"That was the amazing part. The shark was an accomplice after the fact."

"Emma."

"What?"

"The shark's name is Emma. You should know in case you ever meet her."

"I'll be sure to give her a fish or whatever they eat. She took the blame for me. 'All's well that ends well,' as the Bard said."

"It didn't end well for Munson."

He sighed. "Nor for you, I'm afraid. The cistern under this tunnel is going to be your final resting place. Sorry it has to end his way."

He seemed uncertain whether to do me in with the cutlass or the gun. I was hoping for the sword, thinking I might be able to rush him when he raised it to strike. Maybe the same thought occurred to him because he leaned the cutlass against the ladder and raised the pistol.

In my fevered imagination, I saw a red blossom sprout from the muzzle and felt the bullet crash into my chest even before the *bang* hit my eardrums.

But what actually happened was a lot different. The sound I heard was not a gunshot. It was more like someone hitting a watermelon with a hammer. Max went cross-eyed, the pistol fell from his limp fingers, and he collapsed like a ruptured balloon.

What seemed like the voice of almighty Zeus boomed down

from above: "And…Cut!"

CHAPTER 36

The female police officer who'd been at the Big House investigating Yergo's death looked across the table at me.

"Is that all?" she said.

We were sitting in an interrogation room at the police station. For the last couple of hours I had been laying out the story of how I came to be in a dank Prohibition-era rum-runner's tunnel with a homicidal movie director.

"That's it; at least for now," I said.

She looked across the table at Jason, who was sitting next to me. "Do you have anything to add, sir?"

Jason spread his palms wide. "For the first time in my life that I can remember, I am at a loss for words," he said.

She turned back to me. "From what I've heard you are a very lucky man, Mr. Socarides."

"No argument there. I would have been dead if Jason hadn't dropped the bottle of rum on Max's head."

Jason said, "Even more good news. The bottle didn't break."

Luckily, Jason had ignored my advice to stay sober. After I'd left he got into the martinis. When the party broke up and he was the last man standing, he decided to have a nightcap at the gazebo. He noticed that the bar had been shoved aside. Where the bar should have been, the floor was open. In his haste to get into the tunnel ahead of me, Max had left the trap door up. Jason heard every word of Max's confession. Better yet, he recorded it on his cell phone. When the conversation got to the part about dumping my body into the cistern, Jason dropped a full bottle of rum on Max's noggin.

"Thank you for your time, gentlemen," the police officer said, switching off the recording device she'd been using to take down our statements word-for-word.

"Glad to help. What comes next with Max?" I said.

"As soon as Mr. Corman recovers from the egg-sized lump on his head, he will be read his rights and arraigned on charges of murder and attempted murder. The next move will be up to his lawyer, who will listen to the confession recorded on your cell phone, Mr. Kingman, and to your statement, Mr. Socarides, along with any corroborating evidence. I expect there may be an attempt at a plea bargain."

"What about the matter of tax fraud?" I said.

"That issue is being dealt with at the state level. Thanks again for coming in. Please let us know if you are leaving the immediate area."

She ushered us out of the interrogation room to the door of the station. We stepped out into the morning sunshine and I filled my lungs with fresh air that couldn't have been sweeter. Only a few hours before I was close to drawing my last breath in the damp confines of the escape tunnel.

"I owe you big time, Jason. Don't know how I can repay you."

"Buy a bottle of rum to replace the one now sitting in the police evidence room."

"That's easy."

"Something else is of grave concern," he said in his spooky voice.

"I'd be glad to help."

He broke into a smile. "I want you to be the best man when Ana and I get hitched."

"I'd be honored, Jace. Has she said yes?"

"Not yet, but she will. I'll ask the fair lady for her hand after we shoot the scene at Goody Hallett's meadow."

An alarm bell went off in my head. "I thought the last scene was filmed out of sequence a few days ago. The one with Ana standing on the cliffs."

"Remember what I said about artistic differences?"

"Vaguely. You didn't go into detail."

"This scene is a perfect example. Max and I agreed that Goody Hallett standing at the edge of the cliff with her scarlet cloak blowing in the wind was the defining scene, but his version, having her disappear into the mists, milked it of all the drama. I've talked it over with Ana and she's eager for a re-shoot under my direction. It will be a real *zanga-banga*."

"When are you shooting this *zanga-banga*?"

"Later today. When we get back to the Big House I'll bring everyone up to date on Max. After breakfast we'll have an organizational meeting, then we're off to Lucifer Land for fun and games."

I wasn't too sure about that. It was a bad idea for Ana to leave the Big House while Drazik's thugs were still at large. Even if Flagg could arrange an escort for protection, she'd be vulnerable. I was pondering how to talk her into staying put until Azra finished testifying, when out of the corner of my eye I saw a double flash. *Flick-flick.* Then another. A black Ford Taurus parked in the police station lot had blinked its headlights.

The night before, Jason and I had followed the police cruiser to the station in the GMC pickup. I told him to take the Jimmy back to the Big House and said I'd catch up with him later. After he drove off I walked over to the sedan. As I approached the driver's side, the window rolled down and I saw myself reflected in the lenses of Flagg's aviator sunglasses.

"You've been a busy boy again," he said.

"You know what they say, Flagg. Idle hands are the devil's

playthings."

"Never known you to be idle, Soc. Might be better off sometimes if you were."

"I'd be the first to agree after last night. How'd you know where to find me?"

"Ana called and said the town police showed up last night. They arrested the director. You and her actor friend went off to the cop shop. Been waiting for you to come out. Still got some coffee in a thermos. How's about you get in and tell me what happened."

I went around to the passenger side and got into the Taurus. Between sips of coffee I gave him a bare-bones account of my encounter with Max in the tunnel. It's tough to get a laugh out of Flagg. Hell, he hardly ever smiles. But when I told him how Jason had *kayo'd* Max with a rum bottle, he threw his head back and guffawed.

"I've been in lots of weird situations, Soc, but you're constantly up to your chin in crap."

I was in no mood for a lecture, even from a friend. "I'm not the only one who ends up in a big pile of manure from time to time."

"Yeah, but with me it's part of my job description. Correct me if I'm wrong. Last I heard you were running a charter fishing boat, not locking horns with bad guys."

I didn't feel like arguing with Flagg, mostly because I knew he was right. So I changed the subject. "Speaking of bad guys, what's the word on Azra?"

"She's on the other side of the big pond getting ready to sing like a canary."

"Any idea where Drazik's thugs are keeping themselves?"

"They've gone to the mattress. My guys started looking for them after they put Azra on a plane, but there's a lot of ground to cover."

"Maybe they got scared and hightailed it out of here."

"Huh," Flagg said. "What do you really think?"

"My guess is that they are more afraid of Drazik than anything.

Which means they're still around, waiting to grab Ana if she leaves the Big House. I'm worried that they'll get their chance today."

I filled Flagg in on the plans to re-shoot the scene at Goody Hallett's meadow.

"I don't like it. Think we can talk her out of it?" he said.

"Doubtful. She and Jason both have a lot riding on this movie, but I can try."

He pressed the car's ignition button. "I'll give you a ride home."

Flagg dropped me off at the Big House and said he would wait until he heard from me. When I stepped into the dining room, conversation came to a halt. Then Jason stood and began to clap and the rest of the crew joined him in applause. Ana came over to give me a hug; Cait did the same.

I thanked everyone, pulled up a chair and dug into scrambled eggs and toast, washing it down with a gallon of coffee.

After the breakfast plates were cleared away, Jason stood up and said: "Everyone is bursting with curiosity about how you fingered our esteemed director as a murderer."

I had gone over the story again and again at the police station but the crew was entitled to know what had happened. So I sketched out the trail I had followed to the smuggler's tunnel and was rewarded with another round of applause.

When the clapping ended, Jason stood again, and said: "Please accept the thanks of everyone on the crew of *The Pirate's Daughter*. We are all glad that you are safe. Cait informs me that the extras will be on the set in about an hour for the re-shoot. I'd like everyone to leave for the meadow in fifteen minutes."

The dining room emptied out. I pulled Ana aside.

"I talked to Flagg a while ago. We're worried about you leaving the Big House. Drazik's men are still on the loose. You'd be safer staying here."

"You and Mr. Flagg have done so much for Azra and me," she said. "I appreciate your concern, but it's essential that we make the best movie we can."

"Even at the risk of your own life?"

She smiled. "Jason and I died years ago. Or at least our careers did. Even worse, we deserved the mess we made of our lives. We let down everyone who tried to help. We've not been true to our fans. This movie is the only chance we will ever have to show the world that we can still act."

I had seen every movie Ana Roman made. I had watched her take on complicated roles as easily as she slipped on her scarlet cloak. As the biggest Ana Roman fan in the universe, I could say this: Ana's stubborn refusal to live in fear was not an act.

Less than fifteen minutes later I was in the GMC behind Jason and Ana's van. As we pulled out of the driveway, I saw Flagg's Ford sedan parked on the side of the road. After we passed, he got in line. It was reassuring to have him take up the rear. My calmness went up in smoke, however, when a black Cadillac Escalade SUV, parked on the other side of the road, pulled into the lane, did a tight U-turn and joined the parade.

I called Flagg. "Don't mean to ruin your day."

"I know," he said. "We've got company."

CHAPTER 37

Our caravan arrived at Goody Hallett's meadow and pulled up behind the movie production truck near the start of the path that led out to the cliffs. The park ranger assigned to the movie was on hand to keep curious spectators from walking out onto the dunes. The crew was unloading gear from the truck and carrying it out to the set.

Jason had made an amazing transition from a boozy over-the-hill actor to a movie director with fire in his bloodshot eyes. In the few short hours since taking over, he had whipped together cast and crew and written a new closing scene for *The Pirate's Daughter*. He pulled the van in behind the ranger's SUV and I parked the Jimmy behind him. Flagg backed into a small parking lot on the other side of the road. The Escalade that had trailed our caravan kept going toward the Marconi site.

As I got out of my truck, the bus pulled in and six extras got out, dressed in baggy pants, boots and puffy shirts. Cait was the last one off the shuttle.

"Hi, Soc," she said. "These are the only angry villagers I could round up at the last minute. Gentlemen, show Soc how furious you are at Goody."

Pumping their fists in the air, the extras produced a bloodcurdling chorus of shouts. A couple of men who still thought they were playing pirates let out some *arghs* by mistake.

"Pretty scary," I said. "But I thought angry mobs carried pitchforks and torches."

"You've got to be kidding! Sharp implements and fire are the last things these guys need. Talk to you after the shoot."

She herded the extras toward Jason who had taken up a command position near the start of the path.

"Thanks, everyone, for coming out on such short notice," he boomed. "We are here to re-shoot the last scene of *The Pirate's Daughter*." He gestured toward the ocean. "The original shot opened with Ana standing on a cliff gazing out to sea, the wind whipping her cloak and hair. Her figure gets smaller and smaller until it disappears in the mist. The camera slowly angles up into the sky, then comes the scroll of credits. Romantic music. *Ta-da.* Poignant but boring."

Ana stepped to Jason's side and wrapped her arm around his waist. "Jason is exactly right. The shoot we did a few days ago also leaves too many unanswered questions. For example, wouldn't the villagers be angry when they learned that Goody has lured their friends to the island of treasure only to exact her revenge? Wouldn't they want to get back at her?"

"Thank you, Ana," Jason said. "Now listen up, folks. Goody Hallett will be walking along the edge of the cliff, silhouetted against the ocean, when she hears loud voices. She stops, turns, and sees the mob of villagers burst from the woods. Close-up shot. A smile comes to her face. She raises her hands in the air. Although it is sunny, a rolling fog envelopes the villagers. When it drifts away, Goody has vanished. The villagers are left standing at the edge of the cliff looking out to sea. Well?"

The crew and actors burst into applause. Jason looked the happiest I had seen him. Once again, he was the dashing swashbuckler climbing into the rigging, sword in hand. The film crew started moving the camera and lighting equipment out onto the dunes. The fog machines were placed between the cliffs and the woods. Jason ran a test to make sure the breeze carried the mists toward the woods. While the crew was busy getting ready for the shoot, I sidled over to Flagg's car.

He rolled down the window. "Look up the road."

The Escalade that followed us to the set was pulled off the road, facing us.

"I see the SUV that joined our parade sitting where there's an unobstructed view of the set. Any sign of the driver?"

"No one's gotten out. SUV isn't moving. Seem suspicious?"

"Maybe the driver is curious about the movie."

"Then why isn't he hanging with those spectators? I think he's calling his pals in to give him a hand."

"In that case we can expect to see his pals any minute," I said.

"Maybe not. They won't want to make a fuss. Too many witnesses. Escape routes are limited. How would you work it if you wanted to get at Ana?"

"I'd try something after she leaves here. There's only one main road. They can pick the best spot for an ambush."

"Details?"

"My guess is that they'd run the car off the road, shoot Jason and grab Ana, so they can use her as a bargaining chip. Without Azra's testimony the case against Drazik falls apart. He'll deal with the sisters once he's free."

"Yeah, that's pretty much my take on it," Flagg said.

"How do we prevent it from happening?"

"There's protection and there's diversion," Flagg said. "Even if we had my agents riding shotgun, a couple of bad guys with rifles or grenades could neutralize the defense and get to their target."

"Why are we even talking about stuff that won't work?"

"Process of elimination, Soc. We can't protect her. That leaves us with diversion. Maybe I take out the guy in the truck, you grab

Ana and hide somewhere until back-up arrives."

I looked in the distance at the figure in the scarlet cloak making its way toward the cliffs. "I've got another idea. Might be better than a shoot-out on the dunes with all these people around. It's going to be risky and we'll need timing and luck."

He stared at me so I could see my face reflected in his sunglasses. "Sounds like a typical Soc scheme. I'm all ears."

"We start with Ana. We create a diversion so we can take her away before there's any nastiness. The key is that we control the situation, not them. We don't want the bad guys sitting out on the highway waiting for Ana. And we don't want them to get impatient, so that they'll charge in with guns blazing. We get them here at a specific time and place so we can deal with them."

"How do we do that?"

"Witchcraft," I said.

Flagg saw that I was serious. "Make believe I don't have a clue what you're talking about."

"I got an idea from one of the scenes we shot where Ana lured the bad guys to a place where she was able to knock them off one by one."

"I like that," Flagg said. "What kind of spell does the little ol' witch weave to get them here?"

"No spell necessary. Ana calls the hit squad. She'll have their number from the time they called her on Yergo's phone. She will tell them that she is tired of running and wants to make a deal. She says she wants to meet with them here after the filming. She offers them an incredible bribe on the condition that they leave her and her sister alone."

"Think they'll believe her?"

"She's one of the best actresses in the world, Flagg. If anyone can play the part of the desperate and panicked sister, she can. But it doesn't matter." I glanced again at the Escalade, which hadn't moved an inch. "Their scout will report that everyone has left, leaving Ana alone. The thugs will jump at the chance to give Drazik good news."

"Let me think about it." Flagg gazed off at Goody Hallett's meadow. He was silent, but knowing Flagg I surmised he was thinking about defense, offense, position, and what could go wrong.

"We can do it," he said.

"The filming is about to start. You'll see what I have in mind."

Ana was walking along the edge of the cliffs. She heard the shouts of the villagers, stopped and turned to see them burst from the woods. As they advanced on her, the fog machines began cranking at full blast. The villagers disappeared behind a rolling wall of gray mist.

Jason went into the pop-up tent to check the scene on the camera monitor. He came out a minute later, announced that he wanted to shoot the scene again, and told the crew to take a ten-minute break.

I hustled over to Ana, and said, "Looks like Jason is even more of a perfectionist than Max."

She laughed. "Apparently so. Multiple takes are exhausting. Luckily this is the last scene."

"Do you have your cell phone with you?"

"Yes," she said to my relief. "In my cloak. Why?"

"There's been a slight change in the shooting schedule. When you're through with Jason I'd like you to do one more scene," I said.

A puzzled look came to her face. "I don't understand. Jason didn't say anything about shooting another scene after this one."

"Jason doesn't know about it."

"Then I'd better check with him."

She turned to go, but I said, "Keep Jason out of it for now. We'll tell him when the time is right."

"What's this all about?"

"Drazik's men know you're here. They will try to kidnap you to keep Azra from testifying. Once Drazik is free he will come after you and your sister."

She gazed at me with calm eyes. "Tell me what I have to do."

CHAPTER 38

Ana didn't hesitate for a second after I gave her a quick run-through, spelling out what she had to do. She dug her cell phone from the cloak pocket, clicked on the redial list and put the phone to her ear.

"What do you want me to say?" she said in a calm voice.

"Play it any way you want to, but here's what we have to get across."

She nodded as I ran through the main points of the script. Seconds later she was talking on the phone in Croatian. I didn't understand a word, but her voice quivered as she played her role—the frightened woman who would do anything to protect her younger sister.

When Ana hung up her eyes practically glowed in triumph.

"The idiot fell for it," she said. Her nervous phone voice had reverted to its normal smoothness. "He said if we meet face-to-face he'll will negotiate a sum of money to ensure that they all leave me and Azra alone. In return, I agreed that I will convince Azra not to testify against Drazik. How did it sound to you?"

"Perfect, except for the part about you meeting him," I said.

"I don't understand. You asked me to say that."

"Correct. But you won't be the one to greet him."

She pinned me with a green-eyed gaze. "What exactly do you

have in mind?"

"I'll explain the plan but I guarantee you won't like it."

I was right. She didn't like it a bit.

Ana jabbed my chest with her fingertip. "I can't let you risk your life for me or my sister. This is none of your business." When I started laughing, she said, "What's so funny?"

"Remember when I said I'd seen every movie you ever made? Don't mess with an Ana Roman movie buff. You used pretty much the same line when you tried to talk Jason out of risking his life to save your brother in *The Desert Queen*."

A stunned expression came to her face. "*Omigod*, you're right, Soc. I was heavy into Quaaludes at the time. The only thing I remember about that awful movie is how quickly it sank out of sight, taking what was left of our film careers down with it. Damn, Soc, just because you remember movie lines doesn't mean you should stick your neck out."

"Drazik could go free if Azra pulls back. He'll keep his head low until you and Azra let your guards down, then he'll kill you both. But these guys are Drazik's family members. If we can eliminate them today, Drazik will have to use hired guns, which will be tough for him to do after he's tossed into a black hole."

"You're right, of course. I'll go along with your plan. The person on the phone said they will know when today's shoot is ending." She glanced around. "They must have someone watching."

"That's their scout in the SUV parked on the road. He's probably in constant contact with his buddies."

"Won't he tell his friends that I've left?"

"Not if we play it right."

I told her what I had in mind.

"You'll be acting as bait," she said.

"Bait sounds fishy. I'm a lure. I'll be like you, luring the villagers onto the island."

"That was make-believe, Soc, and you don't have the supernatural powers of Goody Hallett. Even if your crazy scheme works, you can't take these people on by yourself."

"I won't be alone. You met my friend John Flagg."

"Yes, he's the government agent who arranged for Azra and me to say goodbye before she left the country."

"That's right. He'll be bringing in other agents to back us up."

She sighed. "Let me tell you something, Mr. Socarides. When you are an actor you can tell when other people are acting. I believe you are not telling the whole truth, but for Azra's sake, I will go along with this insanity. I will die if anything happens to you or your friend because of us. That's not a line from any of my movies, by the way." She saw Jason waving at her. "Please excuse me. I have to get back to work."

Jason shot the scene until he was sure he had it right. Ana walked out on the cliff three more times, pirouetted to face the angry mob, waited until the fog rolled in, then left her perch, leaving the illusion that she had vanished, presumably to join her lover in whatever ghostly realm dead pirates call home.

It was nearing dusk when Jason called it a wrap. Applause echoed over the dunes. The crew started moving equipment back to the truck. Cait herded the extras onto the bus. Before she left, she said she would see me back at the Big House to toast the end of filming.

Jason was ebullient. He slapped me on the back. "Time for another celebration, Soc."

"In a little while," I said. "Why don't you take the GMC?"

"I'd love not to drive that minivan, but are you sure?"

"Very sure. I have a favor to ask in return. Leave the fog machines."

His eyes narrowed. "What on earth are you up to now, Soc?"

"Something of life and death importance to Ana and Azra." I held out the truck keys. "Ana knows what to do. Get the truck. She'll be with you in a minute or two."

He took the keys, we shook hands, and then he headed for the pickup. Ana was waiting on the dunes' side of the equipment truck, shielded her from the view of whoever was in the SUV.

She passed me the folded cloak and tucked her hair under a baseball cap that she pulled low over her eyes. She whispered to be careful, gave me a cheek kiss, and then got into the back of the truck.

I threw the cloak around my shoulders and pulled the hood over my head just before the movie truck pulled out into the road and headed back to the highway. I started off along the dunes' path. At the edge of the cliffs, I stopped and stood there facing the sea in the blue light of dusk. The cloak was too small for my body and I held it together in the front. Had it been daylight my disguise wouldn't have fooled a moron. The fading daylight would help me, at least until they got closer, but most of all, I was banking on the fact that Drazik's men *wanted* to see Ana, and would shove any doubts aside in their zeal.

I guessed Drazik's men would come as soon as the coast was clear. Ten minutes later I heard the sound of an engine and glanced back. Moving slowly along the road was a twin of the SUV that had arrived earlier.

The SUV made a U-turn and parked behind the other Escalade. The car doors opened and three men got out. Another man got out of the scout vehicle. They huddled for a few seconds, then all four men started walking single-file along the path.

I waved at the walkers. Friendly like. No one waved back. They kept on coming. Using the same maneuver they tried the night of the firebombing, they split up and advanced across the dunes—four abreast, a few feet apart. Even in the poor light, my disguise would soon fall apart.

So when they were about halfway between the woods and the cliffs I took the remote control from my pocket and hit the 'on' button. Twin streams of fog poured from the nozzles. The clouds rolled across the dunes from opposite directions and enveloped the walkers.

I hit the 'off' button. The breeze shredded the fog. I slipped the cloak off and waved it around over my head like a matador taunting a bull. That got their attention. They started toward the cliffs again, this time at a trot. They were so intent on me, they didn't even see the five ghostly figures who emerged from the woods. One raised a long object at the sky and the stutter of an automatic weapon echoed across the moors.

Drazik's men stopped and turned. As the fog peeled away, Flagg and his *Men in Black* advanced toward them.

Flagg shouted at Drazik's men to toss their weapons far away and get down on their bellies. They quickly flopped face-down onto the sand. The MIBs tied their hands behind their backs, hoisted the men onto their feet, and pushed them in the direction of the road.

Flagg walked over. "You okay?"

"Better than I was before you showed up. Lucky we had help, because standing up there solo I began to think maybe I'd talked you into something we couldn't handle"

"Communication and timing could be better, but I was ninety-nine percent sure it would work."

"What about the one percent?"

Although the light had faded, I could see the flash of his white teeth. "That's where luck comes in."

"That's what I thought," I said. "I've got one more favor to ask. I'm going to need a hand loading those fog machines."

As we walked across the haunted meadow in the twilight, Flagg said, "Meant to tell you something I noticed while we were waiting in the woods."

"What's that, Flagg?"

"You look real pretty in red."

CHAPTER 39

After the romp on the cliffs of Lucifer Land it was good to be back at the boathouse, especially after seeing lights in the windows and Sally's car parked in the yard. But when I stepped into the house my happy smile vanished. Sitting next to the door was Sally's suitcase. Before I had a second to think about what the bag was doing there, Sally called out.

"Is that you, Soc? I'm out here with Kojak."

I followed her voice to the deck and found her sitting in an Adirondack chair with Kojak curled up in her lap sleeping. The deck lights were on and Sally had changed from the shorts and T-shirt that had been her standard Cape Cod uniform into a pair of light-colored slacks, matching jacket, and button-down blouse. Instead of sandals, she wore casual but dressy leather shoes.

She smiled. "I'd get up and give you a hello hug but I don't want to disturb Kojak."

"That's okay," I said, flopping down in the other chair. "As someone said, better to let sleeping cats lie."

Sally cast a motherly glance down at the snoozing feline. "I'll hate disturbing him when I do get up from the chair."

"Unless your knees are going numb, stay where you are and enjoy the scenery while I mix a couple of cool drinks."

She gazed out at the distant lights reflecting in the puddle of darkness that was the bay at night. The air was redolent with the sweet fragrance of sea air and salt marsh that comes in the early fall.

"It is beautiful," she said. "And so peaceful."

"Too bad you're leaving," I said.

She sighed. "I was waiting for the right time to break the news. You saw my suitcase in the hallway."

"And you're wearing travel clothes."

"That was dumb of me. I was going to put the bag in my car after I made some telephone calls out here, but Kojak jumped onto my lap and I haven't been able to move since." After a pause, she said, "I'm on my way to Florida."

"When will you be back?"

"I don't know. Maybe not for a while."

"I'm surprised. I thought you were going to hang around up here a few months more, maybe make this your base of operations. Why did you change your mind?"

"I've been offered a senior position with the Scripps research organization. I've been working with their facility in Florida."

"Congratulations," I said. "You deserve it. You're smart and you work hard."

"Thank you. But it was your detective work with Emma that made it possible."

"You lost me, Sal. What's Emma got to do with your plans?"

"Everything. Remember back when we first talked about this, I said how important it was to know if a great white shark had killed that man. Specifically, to learn how to deal with the inevitable interaction between sharks and humans."

"Sure. You were worried about the *JAWS* effect. If Emma had killed Munson, beaches would be closed and that would hurt tourism, the number one industry in these parts."

"You'll also recall I said that was only part of the greater picture. By killing thousands of sharks, humans have been damaging the ecosystem. If people could see what sharks really are, important predators who rarely harm people, it would help with all the worldwide efforts in conservation. And by studying their ways, and making our own behavior smarter, we can reduce even those few instances where sharks have attacked humans."

"I remember all that too, but what does my work have to do with you leaving town?"

"Everything. You proved that Emma didn't murder that man. Another human did! Proof that humans are more dangerous to people than sharks. When I reported the results of your investigation to the research group, they were so impressed that they offered me the job. I owe it all to you."

I shook my head. "If I hadn't tracked down the real murderer, you might not have been offered the job, and your bag wouldn't be packed and ready to go."

"I'm disappointed, too. But I should never have led you on. It's been wonderful to see you again, but ever since I arrived I've been on the fence about whether I'd stay or not. I guess I was waiting for a sign. The job offer was it."

Sally's words were like arrows puncturing my Greek male ego. How could she resist my obvious charms and looks and sparkling personality? Just then, the breeze picked up, coming from the east, cooling my fevered brow. Before long, the marsh grass would be painted in copper tones and the red-winged blackbirds would head south along with a sizable percentage of the local population. The winter temperatures would cool down any chance at romantic nights on the deck. We'd be hunkered down in my drafty old boathouse where cabin fever would set in. Sally was made for a bigger world.

"It's okay, Sal. Kojak and I will miss you, but this is what's best for you. Florida's only a few hours away."

"Well, no," she said. "After a visit to Florida, I'll be going to be working the Scripps Institute in California. Soc, I'm sorry."

"Me too." I groped for the right words but they slipped out of my grasp. The best I could come up with was, "When do you have to go?"

She glanced at her watch. "I have to leave now to catch the red-eye out of Providence."

I got up, removed Kojak's semi-conscious body from her lap and carried him inside to his bed. Sally patted him on the head, said goodbye, then gave me a warm hug and a kiss that would have made me dizzy with its promise, if there *were* any promise. I walked her out to the car and watched the red taillights disappear down the driveway.

I felt emptier than I had ever felt before, which might have had something to do with the fact that I hadn't eaten. I opened the refrigerator and found it as empty as my soul, except for a bottle of Cape Cod beer and some evil-looking growths in plastic containers. I wasn't really hungry anyway.

I walked out onto the deck, took a gulp of beer, and looked across the bay at the lights of the resort where I'd signed on to *The Pirate's Daughter*. That gig was over as well. I could pick up my dive gear tomorrow morning, but I didn't want to spend the night in my place with the scent of Sally's perfume still hanging in the air. As much as I liked Kojak, I craved human company. Maybe I would find it at the Big House.

Cait's Mini was the only vehicle in the parking lot when I arrived. I parked next to it and walked around to the lawn entrance. The house was shrouded in darkness, except for a few lights on the first floor. I went inside and made my way to the salon. Cait sat in a chair looking at the screen of her electronic pad.

She was intent on her work, but she looked up when I came in and gave me a smile that lit up some of the darker corners of my soul.

I looked around. "Where's the rest of the gang?"

"I got the night off from chef duty. Everyone was tired from today's shoot and, since they had the wrap party here last night, they decided to go out and celebrate the good news about our stars."

A few more shadows retreated. "Ana accepted Jason's proposal of marriage?"

"You knew? Oh…of course you'd know. You're a detective."

"More important, I'm Jason's rum-drinking buddy."

She put the tablet aside and pointed to two wine glasses and a bottle of champagne in an ice bucket.

"In that case, you can be my drinking buddy as well. Will you do the honors?"

I popped the cork and poured the bubbly; we clinked glasses and toasted the engaged couple. I sat next to her on the sofa, took a sip, and said, "Why aren't you celebrating with everyone else? All work, as they say."

"Oh that. I was just catching up on a few things while I waited for you."

"I'm glad you did. It would have been depressing coming into an empty house."

We clinked again, toasting the end of filming, then refilled our glasses. I was starting to feel better already and my mood improved even more when Cait pressed her body closer to mine, put her arm around my shoulders, and kissed my cheek.

When I turned my head to return the favor, she planted the real thing on my lips.

Pulling back, she giggled. "You look surprised."

"Didn't expect that, roomie."

"Didn't you like it?"

"I liked it a lot, but I thought…well…"

"That I don't dig men?"

"Hell, Cait, you've got me very, very confused. I know you like men, but I didn't know you liked them in, a…um, sensual way."

"Well, you're wrong, Mr. Detective. I told you at the start that not everything is what it seems in the film business. After I got stuck with Munson for a roommate he began to come on to me. I figured I'd put him off, thus the short hair and the baggy men's clothes. It must have worked, because he moved out."

A tickle started in the pit of my stomach where the longing for Sally had made its home. The tickle traveled up my chest and by the time it came out of my mouth, it was a roar. Cait joined in and we laughed until tears came to our eyes.

"What about the snoring?" I said. "Was that part of the act, too?"

"Unfortunately, no. That was authentic. The only time I don't snore in bed is after I've had sex." She hiccupped. "Which usually follows when I've had too much bubbly."

"In that case," I said. "How about I open another bottle?"

CHAPTER 40

Cait was still sleeping peacefully when I slipped out of the bedroom the next morning. Kojak greeted me at the boathouse door with a pussycat frown, but he buried it in the munchies I poured into his bowl. I looked in the refrigerator before I remembered it was empty.

I decided to go to Elsie's for a breakfast of burnt toast and overcooked eggs. But as I was walking out to the GMC, Gill's cammy-wagon bounced down the driveway and came to a stop. Gill got out carrying a bucket of oysters.

"These are the last batch to come off my farm," he said.

I took the bucket and thanked him. "Oyster season can't be over yet."

"It is for me. I sold the shellfishing rights to the farmer who has the grant next to mine. He'll do a good job with it. I'm getting ready to go to the University of Massachusetts at Dartmouth for refresher courses. I've got some teaching fellowships lined up. Hey, who knows where it will go from there?"

"I think it will go as far as you let it," I said. "Good luck with your career change."

"Thanks. Speaking of career changes, as my last job as an assistant Sherlock I passed on the documents I dug up to your friend ADA Martin. It didn't take him long to pick up on the same thing you did."

"That his boss, the DA, was on the list of principals who wanted to develop your land?"

"Yup. Along with Guy Rich and the New Bedford fishing dealer whose business was a cover for a drug operation. The DA has since taken a leave of absence pending an investigation. Mr. Martin has stepped in to take his place."

"That gives me a warm fuzzy feeling all over," I said. "Thanks for the oysters."

"Got something clse. I was going to sell my truck. I won't need anything so, uh, utilitarian once I'm on campus. Wondered if you'd like to drive it until you get something else." He shrugged. "Won't hurt my feelings if you paint it."

'Any port in a storm,' says the old mariner's adage. "Thanks for the generous offer. I may take you up on it."

"One more thing." He reached into his shirt pocket and came out with an envelope. "I talked to the other oyster farmers. Rich had set up a bank account with the reward for information leading to the arrest of the poachers. The oystermen took a vote yesterday, and this is all yours." He handed over the envelope.

Which is how, a few days later, I happened to be out on my charter boat with a very special party. I'd invited my family to meet me at the marina, handed over a check for the money I owed Parthenon Pizza, and took them for a ride around the harbor and out into Nantucket Sound. Chloe was ecstatic, George was reluctant until I explained the trip as checking out the company's investment, and my mother sat in the stern, gazing off at the blue-green sea, and murmured the word, *Thalassa*.

Fair weather followed, and I managed to take out a few more charters, including one with John Flagg as my only customer. We caught some fish, let them go, and hoisted beers while John told me that Azra's testimony not only sent Drazik into a deep, dark hole until the end of his days, but with help from the hit men who'd fallen afoul of the MIB on Lucifer Land, the cops rolled up the entire trafficking organization as well.

After the fishing trip John returned to the sea of intrigue that he swims in, not unlike the sharks that Sally follows. I've heard from her once, to let me know that Emma had left Cape Cod and was last seen off the coast of North Carolina, heading south. I've been busy getting the charter boat out of the water and buttoning her down for the winter.

Frank Martin called to thank me for my help and to say he's running for District Attorney. After I wished him well, he said he had tried to track down the Virginia license plate of the black sedan, as I'd requested, but there was no such number listed. 'Maybe I made a mistake,' he said. 'Yeah,' I said, 'that must be what happened.'

I'll be heading west soon to be the best man at the wedding of Jason and Ana. Sally told me to look her up next time I'm in California. Maybe I'll give her a call. She's probably still getting settled. Cait is back in L.A., where she's got a casting job on a feature film, and she says she'll show me the town after we all attend the premiere of The Pirate's Daughter. Cait was right about the movie business. It was all light and shadows. In the end, the only thing that had any real substance was the story of Goody and Sam.

Sam was real, and I think Goody was real enough. I can't think of any better reason than love for a pretty young woman to persuade a pirate at the top of his game to desert the tropic climate. Maybe Goody really did have a daughter who ran off with a ship captain and had children of her own. Maybe her descendants came back to Cape Cod and some local kid working in a fish market or clam shack can claim genes that go back to the star-crossed couple who vowed to be together again one day.

Was Mary Hallett a witch? Max may have answered that question in his screenplay. Before Goody vanishes forever she drops off a tapestry she has woven, saying it is a gift to the town. When the villagers unroll the work, they witness—woven into a tangled, dark background—the terrified faces of the men who had followed her to Great Island.

She certainly bewitched Sam. And Max, too. He was willing to kill, and kill again to tell her story. Maybe if the prison officials let him see the movie he'll ponder whether he has any regrets. Knowing Max, he'll say it was worth it.

Like I said, I'm no expert on ghosts. It's the live humans who are the real mystery. But if you happen to find yourself in Lucifer Land, with the fog smothering the lonely moors, twisting itself into phantasmagorical shapes, the rumble of the breaking sea echoing in your ears, and the wail of the wind mimicking the sad chorus of a hundred drowned pirates, come by the boathouse and let me know if you *still* think the dead stay dead.

The End

ABOUT THE AUTHOR

My fiction-writing career owes it start to the bad navigation of an 18th century pirate. For it was in 1717 that a ship named *Whydah* went aground off Cape Cod, reportedly carrying a fabulous treasure. Samuel Bellamy, the ship's captain, was drowned along with most of the crew. In the 1980s, three salvage groups went head-to-head, competing to find the wreck. I was working for a newspaper covering the treasure hunt. The controversy over the salvage got hot at times and I thought there might be a book based on the story.

I developed my own detective, an ex-cop, diver, fisherman, and PI named Aristotle "Soc" Socarides. He was more philosophical than hard-boiled. His first appearance was in "Cool Blue Tomb," which won the Shamus award for Best Paperback novel. After many years in the newspaper business, I turned to writing fiction and churned out five more books in the series.

Clive Cussler blurbed: "There can be no better mystery writer in America than Paul Kemprecos."

Despite the accolades, the *Soc* series lingered in mid-list hell. By the time I finished my last book, I was thinking about another career that might make me more money, like working in a 7-11.

Several months after the release of "Bluefin Blues," Clive called and said a spin-off from the *Dirk Pitt* series was in the works. It would be called the *NUMA Files* and he wondered if I would be interested in tackling the job.

I took on the writing of "Serpent" which brought into being Kurt Austin and the NUMA Special Assignments Team. Austin had some carry-over from Soc, and another team member, Paul Trout, had been born on Cape Cod. The book made *The New York Times* bestseller list, as did every one of seven *NUMA Files* that followed, including "Polar Shift," which bumped "The Da Vinci Code" for first place.

After eight *NUMA Files* I went back to writing solo. I wrote an adventure book entitled, "The Emerald Scepter," which introduced a new hero, Matinicus "Matt" Hawkins. I also worked with *Suspense Publishing* on the re-release of my *Soc* series in digital, print and audio. In 2013, responding to numerous requests, I brought Soc back again in a seventh Socarides book entitled, "Grey Lady." After that book I wrote a sequel to the first *Matt Hawkins* book, entitled, "The Minoan Cipher," which was nominated for a Thriller award in the Best Paperback category for 2017 by the International Thriller Writers.

The eighth *Soc* book, "Shark Bait," incorporates the aforementioned story of the *Whydah*, its doomed captain Samuel Bellamy, and his lover, Mary Hallett.

My wife Christi and I live on Cape Cod where she works as a financial advisor. We share a circa 1865 farmhouse with two cats. We have three children and seven granddaughters.

To learn more about Paul Kemprecos, check out his website at www.paulkemprecos.com.

85849386R00166

Made in the USA
Middletown, DE
27 August 2018